"Let me clarify. Yo... lips are the reaso... you've forgotten w... barn last week?"

Something utterly delicious shot through her veins with all the speed of a medical injection. He was here about their kiss? A kiss he felt the need to visit her about?

"I haven't forgotten anything."

"Good. Then I'll plan on picking you up at seven this evening."

"For what?"

"A date."

All the delicious heat coursing through her veins cratered in her stomach with a huge crash. "I'm not going on a date with you."

"Yeah, you kind of are. Consider it payback for cornering me in my own stable and reminding me of how good things used to be between us."

"But I can't go to dinner tonight."

"You have other plans?"

Damn him. "No."

"Then you'd better come up with something else pretty quick."

* * *

We hope you enjoy the Midnight Pass, Texas miniseries

* * *

If you're on Twitter, tell us what you think of Harlequin Romantic Suspense! #harlequinromsuspense

Dear Reader,

I'm so happy to welcome you back to Midnight Pass, Texas. For those of you who've already met the Reynolds family, thanks for joining me once more. If you're new to town, settle in and let me tell you a story. Once upon a time, there was a fifth-generation Texan ranching family...

Actually, all you really need to know is that the Reynolds men are some of the finest cowboys in the state of Texas. Everyone knows this, including large-animal vet Veronica Torres. The gorgeous Doctor Torres had a wild love affair with the eldest Reynolds brother, Ace, nearly a decade ago. But when their volatile personalities ultimately drove them apart and Veronica into the arms of another man, both buried that love way down deep.

Only now, Veronica is back in the Pass. Divorced and determined to pick up the pieces of her life, she's built a strong practice caring for the animals on the various ranches and farms in the area. Her life is just as she wants it—calm, quiet and wildly different from the chaos she experienced during her time in Houston.

Except Veronica doesn't know the danger that had doomed her marriage has been keeping a vigilant eye. Now, just as she and Ace are teetering on the edge of finding one another, that long-quiet enemy makes itself known.

I hope you enjoy *Under the Rancher's Protection*, and I look forward to sharing the final book in the series about Ace's sister, Arden, in the near future.

Best,

Addison Fox

UNDER THE RANCHER'S PROTECTION

Addison Fox

HARLEQUIN®

ROMANTIC SUSPENSE™

Recycling programs
for this product may
not exist in your area.

ISBN-13: 978-1-335-75948-1

Under the Rancher's Protection

Copyright © 2021 by Frances Karkosak

All rights reserved. No part of this book may be used or reproduced in any manner whatsoever without written permission except in the case of brief quotations embodied in critical articles and reviews.

This is a work of fiction. Names, characters, places and incidents are either the product of the author's imagination or are used fictitiously. Any resemblance to actual persons, living or dead, businesses, companies, events or locales is entirely coincidental.

This edition published by arrangement with Harlequin Books S.A.

For questions and comments about the quality of this book, please contact us at CustomerService@Harlequin.com.

Harlequin Enterprises ULC
22 Adelaide St. West, 40th Floor
Toronto, Ontario M5H 4E3, Canada
www.Harlequin.com

Printed in U.S.A.

Addison Fox is a lifelong romance reader, addicted to happy-ever-afters. After discovering she found as much joy writing about romance as she did reading it, she's never looked back. Addison lives in New York with an apartment full of books, a laptop that's rarely out of sight and a wily beagle who keeps her running. You can find her at her home on the web at www.addisonfox.com or on Facebook (www.Facebook.com/addisonfoxauthor) and Twitter (@addisonfox).

Books by Addison Fox

Harlequin Romantic Suspense

Midnight Pass, Texas

The Cowboy's Deadly Mission
Special Ops Cowboy
Under the Rancher's Protection

The Coltons of Grave Gulch

Colton's Covert Witness

The Coltons of Mustang Valley

Deadly Colton Search

The Coltons of Roaring Springs

The Colton Sheriff

The Coltons of Red Ridge

Colton's Deadly Engagement

The Coltons of Shadow Creek

Cold Case Colton

The Coltons of Texas

Colton's Surprise Heir

Visit the Author Profile page at Harlequin.com.

For Beth Gaddis

College might have made us roommates,
but I'd like to think fate (and our shared love of
romance novels!) made us lifelong friends.
I'm so fortunate to have you in my life.

Chapter 1

Ace Reynolds didn't consider himself a particularly superstitious man, but even he couldn't shake the spooked feeling by midafternoon when his horse threw a shoe.

The shoe had been the last in a steady line of increasing problems, starting with the rattler that had curled around his boots that morning as he'd sunned himself on the back porch of the Reynolds ranch house. It was only quick thinking and a stroke of good fortune that had him reaching for a shovel all while getting his bare feet out of striking range. If he were honest with himself, that was purely a stroke of *dumb* luck. He knew better than to blithely stroll around outside the ranch without protection on his feet.

The dead rattler had been followed by a problem with one of their calves, who even now still showed signs of a rapidly progressing problem that had the little guy lethargic and breathing heavily past his lolling tongue. Ace and two of his ranch hands had tried to restrain him and move him on one of their large transport carriers, but the calf's mother was having none of it. Which had resulted in moving the rest of the herd out of range so they could get the vet out to where the calf needed attention.

And then Walter had thrown the shoe.

"Doc Torres is on her way." Ace's youngest brother, Hoyt, came up next to him, his gaze on the calf. "You have any idea what has him down?"

"I'll give the doctor her due, but for my money it's theileriosis."

"He's the right age for it."

"And we've had a bad tick season so far." While a mature cow could handle ticks with little or no side effects, the calves weren't so lucky. And they were most vulnerable in their first three months of life.

"Doc Torres will know."

"That's why we pay her," Ace said, careful to keep any and all traces of, well, *anything* from his voice.

Hoyt shot him a side-eye but didn't respond, for which Ace was grateful. His youngest brother knew how to keep his thoughts to himself—better than most and certainly better than Ace's two other siblings, Tate and Arden. None of it meant Hoyt wasn't sizing up the situation and coming to what was likely a highly accurate conclusion.

Ace dreaded the arrival of their vet, Veronica Torres. The woman was dedicated and competent, one of the best large-animal vets in the entire state of Texas, but he still wished there was someone—*anyone*—else in Midnight Pass they could work with.

Or, more to the point, someone he hadn't seen naked.

Seen. Touched. Tasted.

An electric series of memories that he had the benefit of reliving each and every time he was in the woman's company. Memories that, even after more than eight years, he could still recall at will and in exquisite detail.

"Tate just texted me. She arrived a few minutes ago and he's driving her out here."

Ace's quick calculation meant they had no more than ten minutes based on their distance from the ranch house. Which meant it was time to get his game face on.

Veronica Torres had once been a fixture around the ranch, his girlfriend and if he'd had the chance nearly his fiancée before he fouled it up in a rush of jealousy and temper. She'd deserved neither and the apology he'd attempted last year, after she'd returned to Midnight Pass, had fallen on stone-deaf ears.

Since the apology was nearly eight years overdue, he'd figured it was his responsibility to give it, but she'd had none of it, brushing off their shared past as if it had been little more than a blip in the history of her life.

It had taken him a damn week to screw up the words to give that apology. Between the overwhelming pain of his father's betrayal and the general all-around asinine behavior he'd swaggered about with in his midtwenties, the apology was not only overdue, but the words were as much about seeking forgiveness as it was purging his soul.

He wasn't that same man and he'd spent the last eight years proving it to himself, even if Veronica hadn't been around to see any of it.

He'd loved her once and he'd let the shame of his father's betrayal burn a hole through him. When it only added fuel to the heat that flared between them, fiery passion had eventually incinerated everything they shared.

"You think we're going to lose the calf?" Hoyt asked, interrupting the spears of annoyance that always accompanied the memory of standing in Veronica's clinic, hat in hand.

"I hope not." Ace eyed the calf. "One of the hands spotted him early and I'm hoping we got to this in time."

"And the others?"

"No signs of distress in any of the other calves, which also reinforces the nasty tick theory."

"'Suppose so." Hoyt kneeled down next to the calf, his attention focused on the fast-growing body that had already doubled in size since birth. He ran his hands gently over the heaving chest cavity, and even from fifteen feet away Ace could hear the labored breathing.

And once again, that spooked feeling settled into his bones, a portent he neither believed in nor cared to imagine.

Even if he couldn't shake it.

That odd anticipation ratcheted up another few notches as one of the ranch trucks came bumping toward them in the distance.

Reynolds Station was large—one of the biggest working cattle ranches in the state of Texas—and covered thousands of prime acreage in the Rio Grande Valley, just north of the US-Mexico border. The land had been in his family for generations and he felt the weight of that heritage in every fiber of his being. The Reynolds brand was as stamped on his DNA as it was the cattle they sent to market each year. He cared about his work and the product they produced.

Maybe a little too much, of late.

The thought poked at him, much as it had the last few times it had cropped up at odd moments, and for a few seconds, Ace gave it the room to linger. He wasn't one to mull things over or dwell on his problems—he far preferred action and activity—but something had changed of late. Both his brothers were in relationships—Tate about to marry his old flame, Detective Belle Granger, and Hoyt married to pretty high school teacher Reese Grantham. He'd added two sisters to the fold with Belle and Reese, in addition to Arden, his sister by blood, and the house was full to brimming with new energy.

New *female* energy.

And a shocking amount of hormones, Ace admitted to himself, since Reese was growing by the day in the full bloom of her pregnancy.

Women were plentiful in the Pass, but he wasn't interested in the ones who quickly sidled up at the bar or made flirtatious comments at the town diner. He'd long been aware a pair of jeans and a cowboy hat did something to the female libido and he'd be a liar if he didn't cop to taking full advantage of that fact from time to time, especially in his younger days.

But in the past year, something had changed. It wasn't just his brothers' steady march to the altar, either.

It was him.

The lack of commitment in his personal life had always been a fine thing. He'd had his grand romance and learned a ton from the broken wreckage that came after, ensuring he had no desire to wade into those deep waters ever again. You didn't get perfect twice and he'd long come to accept that. Add on that his business was his life and he'd learned to put women in a category his heart *and* his head could handle.

He respected them. He was up front and honest. And he made it clear that sex and time spent together was a fun distraction. That attitude had been enough. More than enough, for the past eight years.

Until she'd come back.

"Doc Torres is here." Hoyt pointed toward the horizon as a Reynolds Station truck came bouncing over the dirt path.

"So she is."

Ace shook off the weird sensation that he'd been thinking about Veronica Torres's arrival back in his life, only to have her physically appear, but he knew it was more than simple coincidence that they needed her today. She really was the best damn large-animal vet in all of Texas and, in a state where the management and sale of cattle still reigned supreme, there were a lot of good veterinarians.

But she was the best.

And the best was the only thing he wanted for Reynolds Station.

He couldn't see her yet but he knew what to expect when she got out of the truck. Her dark hair would be pulled back in a high ponytail and her long, lithe frame would be covered head to toe in some sort of work shirt and khakis. It was damn near a uniform and he'd never, ever seen a woman who could pull off such drab clothes with Veronica's elegance.

Of course, drab clothes couldn't hide knockout curves, nor could they dim the beauty of her soft, flawless, olive-toned skin.

But it was the competence, Ace had to admit, that wrapped up the whole package. She was smart. Dedicated. And absolutely devoted to the animals under her care. She loved them as much as she did the art and science of treating them.

There was no doubt about it, Dr. Veronica Torres had it all.

And once upon a time, they'd had each other, too.

Veronica appreciated Tate Reynolds's ability to keep up a steady drone of friendly conversation, but even the company of a very attractive cowboy with a big grin couldn't assuage her nerves at what was to come.

Ace Reynolds.

The one man she'd spent most of the last decade doing her level best to forget.

Or, if she was being truly honest, exorcise.

She wasn't a person who looked to the past. Her profession, while steeped in history and reliant on experience, was forward-facing. Science and technology led the way. New ways of examining a problem, new treatments and always—*always*—that focus on the next big breakthrough.

While she'd chosen animals over treating people, the goals of her profession were still in lockstep with all other facets of modern medicine.

Survival.

Comfort.

And the advancement of life.

She'd made it her life's work, even if that had come at the expense of the rest of her existence. Her marriage certainly hadn't managed to survive it, either, and its demise, as well as a shocking act of violence, had had her fleeing Houston as fast as her legs could carry her.

Why she'd picked Midnight Pass as her landing spot still surprised her at times.

It shouldn't have, since she'd taken over the practice of her old mentor, but she had come to realize it was a bit of an ill-conceived decision. The offer of the practice, just as she was trying to escape Houston, had seemed like the perfect answer to her troubles. Instead of running with her proverbial tail tucked between her legs, she'd had a business opportunity that called her to South Texas.

It was only after she arrived and realized just how much time her mentor had spent out at the three largest ranches in the southern portion of the state—all denizens of Midnight Pass and the majority of the practice's clientele—that she'd realized her mistake.

Working with the Vasquez family, no problem. Same with the Crown Ranch. But Reynolds Station?

Was it just her imagination or did they have need of her services more often than the others?

The thought had bugged her so badly she'd made a point to look it up, reviewing all her case files a few weeks back to see how often she'd had appointments at Reynolds Station. Not only was that assumption false— the Crowns had faced a bad patch of infection that had caused considerable issues for their herd and the Vasquez family was still struggling with a bad run of herd births that had reduced their stock for the season—but she'd actually spent far less time at Reynolds Station than she'd have expected for clients of their size.

And even if she didn't see Ace each time she was at the ranch, why did Reynolds Station feel so *present*?

The thought haunted her as Tate turned off the dirt path and onto a rich patch of land, ripe with verdant grass. She took in the lush pasture and already began running through a mental list of things that could be wrong with the small but solid calf laid out on the grass between several watchful ranch hands and their boss.

Ace Reynolds.

Since her body came to life with anticipation at the very thought of him, seeing him was almost painful. Heavy pulse, racing thoughts and shocked-to-the-core nerve endings all lit up in full tempo, like a manic orchestra, as she took in the thick, muscular form, long legs clad in worn jeans and about an acre of chest covered in a white T-shirt under a long-sleeved blue shirt.

If she had a camera, she'd have called the resulting shot the Quintessential American Cowboy.

And then she'd have privately titled it Emotional Train Wreck because that's what resulted every freaking time she saw him.

Goodness, how did he manage it? Every. Single. Time.

She'd seen good-looking men before. Her ex-husband had been an attractive man. Mild-mannered and more refined than Ace, but attractive all the same. Yet neither Mark nor anyone else she'd ever met could leave her feeling quite so breathless.

Those long legs currently bunched beneath him as he kneeled beside the calf. He'd removed the hat he was rarely without, giving him room to bend his dark blond head toward the animal. His hair was close-cropped, sun threading lighter streaks of blond artfully around the crown of his head.

But it was that jaw that got her every time. It looked like it was chiseled out of Texas granite, smooth and hard and, as her memories reminded her far too often, absolutely implacable when he chose to be.

"We've got him comfortable over there." Tate pointed through the windshield. Even with the obvious statement—words that had nothing to do with his brother and everything to do with the small calf who needed her attention—Veronica was grateful for the few extra seconds the man's words provided. "His mama's fretting, but they're keeping her at bay."

Several yards away from the downed calf Veronica could see where the hands had created a makeshift corral for the fretting mother, a large ring of Reynolds Station trucks penning her in, while several of those hands stood on the truck beds, lassoes at the ready. One other held a tranq gun, which she recognized from her inspections on the equipment the past month.

"I'm glad to see she hasn't had to be put under. The little guy's going to need her alert and attentive, assuming we can get him back on his feet."

"Do you think we're going to lose him?"

"Not if I can help it."

With professional determination brimming in her blood, Veronica pushed out of the truck and willed that attitude to carry her through the rushing pulse, maddeningly thudding heart and the mix of glorious and bitter memories that always flooded her mind where Ace Reynolds was concerned.

It was time to do her job.

The ranch hands quickly made room for her, several offering a respectful tip of their hats or a murmured "hello, ma'am" as she came up to the group. She nodded silently to each of them, but it was Ace who held her focus.

"How long has he been like this?"

"Hello to you, too."

She nearly stumbled at that—there was no need to get rude—but goodness, the man made her forget herself. On a firm nod, she added, "Hello, Ace."

When Ace only stared at her, something warm yet speculative in his deep green gaze, she did nearly stomp her foot. Willing the emotion back, she added a smile and hoped like hell it didn't come off as a grimace. "How's the little guy doing?"

Seemingly satisfied with the shift in attitude, Ace dropped to his haunches next to the calf. "We noticed it early this morning that he seemed to have some trouble keeping up. By afternoon he was lagging and we finally pulled him out of the herd." Ace glanced over his shoulder. "His mama's none too happy about the situation."

"I imagine she's not."

Whether it was their attention on the mother or the animal's patience finally slipping its short tether, Veronica didn't know, but the cow cried out, her large body bumping hard into one of the trucks penning her in.

One of the hands shouted, "We need some help!"

Tate rushed off toward the ranch hands, Ace nearly on his heels, when Veronica reached out and laid a hand on his arm. "I need one of you."

"Of course."

The sounds of the angry mama and shouting men echoed from the distance but Veronica drowned it out. She needed to focus and she needed to do it fast before Mama got a dose of the tranq.

Ace had already returned to his position next to the calf and Veronica dropped down beside him, refusing to acknowledge—even to herself—the warm, masculine scent of him. He'd always smelled of leather and fresh air and horse and she was grateful the ground was close by because that particular combination always made her knees weak.

Damn hormones.

She hadn't even felt this rush of lust and longing for her husband, which, in hindsight, was likely a sign their marriage was doomed from the start. She'd shrugged it off at the time—few men were as impressively virile as a cowboy and Ace Reynolds was the very finest of that breed. Strong, strapping build, slim hips and telltale lines at the corners of his eyes from a life spent out in the sun.

Those creases had been faint lines when they'd been together, but even then, he'd been maniacal about moisturizing and protecting his skin. The doctor in her appreciated his diligence, and the woman in her could appreciate the supple smoothness of his skin. Worn but not leathered, and from the looks of it, not much had changed on that front over the past decade.

Frustrated at the train of her thoughts—especially when the calf before her so obviously needed help—Veronica pulled herself back from the abyss. Thoughts of Ace Reynolds were wasted time and effort. He'd made himself more than clear all those years ago and she was smart enough to know a dog didn't change its spots.

"It's okay, little one." She laid a hand on the calf's head, holding him still as she bent closer to breathe him in. While she had a strong suspicion on what ailed him from her initial glance over his body, she knew that looking into his eyes and smelling him would go a long way toward understanding his symptoms.

Side benefit: it also drowned out the scent of Ace, who still hovered so close.

Veronica knew it was odd—she'd been told as much by her colleagues in Houston—but from the start she'd understood that successfully practicing veterinarian medicine was all about using her senses. Animals couldn't communicate what was wrong so it was up to her to use every tool at her disposal to make an accurate diagnosis, from blood work and tests to paying very close attention in the field.

The large brown eyes that stared back at her had grown rheumy with his illness, but even with his lethargic state, she didn't miss the fear. Animals were far more pragmatic about illness than humans, but she also had a strong sense when their spirits weren't ready to move on.

This little guy was a fighter.

Veronica sat back, about to make her assessment, when Ace dived in. "Hoyt and I think it's theileriosis."

"You and Hoyt know your medicine. You're absolutely right. I'll take a blood sample to confirm but I'm going to start him on a course of treatment right away. I'll get in touch later with the test results but you need to get him to a quiet area away from the other calves. Let him rest with his mama."

"You think he'll be okay?" He laid a hand on her forearm, the first notes of anxiety working its way through the light tremble of his fingers.

She stared at that large hand, where it lay over her skin. His fingers were strong, work-roughened and tanned, and without warning, memories of those fingers trailing over her skin assailed her.

Why was it so easy to remember? she thought as a light shudder cratered her stomach.

Or maybe a better question was, why was it so hard to forget?

Ignoring the questions she had no business asking herself, she reached for her medicine bag. The move was enough to have his hand slipping away and it gave her the needed space to focus on the calf. "I think I'm glad you called."

Those strong fingers reached for her forearm once more. "That's not what I asked."

Veronica avoided a heavy exhale from her suspended breath and once more ignored the shot of warmth that her body seemed incapable of suppressing. Like an illness, Ace Reynolds had invaded her system years ago and she'd never fully developed a resistance to him.

Nor had it helped that their businesses would put them into close contact far too often. As a large-animal vet, her practice depended on the work that came from Reynolds Station as well as the Vasquez and Crown families. She needed Ace Reynolds on her side.

"He's a fighter. I can see that when I look at him. Pamper him for a few days and I do think he'll come out the other side of this."

"Thank you."

Tate rejoined them from where he'd worked with the other assembled hands. "We really appreciate your quick attention on this."

"It's okay. I'm just going to get his blood work and get him started on the antibiotics and we'll go from there. I'll plan on swinging by later with the results so I can check on him."

"We'd appreciate that." Tate nodded his head, tipping his hat. "Take your time now. I'll drive you back to the house when you're ready."

Everyone gave her a wide berth as she finished up what she needed to do. It was only once she'd completed the course of treatment and packed everything back up that she began to give orders.

"His mother's getting more and more agitated again. You have a plan for releasing her?"

Ace nodded. "We're going to get you out of here and then we'll move the trucks that have her penned in."

While she'd ignored the distant sounds of distress while working on the calf, Veronica couldn't miss the ever-increasing frustration that came from the direction of the hands who currently surrounded the calf's mother. Her breathing was heavy and her eyes had grown wider with her distress.

"I'd like to watch."

"From the truck."

Veronica had her own tranq gun but thought better of brandishing it around. She was a good shot herself but didn't expect things would come to that. The mother wanted her baby and once they took away the barrier she expected things to return to normal.

"Yes, Ace, from the truck."

In moments, Veronica was back beside Tate in the cab of the truck, the ground near the calf cleared. Each of the ranch hands had taken cover in their vehicles along with Ace and Hoyt. Three remained on guard, one with the tranquilizer and the other two with lassoes, but as Veronica expected, the moment the mother was freed from the barrier of the trucks, she raced to her young.

As Mama bent down to nuzzle her baby, Veronica had a deep shot of satisfaction when the calf lifted his head in response. Oh, yeah, the little guy was on the mend. A few days of rest and the miracle of antibiotics and he would be back to normal.

"You ready to go, Doc?" Tate asked.

Although at least thirty yards separated them, she didn't miss the way Ace stared out of the front window of his truck, his focus on the calf. "I am."

Just before Tate backed the truck up, Ace lifted his

gaze, those vivid green eyes catching hers. She saw his gratitude moments before he lifted the tips of his fingers to the brim of his hat.

But it was the heated look that followed, his gaze never wavering, that haunted her. She remembered that gaze. Remembered all that would follow whenever their eyes met.

Veronica hoped like hell she could keep her distance. She'd done well enough since returning to the Pass, but every woman had her limits. And if the heat that coursed through her body at that simple look was any indication, she was going to have to double her efforts to resist him.

Chapter 2

The scent of steak and onions hit him the moment he walked into the kitchen.

His baby sister, Arden, had always been a stellar cook, but the addition of Hoyt's new wife, Reese, had added an extra dimension to Reynolds family dinners. A high school English teacher, she was more than willing to come home a few days a week and put together a feast for dinner. A glance at the counter at the tortillas and veggies and cheese told him fajitas were on the menu and that put a solidly positive end on a challenging day.

It also meant he got a day off from his usual cooking duty. Since he'd planned his own rousing "feast" of hot dogs in spaghetti, Ace figured the entire family would heave a collective sigh of relief. He certainly wasn't a Neanderthal—and he usually did better than serving a meal well-suited for an eight-year-old—but it was fun to have someone at the ranch who actually enjoyed cooking.

The gently rounded figure standing before the stove fit that bill. Reese turned, her pregnant belly now visible beneath her apron, her smile wide. "Was that a groan of happiness or despair?"

Ace leaned in to buss her cheek. "Happiness. No doubt about it. It smells amazing in here."

"Blame it on the baby. He or she's hungry for steak tonight so I swung by the market for the rest of the fixins' on the drive home from work."

"My niece or nephew has amazing taste."

Ace's gaze dipped to that pregnant stomach before lifting back to the glowing face.

It still amazed him how quickly things had changed. While the baby had been an unexpected blessing for Hoyt and Reese, they were all excited for the child's arrival. Hope, Arden had called the baby, and she was right. After Reese's father had been discovered as a serial killer, brandishing his own form of vigilante justice on the drug dealers who moved their wares through the Pass, she'd had to face the fallout—the censure of the town and the risk of her teaching job, all while still grieving the death of her father. The fact that she and Hoyt had found each other in the midst of that grief was a miracle unto itself.

The addition of a new life had only added to the joy.

Without warning, an image of Veronica pregnant filled his thoughts. Although they'd dated for several years, in all that time, their conversations had never drifted to children or a future.

"Live in the moment" had been their unspoken moniker.

Hadn't that been a big part of the problem in the end?

"Ace?"

He keyed back into Reese's presence, her head cocked slightly to the side in concern. "You okay?"

"Yeah. Sorry." He shook his head. "I'm good."

"Would you mind helping me? I need that large platter up over the fridge."

He saw the curiosity in her eyes and had the strangest urge to tell her about the afternoon with the calf, but held back, turning to the cabinets instead. The platter was where it had been all his life—and it was only when he pulled it down that his knees nearly buckled at the overwhelming sense of stagnation.

His brothers had moved forward. In addition to Hoyt's marriage to Reese and impending fatherhood, Tate was weeks away from marrying his high school sweetheart, Detective Belle Granger. They were building a home on the property and would be out of the ranch house by the end of the year.

Yet here he was.

Life was the same. Unrelentingly so. Even that damn platter, nestled in the same place it had been since he was a small boy, seemed to suggest an odd sense of immobility.

The seasons came and went, each with their own rhythm, and when he looked back over them they seemed to have passed in a blur. The business his father had nearly run into the ground was once again thriving. His family was well.

It was his life that seemed strangely empty.

He handed over the platter and made a few quick excuses to leave. "If you're good, I'm going to go get cleaned up for dinner."

Reese nodded, the subtle sense of expectation and—oddly—understanding in her gaze never wavering. "Of course. I'm nearly done here so dinner'll be on the table in about a half hour."

"Plenty of time."

He turned, anxious to get out of the kitchen, when Reese's voice stopped him.

"Ace?"

He turned at the door, pushing a grin he didn't feel to diffuse the suddenly heavy moment. "What else do you need?"

"Just a question."

"Shoot."

"Hoyt mentioned there was a problem with one of the calves today. Is the little one okay?"

That sense of unease grew stronger when he saw Reese abstractly rub her belly. Once again quelling thoughts of Veronica, he forced his gaze to Reese's. "Looks like he's going to be just fine. When we left him this afternoon he was standing and following his mother."

"Hoyt said Dr. Torres was really good with him. Quick and competent."

"She was."

"That's good." Reese nodded. "Hoyt has always spoken well of her."

"We're lucky to have someone of her skill in the Pass. I know there's a lot of business between us and Crown and Vasquez for a large-animal vet, but not everyone wants to live down here."

"She was gone a long time. It's good to have her back."

"Sure is."

Their conversation hung between them, an ocean of words unsaid, but Ace refrained from saying anything else.

Reese had lived in the Pass her whole life, same as

him. She knew everyone in town and, although she was younger, that included Veronica Torres. He knew his sister-in-law was angling for something, but he'd be dipped in mosquitoes before he was willing to explore whatever it was that had put that thoughtful, musing look on her pretty face.

Reese was quiet, but her still waters ran deep. It made her a great match for his brother but it also meant she saw more than she let on. Well, she could think whatever she wanted in this case.

He knew there hadn't really been anything to see in a very long time.

Veronica took the long drive down the main entrance to Reynolds Station for the second time that day. Knots lined her belly, tightening with every yard she drove closer to the ranch house.

"It's a professional visit," she whispered to herself. "You're just delivering test results like you promised."

The quiet mutter did nothing to ease the knots. In fact, as the ranch house came into view, they only wrapped more tightly around each other. Which in addition to making her feel slightly nauseated, had the secondary effect of pissing her off.

She hated feeling cornered. It was one of the emotions she keyed in on with her animal charges and which made her a good vet. She innately knew how they felt and responded in a way designed to put them at ease. Whether two-legged or four-, no living creature liked the sensation of being boxed in.

It was a lesson life had taught her early—and which her marriage had reinforced—and it had left an indelible mark.

With a focus on deep, even breaths, she tried to will the sensation away. She *wasn't* cornered. She was a professional, here on a professional errand. It would hardly do to walk in with a puss on her face and knocking knees.

Despite her best efforts, the roiling thoughts refused to fade as she parked, walked up to the side door to the kitchen and knocked. It was only as the door swung open, the smiling face of Tate Reynolds there to greet her, that Veronica recognized her mistake.

The distinct scents of dinner wafted past the threshold and five pairs of eyes in addition to Tate's assessed her from inside the kitchen.

"I'm so sorry to disturb you."

"Not at all." Tate waved her in. "In fact, I'd say you're just in time. We're about to dive into a lake of fajitas."

"Oh, no, I can't—"

Belle Granger moved up next to Tate, her smile as welcome as his. Veronica had heard they were engaged and the easy way Belle laid a hand on Tate's shoulder told that story better than any town gossip. "Veronica! It's good to see you again."

"Hi, Belle."

Before she could say anything further, she was pulled in tight for a warm hug. "It's been too long."

While there were some who Veronica would brush off as simply offering polite platitudes, there was nothing facile about Belle. Although they had a few years between them, Veronica had always felt the younger woman was the salt of the earth. Now knowing what she'd been through over the past year—discovering her boss had become a serial killer, taking down drug dealers who flooded Midnight Pass and on into South Texas with any manner of dangerous and illegal substances— Veronica only felt that description to be even more perfect.

"It has been too long." Veronica was touched by the extra squeeze Belle gave her before pulling back.

"Come on in. Your timing is perfect—we're just about to eat. Join us." Belle gestured her fully into the kitchen, which had the distinctly uncomfortable outcome of putting Veronica directly next to Ace.

"Veronica." Ace tipped his head. "It's good to see you again."

"Ace." She nearly stumbled over that lone word. Had there been a day since she was introduced to him twelve years ago that his name hadn't whispered through her mind? She rarely gave it space on her lips, but that hadn't stopped her traitorous memory from thinking of him often.

Too often.

Using that as armor, she kept her smile polite.

"Oh, I don't want to intrude. I just wanted to bring over the results. On the calf. Like I promised." The words felt stilted and her tongue felt too big for her mouth, like she was one of the animals she treated for heat exhaustion, their tongues lolling and drooping toward the ground.

Sexy image, Torres.

Why, oh, why hadn't she just sent her assistant? The Reynolds ranch was on Julie's way home and she could have dropped off the report without incident.

Or a dinner invitation.

"Thanks for doing that," Ace said. "The little guy seems to be improving. A few of the hands kept an eye on him from a distance and I drove out at the end of the day to check myself. He's standing. He's a bit wobbly still, but I figure it's a sign the antibiotics are working if he's up and moving. I even saw him trotting a bit after his mama as I drove away."

"A very good sign."

The urge to prickle up in his presence was always strong, but it was hard to feel anything but a sappy sort of appreciation at his obvious care for his stock. It was one of the things that had attracted her to him from the start—his obvious love for what he did and his abiding commitment to the well-being of the animals they raised. It was a funny juxtaposition, especially since the core of their business was to treat those animals as product, yet she knew without a doubt that Ace had a deep affection for the animals they raised on Reynolds land.

"Please stay." A woman Veronica recognized as Reese Grantham—now Reese Reynolds—turned from the stove. She handed a spatula to her husband, Hoyt, and moved closer. Veronica noticed the woman's pregnancy immediately and felt a wholly unexpected shot of envy light up her stomach, replacing the nerves that had only just settled.

Pregnant and awaiting new life. What must that be like?

As a vet, she was used to the annual foaling of the four-footed variety. While she'd never compare those babies to children, she both understood the mechanics of how babies were made and how they came into the world. She wasn't a woman who reacted to pregnant bellies.

All evidence to the contrary by the wicked green tentacles of envy that still wrapped around her midsection with a tight squeeze.

A pointed stare between Reese and Hoyt had the man jumping up from his seat and gesturing her toward the table. "Sit down here and I'll get another chair from the dining room."

Veronica would have laughed at the funny tableau if she weren't the object of that intense focus. The abject desire to flee still rumbled through her stomach in hard waves, but to refuse now would look rude. Especially since she hadn't been quick or clever enough to give an excuse when she stood on the other side of the kitchen door, the enticing scent of fajitas nearly as big a lure as the large, sexy frame of Ace Reynolds.

"Veronica, tell us all about your practice." Belle eagerly took the opening conversation gambit the moment they were all settled at the table, large tortillas covering their homey, multicolored plates as bowls of meat, cheese, peppers and onions and sour cream passed from hand to hand.

Although she and Ace had dated for several years, the fact that the foundations of his family were crumbling at the time had ensured there were very few shared meals with his parents. His father's disgrace—selling illegal meat from their cattle operations—had nearly railroaded the business, the man's death six months later only adding to the confusion and stress and sadness that had pervaded Ace's life during that period.

"Things are going well. I bought it from Dr. Talente once he decided to retire. We'd kept in touch after I worked for him out of vet school and his offer came at the perfect time."

"Why's that?" The question was innocent enough, but Tate's vivid green eyes quickly narrowed and he barely concealed a hard grunt as Belle's foot connected with his shin.

Or that's what Veronica assumed when his grunt came

mere moments after she'd heard a distinct thud coming from beneath the table. Taking pity on the cute and, at the moment clueless, cowboy Veronica said, "I was going through a divorce at the time."

"I'm sorry to hear that." Tate recovered quickly. "And apologize for the seriously poor judgment of my sex."

"Why do you assume it was her husband's fault?"

Ace asked the question in a deceptively low voice, the green gaze that was an identical match to his brother's nearly smoldering from across the table.

"You'll have to excuse my brother." Tate's smile never wavered, an unholy light filling his eyes. "He nearly got the fang end of a snake this morning curled up in his boots. Clearly some venom found its way in even without a solid bite."

"I was only making an observation," Ace muttered. "Veronica's a smart, ambitious businesswoman. Maybe her ex wasn't worth sticking around for. A woman can make that decision for herself."

While Ace appeared chastened, Veronica couldn't deny the strange turn of the conversation had put her in a rather favorable light. While she wasn't ready to call a truce, she was in Ace's house eating his dinner. The least she could do was hold up her side of the conversation.

"A lovely thing to say and, in the end, there was little blame and just the sad acknowledgment on both sides it was time to move on." The exact opposite, she admitted to herself, of her raging, smoking, incendiary breakup with Ace.

Of course, she could say all this now, but there had still been moments in the marriage when watching it dissolve before her eyes had caused immeasurable pain. What Veronica hadn't quite figured out was how that pain had seemingly vanished over the past year since returning to the Pass, leaving nothing behind but an empty void. No sadness. No grief.

And such little feeling it scared her sometimes.

Shouldn't a person *feel* more?

Because if you didn't feel anything, didn't that somehow mean it had never meant all that much in the first place?

Conversation shifted to a funny story that had happened to Reese with a few of her students and it gave Veronica a respite from the questions. It also gave her a chance to catch up on all that had happened since the last time she'd lived here.

The discussion moved on from teenage hormones, the table full of easy conversation and laughter. Belle and Tate were in high spirits as they discussed their upcoming wedding and their plans for a honeymoon in Hawaii. Hoyt talked of a particularly inventive herd rotation he'd been studying and asked her opinion on it, and Arden spoke of a few Pilates classes she was looking to pilot at a studio in town where she already taught yoga class.

Everyone had plans and activities, not to mention the ever-present hum of excitement that a new baby was on the way.

Only Ace remained quiet.

Oh, sure, she was likely the last person he'd expected at his dinner table that evening, but she was unable to shake the sensation that there was something else hovering just beneath the surface. Something more than the simple discomfort of spending dinner with an ex.

Because, as the conversation had continued, each adult around the table contributing some story or anecdote, Ace grew quiet. He was physically there, but it seemed the conversation flowed around him, rather than including him.

For all her memories of Ace Reynolds as a larger-than-life figure, it was almost as if he'd faded into the background, still there in solid form yet quietly growing invisible. But what really bothered her was the fact that she recognized the look.

Hell, she'd lived it.

The feeling that conversation and plans and life were happening around you, not to you.

While she loved her career, working with animals, publishing papers and even contributing to a new drug trial with a major pharmaceutical company, she couldn't deny there was something missing. She'd excused it for far too long as the aftereffects of a divorce, but as the memories of day-to-day life with Mark had faded, Veronica had to admit there was more to it. Something had been missing for a lot longer than the dissolution of her marriage.

Something, she thought, a lot like Ace Reynolds.

Ace had never considered himself a particularly philosophical man. He didn't have those quiet depths like Hoyt or the easy laugher like Tate or the carefree attitude that Arden possessed as youngest and only girl of the family. No, he'd always carried his role as oldest son with a mix of gravitas and wry good humor. That subtle knowledge that he could handle whatever came his way because, whether he liked it or not, he had little choice in the matter.

It had been true of Ace's father's professional ruin, followed on quickly by his subsequent failed health. His mother's death had been equally hard, for entirely different reasons. And even the pressure of running the business—of bringing it back from the very brink of failure—had simply been something he'd done.

No, he amended to himself, something he'd *handled*.

He was the oldest and he'd had damn near thirty-five years of being good at it.

But the sad truth was, you didn't handle a person. And it had taken him far too long to realize that the same approach he took to life—taking charge and getting things done—didn't apply to relationships.

Shrugging off the town's words and the cutting remarks of your suppliers was something you got through. Not sharing the pain of that with your partner, when it happened at a town barbecue in earshot of her, simply did not work. Neither did working yourself near to death as an excuse to miss family events. And it sure as hell didn't work when the person who claimed to love you was brushed off time and again when she had both a well of love and unending patience *and* the professional wherewithal to help.

At the time, he'd comforted himself with the idea that Veronica was equally at fault. That their matched tempers and fiery personalities were as volatile and risk-prone as a lit match in the barn.

But with time, he'd understood something else.

The fault had sat squarely with him.

He'd come to accept it long ago. Hell, it was why he'd tried to make that damn apology after she'd returned to town. Only she'd ignored it, offering up a small smile that smacked of pity and the clear indication she'd long ago moved on.

Which was why, after he'd walked his plate to the

sink, he'd decided his evening of making nice was over. "I need to go out and check on Walter."

"What happened to him?" Arden sat up, alarmed.

Ace ran a hand over a day's worth of stubble, the sudden spotlight making him want to fidget. Forcing a casual note into his tone—one that did not convey his true feelings of "let me out of here as fast as possible"—he played it cool. "He threw a shoe this morning and the farrier can't get out until tomorrow. I want to check on him and give him an extra bit of attention."

"Can I take a look at him?" Veronica asked before adding on, "I'll make sure nothing's bothering him."

"The farrier'll check him out when he adds a new shoe."

"And if he finds something, I'll be right back out here. Let me look now."

Since Veronica was already out of her seat, Ace fought the urge to shrug and extended a hand toward the door. "The barn's out this way."

Which she already knew but it was too late to pull back the inane comment or the subtle heat creeping up the back of his neck as a kitchen full of his nearest and dearest watched him walk out the door with his old flame.

Ignoring them all, Ace let the door slam heavy in his wake. An action that only got a laugh out of Tate, evident even on the other side. If she'd heard the laugh or felt the underlying tension, Veronica ignored it—instead, walking on ahead, her focus determinedly on the barn.

Oh, yeah, she heard it. Which meant she'd also heard the unspoken subtext, too.

"Sorry to cut your dinner short. I do appreciate you taking a look at Walter."

"It's no problem. And like I said, it'll save me a trip

out tomorrow if Tom Statler does find something when he's putting on the new shoe."

"Suppose so."

"Excuse me?" Veronica asked as she swung the barn door wide.

"Just that you're always right. And efficient. No use in making two trips when you can make one."

The dim yellow lights of the barn backlit her against the halo of the strong overhead that came on as they'd crossed the back parking area in the darkness. That confluence of light made a strange sort of half mask over her face. Was she angry? Confused? Irritated?

All of the above?

And all valid since he'd suddenly opted to make an ass of himself in the face of a professional courtesy.

Ace swatted at the creeping heat at the back of his neck, rubbing at the base and the growing tension there, before tapping in the code to open the barn door. Their newly installed security system matched the scent of fresh wood, both the result of the fire that had swept through a few months back.

"The barn looks great." Veronica glanced around, the seeds of their argument vanishing into mist. "I can't believe how fast you've gotten it done."

"It was a priority. And it's amazing what you can do if you pay a premium. As it always has, money talks."

"I guess it does." Veronica continued to look around at the updated interior, her concern for the horses evident as she checked out the neat rows of stall doors. A light pat here and sweet words floated into the air as she talked to each horse in turn.

"How has Reese handled it all?"

The question was casual but Ace didn't miss the

deeper meaning behind it all. The months since Reese had been terrorized by her late brother's ex-girlfriend had given her time to heal, but that tense and frightening time had taken a toll.

That was part of why they'd pushed so hard to have the barn completed. The burned, hulled-out husk that had stood before had only served as a dark reminder of the fire that had been deliberately set. Hoyt had been adamant that they remove the blight as fast as humanly possible and Ace, Tate and Arden had all agreed.

"She'd doing well," Ace finally said. "That time was scary, but Loretta Chapel is getting the help she needs and I think that's let Reese rest easier."

"I'd say it's a testament to how kind and caring your sister-in-law is. Few people would find forgiveness so quickly."

"Few people are Reese."

It was true and a very real testament to the woman Hoyt had found to share his life with. Reese Grantham Reynolds had faced more hardship in her life than anyone should, yet she'd managed to come out the other side whole and as deeply caring as anyone Ace knew.

He was happy for his brother and it was moments like this when he remembered how much he enjoyed seeing his family happy and looking toward the future. And how little he cared for the more maudlin moments that had dogged him earlier.

He'd always pictured his own forever as some sort of distant future in his mind's eye. Someday he'd settle down. Someday he'd have a family of his own. Someday he'd look out over the land that made up Reynolds Station and pass it on to his children.

Only someday had never come.

There was only now. And the very real truth that the one woman who had made him think of *someday* had left. Her reasons had been fair—and the fault lay more with him than her—but she was the one who'd moved on with another.

So damn quickly his head had spun.

"Few people are." Veronica smiled, her solid affirmation about Reese proof she was oblivious to his thoughts.

She'd always had that, he mused. The ready ability to see the good in others and a willingness to say so. So many seemed to worry that praising another was somehow minimalizing themselves. But not Veronica.

She looked for the best and found it. Why hadn't that carried over to the way she'd felt about him?

"It's good work in here," Veronica added. "I can see the additional security and I'm assuming you've got all this hardwired to your phone."

"Phone, tablet and devices in all the trucks."

"Well done." She looked around once more. "Let's go see Walter."

"He's down the end on the left."

The horses whickered lightly as they passed and Ace distributed the handful of snatched sugar cubes he'd secreted when he walked in. The trauma to the barn had affected their four-legged family, as well, and he'd been the first to find ways to make their transition back into the space as easy as possible. A few sweet treats had made the assimilation to their updated home go a bit smoother.

Veronica turned at Walter's stall and caught him as he gave a cube to Tate's horse, Tot, in the next stall. "They all seem pretty fond of the Willy Wonka routine."

Once again, that damnable heat crept up his neck. He might have been able to hide it in the dark outside but there was no hiding in the fluorescent overheads. "It's just a little something to make them happy."

"I didn't say I don't approve. Especially as this is good working stock that gets regular exercise. It's just cute, is all." She opened Walter's stall door and stepped in. "Sweet, I'd say."

"Do bad puns come with the checkup?"

Veronica didn't miss a beat. "They do when it's free."

Although the rebuild had given them a chance to expand the stall sizes, the space was still small and narrow and Ace couldn't miss the fresh scent he always associated with Veronica. She was of the earth. It was the only way he'd ever been able to think of it, with a tantalizing hint of spring always floating in her wake.

It made no sense since the woman spent her day with large animals but it was undeniably true, he acknowledged to himself as the distinct hints of fresh meadow and honeysuckle filled his head with fanciful thoughts.

"He looks good." She stood back up to her full height from where she'd bent over Walter's foreleg. "He's strong and healthy and in beautiful condition."

"Walter's an amazing horse."

"He also gets amazing care. That's a testament to you."

With her passion for animals, there was no higher praise a person could receive from Veronica Torres.

"Thank you." Despite the fresh air they pumped in with a brand-new filtration system, something seemed to still, hovering between the two of them. Even Walter recognized it, his ears perking up as he stood completely still, watching them both.

"Thank you for dinner. I didn't plan to stay but—" She broke off, her brown eyes wide-open windows to memories he knew were best left buried.

They'd been down this road before. Had spent their relationship in a heated, fiery passion that had ultimately left them both raw and shell-shocked. Or it had left *him* that way. She'd moved on pretty quickly, marrying barely a year later.

Which had only reopened a wound he'd believed healed but had to admit hadn't even closed.

So why was all of that so hard to remember as they stood close together, the stall door at his back? Why was it even harder to remember as she took a step closer, her hand lifting to rest on his chest?

And then Veronica was the only thing he could remember—the only thing he could *feel*—as she lifted her head, pressing her lips to his and forcing the rest of the world to fall away.

Chapter 3

What was she doing?

That lone thought whispered over and over as Veronica continued to kiss Ace. A kiss she'd started but which he'd rapidly caught up with, his strong arms wrapping around her with all the strength of forged steel. Steel that layered over one impressively built cowboy, with muscles that bunched and banded and *held*.

God, how she remembered this. How she remembered *him*. And how she remembered how good everything felt with him.

The man knew how to kiss. Hard and strong or soft and lazy, it didn't matter. He managed a powerful mix of all of that, his tongue sweeping through her mouth, forceful at times, only to take her to new heights when he nibbled her lower lip with his teeth. She struggled to keep up—to ride the roller coaster of emotion Ace Reynolds could dish up even after all this time.

This was why she'd stayed away from him since returning to Midnight Pass. Why she'd kept her distance, well aware their past could only cloud her future. Why she'd given him a polite, vague smile that day he'd come to apologize, leaving her heart cracked in two at the sweetness once he drove away.

And it was why, like moth to flame, she was right back here in his arms.

The thought was enough to pull her from the spell and she tore herself away from Ace—and the steady flame that hadn't ever really died out.

"Well. If you wanted to get me alone, darlin'." The grin that accompanied the lazy words was altogether too cocky and she nearly rose to the bait—and the verbal urge to slap back—until she saw the blown pupils in the midst of his green eyes.

He was as shell-shocked as she was and, if she wasn't misreading the signs, was equally affected by that kiss.

"I came out here to do my job," she muttered. "It's time I left."

"What's your hurry?"

"It looks like you were right all along. Walter's fine, just a thrown shoe."

"Yet you came out here, anyway."

"I know my way around a barn." She pushed away from him, the heat of his body as delicious as it was oppressive. "I could have easily come out to check on him on my own."

"And what sort of host would I be?"

Satisfied she'd put enough distance between them as she stood on the opposite side of the hall that bisected the stalls, Veronica stared at him. "The sort that lets the hired help do their job."

"Hired help?"

"You have a different definition?"

"You're a highly paid professional, whose services this ranch depends on. What sort of crap is this, calling yourself the hired help?"

As arguments went she'd picked a lame one, but Veronica was working off pure adrenaline. And the knowledge that she was solely responsible for getting herself into this situation.

She'd insisted on coming to the barn. And she was the one who'd decided to see if her heated memories of kissing him were as sweet and sexy as the ones that lived in her mind, even if she had compressed and suppressed them to the point that she'd wondered from time to time if they'd actually happened.

Newsflash, Torres. They were even better than you remembered.

And they were *real.*

Hot and sexy, with nearly a decade more maturity on those lips, Ace Reynolds was positively lethal. And he had been more than adequate before.

"I'm waiting," Ace pressed.

"I shouldn't have done that. Okay?"

She saw the moment of calculation in his eyes and should have known he'd never let it go, but for the briefest interlude, Veronica thought she'd escape unscathed. That she could go home, relive those amazing moments alone with her private thoughts and do her damnedest to ignore the mortification of what had come next.

"Fine." He stepped out of Walter's stall door and swung it closed, flipping the lock with quick, firm movements, before returning his attention to her. "Then I'll save you any further embarrassment and be the one to do it next time."

He hadn't let it go.

And somewhere deep down inside, in a place Veronica had kept solidly buried since walking out of Midnight Pass nearly eight years ago, she thrilled at his words.

The next time.

Ace rode the pasture on the south side of the ranch, inspecting fence line, and thought about Veronica Torres's lips. He'd thought of little else since their after-dinner interlude a week ago. Except when he was thinking of her face, color riding high on those slashes of cheekbone. Or when he imagined the way his hands fit so neatly at her hips, grasping those slim lines as the pads of his fingers skimmed her waist, just like he'd done a million time in his memories.

He'd long since avoided thinking of her, except for odd snatches of remembrance that would leap up and grab him around the throat, the result of a familiar sight or a reminder of an experience they'd had together. Hell, until she'd returned to the Pass about eighteen months ago, he'd considered himself well and truly over her.

While dates were hardly plentiful in a town of fewer than five thousand, he did go out. There was a watering hole a few towns north he enjoyed a few weekends a month and there were always many lovely women to meet and spend time with.

None were Veronica but none of them had to be. He'd moved on after Veronica had left. The news of her marriage had been enough to push him forward and recognize she was never going to be his—was never coming back—and he'd done what he'd had to do.

So why had the ability to move on seem to have vanished?

And why had his world turned upside down since she'd returned to the Pass?

The flick of Walter's ears alerted Ace half a second before he heard his sister's voice, calling out from about a hundred yards away. She sat her own horse, a handsome bay she insisted on calling Sweet Baboo, an affectionate Peanuts reference to the horse's given name of Linus. With subtle pressure from his left knee that Walter read easily, Ace swung around and headed for his sister.

Arden often surprised him, but rarely caught him totally off guard. Which made the way she sat Linus, her back arrow straight and no hint of a smile on her face, that much more concerning.

"What's wrong?" he asked the moment he got closer.

"Nothing."

"Why do you look like you've been sucking lemons all morning *and* missed your favorite yoga class?"

"How many times do I have to tell you it's practice, not class. Class suggests there's a grade."

"Fine. Practice. Did you miss it?"

"No." Arden shook her head but the firm line of her mouth never shifted.

"Then what has you so upset?"

"I'm not upset."

Ace nudged Walter slightly forward until he'd pulled up fully beside Arden. "Come on, Ards. What's going on?"

"*You* is what's going on. You and your stupid, thick, stubborn skull."

"What did I do?"

"You have a beautiful woman who came to dinner at our kitchen table and you've ignored her. For a week!"

"I've done no such thing." Even if he sort of had ignored Veronica, the fact she'd occupied his thoughts nearly 24/7 made it feel like he hadn't ignored her.

"Yes, you have. She's been out to the stable three times this week and you've been nowhere in sight."

He refused to question why his sister was so interested in this subject and instead focused on the animals. "Out at the stables for what? She checked Walter last week and I haven't heard about any other problems."

"Well, there are some. She was here twice to look at the horses and then once more to check on that little calf. Who's doing fine, by the way."

Reynolds Station was a large, working cattle ranch. Ace knew most everything that went on but he also depended on his brothers to keep up their sides of the overarching partnership. They had little need to tell each other the minutia of their days, but they did connect on the big items. Animal health was one of the biggest, to his mind.

"Who called her out here?"

"I thought you."

"I've been out on property all week. And—" He cut her off before Arden could argue. "I had no idea there've been any calls put in to the vet. Tate or Hoyt probably handled it. Or one of the hands, if the situation was dire enough."

"You really didn't know she was here?" The line of Arden's back was still firm but her mouth did soften.

"No."

"Oh."

Although he avoided discussing his personal life with his family—and certainly not his baby sister—curiosity had him pressing the subject. "Why do you care about this so much?"

"I like her. And I think you do, too."

"I do like her. She's an outstanding large-animal vet and she is an asset to this ranch." Ace knew it was a cop-out—Arden meant a different sort of "like," of that he was certain—but he'd hold on to this ship no matter how close it was to sinking.

"That's not what I meant."

"What you meant has no place on a busy morning. Or anywhere else for that matter," he finished up on a mutter.

"Tate and Hoyt haven't had any problem expressing their feelings for women they care about. I'd think you'd look to their example."

If she hadn't been mounted on Linus, Ace could have imagined Arden standing before him, hands on hips as she delivered her edict on love and commitment.

"This isn't the same. It isn't even in the orbit of the same."

"I think it's exactly the same. Which is why you're hiding here, on the far side of the ranch, inspecting fence, which any of our hands is well able to do."

Although he wanted to argue, he wasn't a liar. The fact Veronica Torres had filled his thoughts nearly nonstop since her visit last week meant Arden was not only in the proper orbit, but she'd pretty much zeroed in on the correct zip code. So he did the only thing he could think of and went on the defensive.

"What has gotten into you this morning?"

"I'm done seeing you roam around out here and hide."

"I'm not hiding. And now you're just pissing me off."

"Good."

"What's that supposed to mean?"

"Not only are you out here physically hiding, but you've been hiding from your feelings for way too long. I get it after she left, but she's back now. Has been back for well over a year. It's about damn time you did something to go after her."

"The woman left and got married. I moved on. Why should I go backward now?" Heat and venom had spilled out with the words and all Ace could think of was putting distance between the way those words clouded the air between him and his little sister. With subtle pressure on Walter's reins, he backed away. "And I'd appreciate it if you'd leave this subject alone."

"She's single. You're eternally single. Do some damn thing about it."

Before he could press the issue, Arden swung around on Linus and hightailed it out of the southern pasture. He thought to give chase—had he been less confused and surly he might have—but instead he simply sat there, high atop Walter, and stared at his sister's retreating form.

What had gotten into her? What in the ever-loving hell did "*eternally* single" even mean? And why did he have the overwhelming urge to settle Walter back in the stables, jump in his truck and go give Dr. Veronica Torres a piece of his mind?

It was Arden he should be mad at.

But as he swung Walter around and followed the same path his sister had ridden, Ace knew the truth.

A week was too damn long. And it was high time he did something about it.

Veronica closed the large manila file and tapped her pen on the cover. She'd spent the morning over at the Vasquez ranch and still hadn't figured out what was wrong with two of their smallest calves. As a vet, she knew she couldn't save them all, but nothing in either animal's symptoms seemed to make sense.

Her first instinct had been theileriosis, just like the Reynolds calf, but the diagnosis hadn't tested out in either case. She'd also checked for fog fever, since the Vasquez foreman had confirmed the calves had been moved to fresh pastures in the past week. All that ripe grass could wreck havoc on the still-developing systems of the calves and caused the most trouble in spring and fall.

"Poor babies." She crooned the words as she switched over to her computer and tapped out a quick note to one of her colleagues from vet school. The man had grown up on a farm and could diagnose most illnesses faster than a Google search—or her tests. She'd hate to see either animal not make it to winter.

Shaking off the shot of sadness that accompanied the thought, she hit Send on the email to Tyler and tried to focus on her other priorities for the day. She had a drug shipment due in late afternoon and needed to be here to accept it herself, catalog all she'd ordered and then lock it all up. She'd toyed with asking for police protection on the days the shipments came in but so far had resisted the urge.

Which was silly, she admonished herself for about the tenth time over the past week, even as the thought continued to swirl.

This isn't Houston.

There'd been a police escort there, provided by the drug companies who supplied the lifesaving medicines she prescribed. As far west as the Pass, she had to manage those things for herself.

"Paranoid much?" she muttered, before standing to pace the small confines of her office.

Her assistant, Julie, would be here for the shipment's arrival and the two workmen she'd hired to build an addition to the back shed would be here later, as well. The men were large and strapping, former ranch hands who'd decided to go into business for themselves. While she kept them and anyone else who visited the property away from the medicine—or the knowledge of just how much a large-animal vet had on the premises—it was nice to know they were around.

Which still didn't explain why she was so jumpy.

Earlier in the week she'd have laid all the excess energy squarely at the feet of Ace Reynolds, the broody, sexy cowboy with the still-outstanding lips, but she'd worked hard to put their intimate moments from the prior week behind her. Kissing him had been a mistake and it was essential she accept those reckless moments as such and push them aside.

The medical delivery had her jumpy all in its own right. As it always did.

It was silly, really, but the past few deliveries had made her feel as if she was being watched. Which was entirely possible since her practice sat at the edge of Main Street, in clear visibility to half the town. Which, Veronica decided on a brisk spurt of action as she hightailed it from her small office to her equally small kitchenette for coffee, was the only answer she was going to accept.

The coffee was hot, rich and thick when it hit her tongue, the only way she'd drink it. She'd developed a connoisseur's love—and attitude—toward coffee during veterinary school and had only allowed it to grow stronger in the ensuing years. Considering the Vasquez calves again, she walked back to her office, anxious to see if her vet school friend had responded.

Wrapped in her thoughts—and that's the reason she'd give herself later—she didn't fully register the bell over the front door. It was only when the heavy footsteps thudded her way on the carpet did she register that Julie had sent their new arrival to her office.

Which meant Ace Reynolds was nearly standing in front of her before she took in his large frame, distinct musky, hint-of-fall scent and impressively narrow hips clad in faded jeans.

Why was it always the jeans that did her in?

Faded and well-worn, with white stress points scattered from thigh to knee.

"Ace."

"Hello." He nodded, the hat he perpetually wore already in his hands from what she could only assume was his first hello to Julie.

She nearly had the words out to ask why he was there when images of the Vasquez calves and their labored breathing came to mind. Had the same problem affected Reynolds Station? "Is everything okay? Is it the calves?"

"The calves are fine. Growing every day."

"Good." Relief filled her, even as confusion grew. "Is something else wrong? Is it Walter?"

A small smile played at the corner of his lips, the first sign she'd seen that gave her a little ease. "He's fine, too. So's the rest of the stable best as anyone can tell."

"Okay. Well, good, then." Well aware it was rude but unable to think of anything else, she blurted what she'd wanted to from the start. "Why are you here, then?"

"You're why I'm here."

Her?

Like a story where she'd clearly lost the thread, she took a moment to consider it all as she took him in. Despite the small smile, he seemed stoic and stilted, his usual state around her. Which was nothing new, so what had she possibly done that had him coming off the ranch in the middle of the day to head into town and her office?

"Let me clarify. You and your damned lips are the reason I'm here. Or maybe you've forgotten what happened in my barn last week?"

Something utterly delicious shot through her veins with all the speed of a medical injection. He was here about their kiss? A kiss he felt the need to visit her about?

"I haven't forgotten anything."

"Good. Then I'll plan on picking you up at seven this evening."

"For what?"

"A date."

All the delicious heat coursing through her veins cratered in her stomach with a huge crash. "I'm not going on a date with you."

"Yeah, you kind of are. Consider it payback for cornering me in my own stable and reminding me of how good things used to be between us."

"But I can't go to dinner tonight."

"You have other plans?"

Damn him. "No."

"Then you'd better come up with something else pretty quick."

"I don't want to go."

"You sure about that?" He tapped his nose, that small

smile that hadn't fully faded growing broader as she protested. "Your nose is growing."

Her fingers touched her nose before she could stop them. "Stop it."

"Seven. I'll swing by your place, then."

"How do you know where I live?"

"This is Midnight Pass. I know where everyone lives."

"But you've never been there."

"You live in the new Parrish Grove development. Middle house on the first cul-de-sac."

She knew the Pass was small and she also knew very little was secret, but she had to admit his knowledge was a surprise. "How do you know that?"

"Arden mentioned it. One of her yoga students lives on the same cul-de-sac."

It was silly to be disappointed. That he'd found out where she lived in such an innocuous way instead of seeking out the information.

Which was just dumb.

And a ridiculous by-product of this weird push-pull of attraction for the damn man.

"Oh. Well, yes." She nodded. "Jodie Michaels raves about Arden's classes so that makes sense."

"Seven. Tonight."

"Tonight."

As he strolled out her door that hat went unerringly on top of his head. Just as her gaze went unerringly to that delectable backside, clad in distressed denim. She wanted to be angry. Or frustrated. Or…something that felt less buffeted by winds she couldn't control. But some things, Veronica admitted to herself, just *were*.

Cowboy hats and the cocky men who stood beneath them.

And the simple beauty of distressed jeans.

* * *

Ray Barnett, better known by all as "the Rat King," watched the cowboy saunter out of the office, stopping only to tip the large gray hat on his head to an elderly woman passing by. While there was nothing in the man's demeanor to suggest he'd done anything but stop in to talk to the vet, something nagged at Ray.

The cowboy was familiar.

He'd done his homework on the people who lived in and around Midnight Pass and knew the town to be dominated by ranching, a few nature companies who took advantage of the rocky, craggy land for outdoor adventures and a police presence that seemed perpetually outmaneuvered against the pervasive drug trade that occupied the entire region.

The big cowboy coming and going in Veronica's office wasn't a complication he'd anticipated, but it wasn't entirely insurmountable. Veronica was out and about a lot, her office locked up tighter than the proverbial drum. But she'd done the same in Houston and they'd found a way around it.

Him and Rocky.

He'd find a way around it now.

In the meantime, he'd find out more about that cowboy. The man was likely just one of her clients, but it paid to be prepared. And to soothe the nagging ache that had settled in his gut when he watched the man stride into Veronica's office, determination in every step.

He knew what was said about him. That he was a hothead who acted on impulse. That he could never run the gang effectively if he didn't check his temper. They'd even given him the Rat King nickname, thinking it was an insult.

But he knew different.

He was far more methodical than anyone gave him credit for. Hadn't he used Google and a crap-ton of social media to get the lay of the land down here? And hadn't he planned this all out himself, unwilling to pull his brotherhood into it before he had a full plan mapped out? Wasn't *he* the one who knew what it was to wait two long years for revenge?

In the end, Ray knew all of them underestimated him. Rocky was the only one who never had. Which was why he was going to do this.

And he had no plan to fail.

Chapter 4

Damn his baby sister.

That thought had kept Ace steady company throughout his shower, his ridiculous and far-too-frustrating selection of clothing for the evening and the ride over to the Parrish Grove housing development.

His visit to Veronica's office earlier that day had been driven by impulse and lingering anger over the way things had ended between them the week before. Arden's poking around that sore spot hadn't helped and he'd headed into downtown with some vague determination to make it right. Or to finally get the movie reel of their heated kiss out of his head. The idea of a date had caught him unaware up to the very moment the suggestion came out of his mouth, but at Veronica's shock and surprise, he'd gone with the impulse, pleased to see her ruffled.

Hell, pleased someone in this situation besides *him* was ruffled.

Only now he'd had time to think about it. And he wasn't sure what had possibly possessed him beyond some unreasonable demon who was determined to saw open old wounds that hadn't ever fully healed.

Hell and damn, when had he gotten so melodramatic?

Since the only other option was to buck up and deal with his impulses, he turned into Veronica's driveway and forced himself to do just that. Ace cut the ignition and nearly had the door open when he sat back heavily against the seat.

What had *he been thinking?*

Things had ended with him and Veronica for a reason. Mostly the sad yet all-too-real fact they couldn't coexist with each other very successfully. They had all the basics.

Chemistry.

Mutual interests.

Explosive sex.

But somehow none of those attributes had made for a successful relationship.

Not that they hadn't tried. But after the endless rounds of fighting and arguing about all the feelings he didn't share and all the angered responses over how she wanted him to, Ace had finally given in.

He'd indulged that small thought that had taken root and sprouted to life, questioning if they'd be better off apart. In the process, he'd allowed his pride—and his stubborn refusal to discuss his father—to take away the one person who could have seen him through it all. It was only then, after they'd finally pushed each other so far and so hard that the only option was to run away from each other as far and as fast as their legs would carry them, had he realized his mistake.

But it was too late. He'd shoved himself so far into the

business, traveling out of town week after week to court new distribution channels. And she'd up and moved to Houston to marry some douche. Or what Ace could only assume was a douche because the jerk had let Veronica go.

The reality of that fact—and the idea that she had moved on with someone else, even if it hadn't been fully permanent in the end—cratered something inside him. He rubbed at the center of his chest at the way that reality settled there and let it take root. It would be his only defense as he looked to get through the evening.

Ace knocked on the door, taking in the wide oak door and pretty wreath she'd hung. The wreath was elaborately woven, but what struck him was the whimsy of small cat and dog figurines embedded in the boughs. His hand was already out, reaching to touch what looked to be a small poodle, when the door swung open.

"Ace. Hi."

"Hey." All conversation left him at the statuesque figure that stood on the other side of the door. Her slim frame was clad in a wrap dress that made his fingers itch to reach for the small closure at her hip. It was a gesture that would have been appropriate—and welcome—once between them.

Recognizing his pep talk in the car had done him little good, he latched on to the first thought he could find. "I like the wreath."

She smiled. "My version of cats and dogs living in harmony."

"Arden claims that's a bit of an old wives' tale. She's seen plenty of households where cats and dogs do just fine."

"So have I. But since I'm neither old, nor a wife, I can also give you my professional opinion on the matter. There are plenty of households where the cats and dogs do not get along. I've closed up any number of stitches that prove that."

He diligently ignored the reference to her being a wife—and the fact she no longer was one—and gestured toward the car. "You ready to go?"

"Actually, I need a few more minutes. Why don't you come in?"

"Sure."

He followed her into the house, feeling like he crossed some inexplicable threshold. It had been strange enough to go to her office, and despite the fact that was a place she clearly loved, it didn't have the same sort of intimacy as coming to her home.

Nor did he expect the memories when several familiar pieces flashbacked at him. The small table that held a lamp in her hallway had been in her apartment the last time she lived in the Pass. The large painting that sat over the fireplace—one of a southwest landscape with mustangs running free—she'd purchased with him while at an art fair near El Paso. And the small chair in the corner that had been her grandmother's still held a place of honor, with a small stitched pillow on the seat reading Home Sweet Home.

He remembered those things. Just like he remembered her.

That continued sense of being off balance—the one that had followed him since her visit and the kiss between them the week before—battered at him again. He rarely questioned his actions, but what was he doing here? What was the endgame?

Or maybe a better question: What was *his* endgame?

Before he had a chance to come up with any answers, Veronica swept back into the room. She'd added a chunky necklace to the wrap dress and a pair of sexy hoop earrings that set off her elegant neck.

With the same determination he faced calf-branding day or some of the long nights when his stock foaled, he braced himself for what was to come. And while hot pokers and childbirth weren't exactly the thoughts that usually accompanied him on a date, he figured he'd do well to keep them in the forefront of his mind.

And decidedly *off* the long length of Veronica Torres's gorgeous legs.

As he extended the crook of his arm to walk her from the house, that subtle scent—the one that had always just been Veronica—made everything else fade away.

Good Lord, was he in trouble.

Veronica took in the neat confines of Ace's truck and was instantly transported to a place nearly ten years ago. They'd regularly tooled around in his truck, seeking out everything from the mundane to the adventurous. She still remembered a long weekend they took to go hiking in Big Bend National Park. By day they'd explored the various rock formations and outcroppings, pushing one another to climb one more hill or descend one more pass. They'd spent each night curled up in each other, snuggled tight in their pitched tent. For as romantic as it had been, she equally remembered the simple joy of spending an idle Saturday together, running errands or doing nothing more than strolling through the mall.

It seemed so bucolic now, when she looked back on it. So simple and well-matched and…well, just nice. Which only further reinforced a question she'd asked herself much too often of late.

How had it all gone so wrong that she'd just up and left?

For as simple as her memories seemed, she and Ace had exhibited a solid streak of battle between them. It had been there from the start, and whether it was a personality defect between them or the consequence of two strong-willed people battling through a shocking mix of chemistry, she wasn't sure.

But they'd fought far worse than the cats and dogs Ace had commented on when he picked her up. Their chemistry had borne the distinct overtones of bulls and red flags.

Ace climbed into the truck and started the engine. His smile was genuine when he turned to her. "You look pretty."

His words and the appreciation evident way down deep in his green eyes touched her, a warm shot of heat curling in her belly. "Thank you."

He used to say those things to her all the time. Simple compliments that were genuine, sweet and often given at the most unexpected times.

When she was covered in daubs of peacock blue and good old-fashioned August sweat as they painted her living room walls in the old apartment she used to rent over the town Laundromat.

Or the time they ran the three-legged race in the Midnight Pass Memorial Day party on the town square. She was covered in grass stains and a layer of mud from when they'd stumbled in the race, but he'd still kissed her and told her she was beautiful.

And then there was the time when he drove her to a dinner held by one of the leading veterinarian pharmaceutical companies. He'd put on a tux and she had worn a fancy dress and he'd spent the evening looking at her as if she was the only woman in the world.

"Where are we going tonight?" Veronica had selected

the vibrant print dress on a whim and hoped she wasn't overdressed for whatever Ace had planned.

"There's an Italian place up in Riverbend. Tate and Belle checked it out a few months ago and seem to hit it at least once a week. My brother is a fan of their chicken parmesan."

"A rather ringing endorsement."

He shot her a quick side-eye before returning his gaze to the road. "You have met my brother, right? He would eat raw chicken if you smother it with cheese."

"Fair point. What does Belle say about the place?"

"She not only endorsed the chicken parm, but she hasn't shut up about the lobster ravioli. She was the clincher."

"Sounds good, then."

The briefest thought toyed with the edges of her consciousness. He'd known about the place for a few months? Had Ace not considered bringing another date here? Did he go on dates often?

Questions she had no business wondering.

Ace made the last turn out of the Pass and onto the interstate that would lead them up to Riverbend. They were both quiet, but for the first time since returning to town she couldn't say that there was tension between them. Instead, there was a subtle anticipation that seemed to fill the air between them.

"How's the baby calf doing, by the way?"

"Really well. If we hadn't marked him he'd be hard to find within the herd."

"I'm glad to hear that. With the right treatment they really are amazingly resilient."

"The calf may be resilient but having a vet who knows what they're doing means something, too."

"I appreciate the endorsement, but in this case I just

helped Mother Nature along a little bit with a diagnosis and a shot. You were the quick thinker who called me out in the first place."

"My family and I don't mess around with the stock."

If she didn't know the history, Veronica would have assumed he was simply addressing his ranching practices and way of handling his cattle. But she knew better. The legacy of Ace's father's bad behavior—a move that had nearly taken down Reynolds Station forever—had obviously left scars.

"And you're well respected because of it."

"It took a long time to claw our reputation back out of that trough. I'm not going to do anything that might put us back down there. Taking care of our stock is a big part of that."

Although Andrew Reynolds's sins had faded, replaced with the diligence and hard work of his children, old memories died hard in Midnight Pass. The illegal ranching practice of rendering—feeding their stock from the by-product of other animals—had left a stain on the name of Reynolds.

Oddly enough, that perceived "stain" had been one of the things she and Ace had fought the most bitterly about.

After some of the immediate embarrassment faded—and the hard work had been done to get the ranch back into optimal practice and out of debt—Ace had continued to behave as if he had something to apologize for. As a large-animal vet she understood the dangers of rendering, including the risk of mad cow disease among other things, but she also understood the deliberate care and sustainable practices Ace had implemented at Reynolds Station.

Yet it hadn't been enough.

His near-manic insistence on proving to all that the name Reynolds equated to quality beef. His lingering embarrassment over his father's betrayal, of their family and all those they did business with. And his seeming inability to see past it all, curling into himself until the man she knew had become a shell.

Oh, how they had argued about all of it.

She knew quality animal husbandry and she knew Ace and his siblings. She'd always believed hard work and determination had a place in the world—one deserving of respect and admiration—and she hadn't understood his continued determination to rehash the past.

In the end, her love for a man who was stubborn and honorable became the qualities that drove them apart.

"Veronica?"

She keyed back into Ace's voice and the obvious question there. "Yes?"

If he thought her behavior strange he didn't say anything, instead pointing toward their exit. "Riverbend is the next exit. It's a nice night. Maybe they'll seat us outside."

"That'd be nice."

More than nice, if she were honest with herself. For all the memories, far too many of them bitter, the two of them had a connection. Even now, past the acrimony that had marred their interactions since she'd returned to town, it was easy to be with him. Comfortable.

And tantalizingly simple on the surface.

It was that surface part she had to keep at the forefront of her thoughts. No matter how tempting it was to brush off the past and only pull out the good parts, she knew how bad things had been at times. Funny how quickly she was willing to brush it all aside, when the only things she could remember of her marriage were the bad.

Had she ever really loved Mark?

She'd believed so on their wedding day—that was the

one thing she was sure of. No matter how much she and Ace had hurt each other, she hadn't married with the intention of divorcing. But even with the best of intentions, things had turned sour quickly.

Was it her? Was she unable to be in a healthy, functioning relationship?

She hadn't been raised that way. Her parents and both sets of grandparents had all presented evidence of good marriages. Both her sisters had made good matches, as well. All had set examples of what love looked like, day in and day out—when things were easy and when they were inevitably hard. Her parents still did that. And they still looked at each other with love shining in their eyes.

Ace pulled into the parking lot, a small wooden sign welcoming them to Cannoli's.

"The place is named after dessert?"

"Sort of." Ace cut the engine and turned to her. "From what Tate tells me, the owner is nicknamed Cannoli."

"A beagle I care for is named Cannoli."

Ace's green eyes crinkled at the corners. "Because he likes dessert."

"Do bones count?"

"I suppose that one falls into the old saying 'to each his own.'"

"His owner is pretty diligent about knowing what dogs can and can't have—dessert sitting at the top of that list. But since I'm also usually scolding him to ensure Cannoli loses some weight, I'd say you're on the money."

"Why don't we go see if the human version can tempt us with something equally tasty."

Veronica eyed Ace across the truck cab. "If you've driven me all the way down here with the promise of chicken parm and don't deliver, I may have to sic one of my patients on you."

"That Cannoli sounds fierce."

"I was actually thinking more of Powder Puff."

"Powder Puff?"

"Yep." Veronica reached for the door handle, the cool night air swirling in as she opened it. "My favorite rottweiler."

A half hour later, Ace still couldn't get the image of a Rottweiler named Powder Puff out of his mind. It made a strange counterpoint to the intoxicating woman sharing his evening. How he could have thoughts of a large, imposing dog in his mind's eye, along with heated memories of making love with the woman sitting next to him, he had no idea.

Yet, oddly, both images fit.

Her love of animals was one of her defining characteristics. When she spoke of them, be they overweight beagles, oddly named rottweilers or even a parrot that a panicked nursery school teacher had brought in the prior week, he was entranced.

And all too easily enamored with her

Again.

"I thought you were a large-animal vet?" Ace asked.

"I am, but I'm trained to treat all animals. And while Zeke Carpenter does well enough for himself as the town vet, he often needs help." She frowned into her wine. "We haven't been nearly as successful recruiting students out of school as we'd like."

"The Pass isn't for everyone. Small-town living with some very high-stakes clients with demanding businesses. For those who want that, we're perfect. For those who don't, I can see where other towns would be more enticing."

"I suppose you're right."

Although he'd avoided thinking too much about the seeming crime wave that had hit the Pass—and his family in particular—he found himself going there, anyway. "The crime over the past year hasn't helped."

"Right again." She swirled her wine, seeming lost in the contents before she lifted her eyes. "I know I haven't said much, but I am sorry for all you and your family have dealt with. First the body on the property, then Belle's kidnapping and then Reese's troubles at the school."

"Thank you. I'm not one to wish time away, but I think I speak for the whole family when I say we're ready to put this year behind us. And then with Hoyt and Reese's baby coming, it makes even more to look forward to."

"It's nice to see them together."

"A true match if I've ever seen one."

"I know Reese mentioned in passing the other night at dinner that they hadn't known each other well, but seeing them together…" Veronica shrugged. "True match is the perfect description."

Ace thought so, too. He and Arden had marveled at it more than a few times. While he'd been happy for Tate and Belle to find their way back to one another, once they did there was a sort of inevitability in their coupling. The two had danced around each other for years, backs up like two cats, but underneath it all, everyone knew how much they longed for each other. Hoyt and Reese, on the other hand, were something of a surprise to everyone. Absolutely obvious once you saw it in person, but neither had been guaranteed to find the other.

A happy accident, Arden had called it.

Ace just figured his little brother had finally gotten

what he deserved: happiness and a woman to love his whole life long.

"Reynolds Station is pretty amazing. I saw a write-up in the Houston paper a few years ago about all the ways you've built sustainability into your ranching practices."

"It's come along. Hoyt, Tate and I have been on board from the beginning, but Arden's been a huge driver of the work. She's done most of the research and run the numbers so we could get up and running."

"Were there concerns about profits?"

"Less overall profits and more how long it takes until the investment begins to flow into the running of the ranch. We focused first on maintaining healthy ground and our overall water management and have worked from there. We had to do a lot of retrofitting and even had to cull out a few of our suppliers because they didn't meet new standards."

"I've done the same. Several food providers simply don't meet my standards and I won't recommend their products."

"I bet those conversations made for some interesting sales calls."

Veronica glanced up from where she delicately sliced off a piece of manicotti, a fierce smile filling her face. "You're not kidding. I had to practically chase one of Doc Talente's old geezer sales guys out with the shovel we use for animal cleanup."

"Let me guess? He didn't care for your attitude or your insistence on making a change?"

"How'd you know?" she asked.

"The same sales guys that call on you make calls on us, too. This is an important territory for them and the feed guys from the big husbandry companies usually glom on to the pharma guys to make us feel that we're key customers."

"Account-based marketing, I've heard them call it."

"Yep. Even though you know each member of the sales team would shank the other if it gave them another few points on their end-of-the-year numbers."

Ace was rewarded by Veronica's light laughter and ready agreement.

God, he remembered this. How much they could talk about and how easily she understood his work. Even better, how much that understanding allowed him to get things off his mind, from the pressing to the mundane, the urgent to the purely silly.

A shot of longing speared his midsection, having nothing to do with the chicken parm he'd been steadily clearing from his plate and everything to do with the woman sitting beside him.

And the startling realization of just how much he'd missed her.

Since she'd been back in the Pass he'd recalled in vivid detail their heated lovemaking and the ready chemistry between them, but he hadn't given enough credence to the memories of how much they'd shared beyond the physical.

"Ace?"

Her smile was still firmly in place, but he saw the question hovering there, too.

With a slight shake of his head, he willed away the memories that filled his brain like cobwebs and tried to remember the thread of their conversation.

"Sorry. Mental image of cleaning up clueless salesman blood on my office floor."

The excuse seemed to satisfy and he pressed on. "The big providers who sell to us want to make sure we know the latest offerings and how to care for our stock, too. Old guy named Bruce the one who called on you?"

"That's the one."

"You ask Arden about him sometime."

"Bruce start calling her 'little lady' and mansplaining to her how important it is to vaccinate stock?" Veronica asked, a vision of Arden's response to that approach already filling her mind's eye.

"Better." Ace got into the story. "Arden pointed toward the poster in her office of a steer's body mass. Told Bruce and his sales buddy if either one of them could correctly point out the reticulum, the rumen, the omasum or the abomasum she'd buy a year's worth of feed."

"They couldn't point to the stomach?"

"Nope."

"And Bruce sells veterinarian medicine. For cows?"

"That was Arden's point." Ace couldn't hold back the smile as he thought of his baby sister, all spit and vinegar as she worked over the clueless Bruce. "I believe the term she used as she shooed them out of her office was that they didn't give a rat's ass about animal welfare."

"I'd say Arden was being far too generous in estimating the size of the rat."

Ace laughed at that, the good-natured retort hitting him just right. She'd always had that ability— to get to the heart of the matter with a slightly cheeky edge.

How had he forgotten it in the midst of all he'd remembered about the two of them?

Only as the laughter continued, Ace had a sneaking suspicion why his subconscious had buried the memories.

A beautiful woman was dangerous to a man's heart. But a beautiful woman who could laugh with you?

She was deadly.

Chapter 5

Ace drove the last quarter mile into town with Carrie Underwood's pretty voice keeping him company. Her pissed-off anthem to scorned womanhood and keyed cars couldn't quite put him off his day and he hummed along without a moment of remorse for his gender.

He pulled his truck into the feed parking lot and cut the engine, recognizing a few other trucks as he did. There was Jackson Crown's big F-150 with the Crown Ranch emblem emblazoned on the side. Right beside it was Tabasco's small beater that still chugged along despite being older than Arden *and* that managed to pass inspection each year. A feat Tabasco regularly boasted about behind the counter at the Border Line. Ace noted a few more familiar vehicles as he climbed out of his truck, remembering at the last moment to snag his list of needed items from the front passenger seat.

The parking lot was large by Midnight Pass standards but still put him in full view of downtown. It was with no small measure of restraint that he avoided looking at Veronica's practice, nestled at the far end of Main Street. His thoughts hadn't strayed far from their dinner date almost a week ago and he was still working through his next move.

Or if he should even make one at all.

He was confused enough—a state that pissed him off more than he could say. There was no way he wanted to add on mooning over the woman to his current list of problems.

Dinner had been better than he'd expected. And way more bittersweet. The animosity that had flared between them since her return to the Pass was nowhere in evidence. Instead, they'd talked easily, with no shortage of conversation. Which had made the end of the evening an exercise in mental torture.

Kiss her?

Don't kiss her?

Wait for *her* to kiss *him*?

All of it had brewed and bubbled in his mind as he drove them back to her place after Cannoli's, and by the time he'd gotten to her driveway he'd been loaded for bear.

And had all the finesse of a fifteen-year-old boy as he fumbled through their after-dinner conversation.

Ace rubbed at the back of his neck and the heat that still crept up even though five days had passed since their date. Had he really told her to have a nice day?

When his neck only grew warmer beneath his fingertips Ace had to admit to himself that he had.

It was also the reason he'd avoided his brothers like the

proverbial plague. Tate and Hoyt were as curious as the next person, despite their ready protests to the contrary, and he knew both wanted to hear how the date went. He also knew the waiting peanut gallery of the expanding circle of women in his life were insistent on getting the details, as well.

Which meant he'd gone out early each morning, come home late and had avoided eating any of his meals at home. And damn, Reese had made lasagna the night before and he'd missed it, homemade noodles and all.

"Ace!"

He was so lost in his thoughts he'd nearly tumbled over Veronica's office assistant, Julie. "Hey, there."

"I'd say penny for your thoughts but those look like they're worth quarters."

Ace smiled at the older woman and knew she meant well. Julie had been about a decade ahead of him at the high school and had even babysat the Reynolds siblings a few times when they were kids. She'd made no secret of her interest in him and Veronica picking up where they'd left off all those years ago and he mentally added her to his avoid-like-the-plague list.

Grasping for some response, Ace settled on the one thing he figured would get him off the hook. "Just making sure I don't forget anything on the list. Hoyt usually prefers managing the chores, but he and Reese had an appointment at the obstetrician this morning."

Just as he planned, the mention of the baby shifted the conversation firmly off his indecision and on to talk of the future. He got his chance to escape after speculating on the sex of his future niece or nephew and what names he thought Reese and Hoyt were considering.

And was left with the image of his little brother holding a newborn infant in his arms in a few short months.

Empirically, Ace knew Hoyt was about to become a father. It was the reality of it that reared up and struck him at odd times. There would be a baby in the house.

Hoyt had already begun construction on the section of property where he wanted to build a house for his growing family. He was making good progress but the day-to-day requirements of running the ranch and planning for the baby meant they'd live in the main house for a while, especially since Reese's house sold more quickly than they'd expected.

Although he wanted his brother to have his own life, Ace couldn't deny how good it felt to think of them all under one roof, a new generation of Reynoldses coming home to the house his great-grandfather had built. And while they'd be nearby, it wasn't the same as being under the same roof.

"And aren't you a mushy mess, Reynolds," he muttered low under his breath before he even realized the words were out. A quick glance around the high shelves confirmed he was alone, but he'd still do better to watch his thoughts. Gossip ran high in the Pass and nothing would fly through the town grapevine faster than the news that Ace Reynolds had taken up talking to himself.

Hurrying through the rest of his list, he had his oversize pallet full of the things he'd carry home in his truck and then went to the front counter to put in the rest of his order for delivery. The wide, floor-to-ceiling windows that made up the front of the store filtered in the bright sunlight and, just like the muttered words, Ace's gaze flew to Veronica's practice before he could stop himself.

He'd nearly pulled his gaze away when he saw the

lone figure who peered in Veronica's front window before moving to try the front door. Since Ace had just seen Julie it stood to reason the practice was locked, but something in the man's furtive movements struck Ace as off.

"Ace?" Dan, the store manager, stared at him.

"Sorry, Dan." Ace grabbed his credit card from the card reader and tucked it in his back pocket before pointing toward the window. "Would you give me a minute?"

"Sure."

Ace felt Dan's gaze on his back as he moved past the edge of the counter and on to the wide window. The guy still stood in front of Veronica's practice but he was back to the window, peering in again.

"Anything the matter?" Dan asked.

"I'm not sure. Watch my stuff, would you?"

Ace didn't wait for Dan's response.

Ace made it across the town square and down Main Street in a time that would have made his high school track coach proud. He'd kept a steady eye on the man peeking in windows, but the dude had moved off around the side of the building as Ace was crossing the square and had disappeared around back. He'd abstractly recognized Julie's car as he raced across the feed lot, which meant she was still safe inside.

But where was Veronica?

A loud honk sounded and he nearly stumbled over the front edge of an SUV as he ran across the street toward Veronica's veterinary practice. With a halfhearted wave for the driver's understanding, Ace closed the last few feet. The light inside the windows was still dark and Ace didn't waste any time looking for signs of activity. He headed for the back.

Although she was a large-animal vet, true to Veronica's discussion over dinner, she took care of the occasional pet, as well. A large dog run was fenced off in the back of the property, abutted against a gravel parking lot. Ace scanned the entire area, frustrated when he saw no one nearby or loping off through the back side of the property or on past the other businesses that lined Main Street beside hers.

Damn it, where had the Peeping Tom gone?

Ace did one more scan, making a slow, three-hundred-and-sixty-degree turn, before he headed for Veronica's back door. The same dark interior he'd observed from the front was true back here, further reassurance that no one was inside.

What had that guy been doing?

Ace knew full well it could have been as simple as that he'd needed vet services, but if that were the case, where was the guy's pet? And why had he looked so furtive, staring in the windows?

He'd nearly turned away, ready to head back to the feed store and his waiting order, when his gaze landed on the doorknob.

And the distinct signs of damage where something sharp had clearly been used to pick at the lock.

Veronica took the turn out of her development and headed for her parents' house. It had been five days since she'd seen Ace—long, torturous days when she questioned everything about the evening they'd spent together—and she was no closer to any answers.

Why hadn't she invited him in? Why hadn't he asked to come in? Why was it so easy to pick up where they'd left off? Why did talking to him make her remember all the things they used to dream about?

And why, for the love of God and all that was holy, could she not stop thinking about the way his shoulders filled out his dress shirt as he sat opposite her at that table in Cannoli's?

Why, why, why.

She was so sick of the whys she was ready to implode and figured she'd commiserate with her mother over the kitchen table and a plate of warm tamales.

After, of course, she forced her mother to give her a stern talking-to about giving no space in her mind to stupid fantasies over a man who clearly didn't have a place in her life.

Hell, he'd proven that when he'd dropped her off, leaving her with the pithy departing line to "have a nice day."

What the hell sort of end-of-evening goodbye was *that*?

The sad truth was that it wasn't one.

Although if she wanted to complain about the unsatisfactory end of her date, she might not have selected the best place to find a listening ear. The tamales were worth the drive, and time with her parents was always time well spent, but Marcelita Torres had carried a soft spot for Ace Reynolds since the very first day Veronica had brought him home for a Friday evening meal and nothing had changed that.

Ever.

Not her and Ace's breakup. Not her marriage to Mark and move to Houston. Not even her move back to the Pass, tail between her legs and pride damaged beyond belief. It had taken two long years since her divorce was finalized but she'd finally begun to believe that she'd come out the other side. Past the shame and the pain of breaking her vow of forever.

And the final acceptance that there was nothing between her and Mark beyond a mortgage and shared wedding photos.

Had there ever been much beyond that?

She'd believed so once, but had regularly questioned that fact ever since it became obvious that her marriage was over. She didn't love her husband and he didn't love her. Marriage had only taken the genuine affection they felt for each other and pulverized it to dust.

So after riding the emotional roller coaster of shame and guilt and failure, she'd come off at the end of the ride still standing and had believed herself ready to move on.

Then she'd gone and messed up all that emotional healing by kissing Ace. And *then* she'd been out of her freaking mind and gone to dinner with him.

All of which had put her right back in the front seat of the roller coaster, remembering how good things had been between them and how stupid she'd been to marry Mark in the first place.

The knock on her window startled her from her thoughts and she turned to see her father on the other side of her door. She cut the engine and climbed out of her SUV into the waiting arms that had never once let her down.

"Papi!"

"My Ronnie." Esteban Torres pulled her into a tight hug, his hold as firm and solid as it had been when he'd held her seat steady as she wobbled along learning to ride her two-wheeled bike.

"It's good to see you." She squeezed once more before pulling back to look at him. His thick black hair had more threads of silver, but the warm brown eyes that stared back at her were as familiar as her own.

"You looked lost in thought, *mija*. Everything okay?"

"Sure, Papi. I had a rare afternoon free and just wanted to come out and say hello."

"Then it's my lucky day."

Her father kept his smile bright and his dark gaze warm and focused. Veronica suspected he sensed her distress, but as the father of four girls, Esteban Torres had long since learned to wait for the inevitable deluge— of tears, of words or of laughter—and adjusted to the needed outcome.

"I heard the Vasquez ranch has been dealing with a bad bout of fog fever."

"Are they ever. I've been out there for the past two days helping out and doing what I can." The tests had come back as she'd guessed and the past few days had been exhausting as they'd worked to save the calves.

"The herd must be on the move."

"Yep. All the rain we've had has been hell on their fall grazing rotation."

"And keeping the cows away from all that lush grass is a tough job."

Veronica wrapped an arm around her father's waist as they walked toward the house, the work conversation a good way to get her mind off Ace.

Esteban Torres's understanding of her work never failed to amaze her. Although he wasn't a formally educated man, her father read everything he could get his hands on and was fascinated by an endless array of topics. When she'd shown an interest in veterinary medicine around the age of twelve he'd dived into the learning with her, buying books and finding articles on the internet, all while working his friendships in town to get her visiting privileges at the local ranches. By the time she was getting ready for vet school, he quizzed her for her entrance exams and pushed her toward several challenging topics for her research projects.

In the years since she'd first demonstrated an interest, he had made himself something of a local expert on their region's grasses, natural predators and airborne illnesses affecting large animals. The fog fever her father spoke of was an unpleasant side effect of too much amino acid in lush green grass and the Vazquez foreman was currently facing hell for not managing the herd rotation better. The fact her dad knew the side effects better than the foreman was proof the Vasquez clan needed to do a bit more interviewing next time they hired for the job.

"Heard you've also been spending a fair amount of time over at Reynolds Station." Despite the simple statement, Veronica heard the question underneath loud and clear. "Now there's a well-run ranch."

"That it is."

"The current generation of Reynolds family are good people. They care about those animals and it shows in the product they take to market."

Since she'd observed the same she could hardly argue, but it still stuck in her throat that they'd somehow managed to swing the conversation around to Ace.

Wasn't she allowed any peace from thoughts of the man?

"Ronnie!"

Her mother's shout from the kitchen echoed down the hall and the subject of Ace and the Reynolds family and ranching and sick cows all vanished in an instant. Veronica crossed the large open living room straight to the equally open kitchen. Her mother pulled her close, the slim arms as tight as her father's had been in the driveway.

"My baby."

Her mother's face still held much of the smoothness of youth, the light fans around her eyes the only indication she had experienced more years than her daughters. But it was her ready smile and open arms that truly lit her up, from the inside out. Veronica sunk into the hug and fought back the tears that smarted at the warm embrace.

Goodness, what was wrong with her? Although she didn't see her parents every day since returning to Midnight Pass she did visit them regularly. So why had she felt such a distance lately?

Even if she had been slowly pulling away, doing that same "fade out" she'd observed in Ace.

If she were fair, it was a circumstance purely of her own making. She'd done the same that last year in Houston, using texts as a way to avoid calls and work as a way to avoid events.

Which made the truth that much harder to fight. There was nowhere on the planet that made her feel as safe and secure as this house with these two people.

Except Ace's arms.

The sly whisper floated through her mind, churning up feelings she didn't want for a man she should have long since gotten over. Which was the worst part of it.

Years apart hadn't erased these feelings.

Ignoring him hadn't erased them, either.

Her mother pulled back from the hug but never broke the contact of their hands. "What is it, sweetie?"

"Oh, Mom."

The tears she'd hardly known she needed to shed fell with the force of a pent-up dam.

And as that proverbial deluge fell, she heard her father quietly leave the kitchen.

Rocky Anders hunched his shoulders and shoved his hands in his pockets, willing himself into what he'd mentally dubbed "sullen young man pose." It was basically his personality, anyway, but he'd found over the years a good shoulder hunch could scare off most of the well-intentioned.

Or the pose had done the job pretty well until he'd come *here*.

God, Midnight Pass was such a pile of crap. That thought had kept him steady company for the past few days and nothing had suddenly popped up to change his opinion. The people were a bit too friendly, a situation he'd quickly learned was just a way to figure out who he was. Casual conversation soon morphed into asking his name and where he was from and if he had kin in "the Pass," as the locals called it.

He'd just as soon pass, thank you very much.

Small towns didn't know what to do with strangers. He'd known that forever and it was why he'd chosen to make his life in Houston. In cities, people minded their own business. If they didn't, it didn't take 'em too damn long to learn how. And besides, in the big city, opportunities really did lurk around every corner.

Like this one.

So here he was, with a job to do and a woman to report back on. A job Ray had given him, suggesting his ability to manage this op would put him in good for a promotion, all while proving his loyalty. Or that's what Ray thought.

Rocky had already parlayed this into a *much* bigger job.

But Ray didn't need to know that.

He'd hit rock bottom a few years back, a homeless punk seventeen-year-old living on the streets. He'd narrowly avoided touching the crap that would take him away from it all, but he'd been sorely tempted. All those small bags of no-good, promising an escape from it all.

And then Ray had shown up.

It was Ray who'd seen his abilities and given him a job. Ray understood he was smart. Real smart, which was why his mother eventually got frustrated and up and left him one day. Said his know-it-all attitude and inability to forget anything had finally caught up with her. She didn't need a kid who was smarter than her telling her what to do.

Like it had done any good, anyway.

But Ray had understood. *Keep your eyes and ears open*, Ray had said the day he found him swiping a sandwich off the front seat of an unlocked car. The car had belonged to a local dealer and Ray wanted some details on the guy's traffic patterns. The crisp Benji had helped seal the deal and Rocky had taken the job.

When he'd shared back some details on another drug runner, Ray had made good on his initial promise to make it worth the effort and Rocky had realized there were much better--and healthier—ways to profit off drugs than shoving them under his skin.

And damn, the Rat King had seen to that.

Rocky hadn't quite gotten used to Ray's endless ranting about being a "criminal mastermind," but Rocky had figured it was a small price to pay for steady work and an opportunity to move up.

Rocky Anders had dreams of the big time and if he

ultimately defeated the Rat King, he'd be a king all on his own. That's how things worked. How you got ahead.

But in the meantime, he'd play the part.

Ray got him off the street and made sure he had a place to live and three squares. He even had a bit of money in his pocket now, and a girlfriend back in Houston and a hot little sidepiece to boot. So he'd stuck close to Ray and done all the man asked.

And then it had paid off. Bigger than Ray would ever know.

But for now, he bided his time. And if it meant roaming around this dump of a town and keeping an eye on things, he'd do that.

It also meant playing it casual. The footsteps he'd heard while trying to break in were a problem. He crouched down low and ran and was now hunkered down behind one of the large dumpsters that sat behind the businesses on Main Street. No one was back here but he'd kept his hands near his feet in the event he had to pretend to tie his shoe, all the while listening for those footsteps. As strategies went it wasn't a great one but he'd take his chances. He hadn't done anything wrong but look around. And if anyone did see him, all it would mean was he'd need to lay low for a few days.

Ray kept saying he wanted this done right. That he'd had patience for two years and a few more weeks was a small price to pay. It was only when the footsteps never came closer that Rocky edged forward to peek around the dumpster. He didn't have a clear view of the doc's office but what he could see looked empty.

Except for the big guy with the cell phone against his ear, pacing back and forth in front of the practice, his jeans and boots suggesting a cowboy.

A protector? A boyfriend?

He didn't think the pretty doc was dating, but she was hot enough, so why wouldn't she be?

But who was the guy?

Vowing to figure it out but well aware he needed to get moving, he turned, shoved his hands in his pockets and took off through the alley toward a small side street where he'd parked earlier. He'd make a full report and then wait for orders. Besides, now he had the pretty doc's schedule and knew when she made her rounds. Midnight Pass might be a dump, but it was a large sprawling dump.

And a bit of roaming around might get him some details on the big cowboy with the cell phone.

Knowing how to find her was an important part of the big score. And once he did, he was going back to Houston with his victory prize.

He could see it all now.

With that thought in the front of his mind, he ignored the small stab of guilt. He came from nothing and he had to make his way in the world. Ray was a stepping stone. Nothing wrong with that. Rocky dragged his car door open, the guilt vanishing on the light breeze that flowed around him.

Nope. Nothing wrong at all.

Chapter 6

Veronica drove the last mile back into the Pass as confused as ever. The time with her parents had been great while she was there, but their loving attitudes couldn't fix the root of her problem.

She wanted Ace. Again.

Had she ever really stopped?

The lies she'd told herself suggested she had. Those lies were powerful enough that she might have even believed them for a while in the early days of her marriage.

It was only when faced with the all-encompassing, all-consuming presence of Ace Reynolds once more that she'd had to admit the truth. The man still held a piece of her heart and always had. She'd drifted from the ashes of their broken relationship straight into marriage with Mark. Only unlike a phoenix rising, her choices had been a desperate effort to hide like a wounded animal.

Her mother had listened to all that pour out of her with a soft smile and soothing embrace and, as Veronica well knew, a slight sense of victory hovering underneath the gentle crooning.

At least the tamales had been as perfect as always. She might be a walking mess, as clueless about life and men and love at thirty-four as she had been at eighteen, but she'd had an outstanding meal. And she'd take that fortification and use it to help embrace the stark reality that the only way to fix this mess was to address it. Much as she'd love to pull the mental covers up over her head and pretend otherwise, Veronica knew the truth.

She *wasn't* eighteen and clueless any longer.

With visions of driving out to Reynolds Station after she checked back in at the office, Veronica took the last turn onto Main Street and saw Ace's truck parked in front of her practice. Had she conjured him up? Because there he was, arms folded and pacing along the small walkway that led up to her door.

She'd barely parked and cut her engine before those long strides had caught up to her, dragging open her door.

"Where have you been?"

"What?"

"I've been calling you and texting you and you haven't answered any of it."

Although her first instinct was to demand what had him so riled up and yelling, there was just enough fear and relief hollowing out his cheekbones that she held back. Flipping the button on her seat belt, she grabbed her large bag from the passenger seat and climbed out.

Only to be crushed into his arms the second her feet hit the pavement.

"What is it?" The question came out muffled against

his chest, but after the way her thoughts had roiled for the past five days she couldn't argue with the absolute sense of rightness she felt in that moment.

"You're okay."

"Ace?" She lifted her head, shocked to see those hollows had only grown deeper. "What's wrong?"

"There was someone here."

"Where?"

"Here. Poking around your practice before they tried to break into the back."

Every ounce of warmth that had built at his touch vanished, replaced with an icy cold that started in her stomach and spread with the speed of her heartbeat.

Just like Houston.

Wasn't that part of why she'd come back? Why there had been such a deep-seated appeal to owning a practice in a small town in a small corner of Texas.

She knew the Pass had problems. Their town was an unfortunate path on the drug trade and no government entity had been able to stop it. She'd been blessedly sheltered from it—she and her siblings all managing to get to adulthood without finding their way to drug use—but she knew others weren't as lucky. A second cousin still battled the demons of addiction. Reese's brother had, as well, before succumbing to them. And there were several others she knew of in town.

Without warning, that discomfort she'd had the prior week reared up and choked her.

Had there been someone lurking outside when she got her drug shipment last week? Someone watching, lying in wait? She'd convinced herself that her unease was due to her prior experiences, but what if she'd sensed a problem and had been brushing it off?

Focus on the problem at hand. Don't jump to conclusions.

"I'm sorry I scared you. I was at my parents all afternoon and didn't have my phone out."

It would be so easy to stand there, taking comfort in Ace and hoping he could make it all go away, but she knew better. This was her practice, her drug dispensary and, therefore, her mess. "Where's Julie?"

"Inside. I asked Belle to come out and Julie's showing her around."

"But she's okay?" Veronica stepped back, putting some distance between them as her head cleared. "And no one got inside?"

He folded his arms, the ready comfort he'd offered vanishing as he took a few steps back of his own. "No. Nothing like that."

Even as his affirmation soothed, snippets of needed action continued to ping through her mind.

Get to Julie.

Check the office.

Talk to Belle and see what the detective had uncovered.

Each struggled for purchase until one thought surfaced from beneath all the others.

"What are you doing here?"

"I was over at the feed store. I saw some guy lurking around when I was checking out."

"Lurking how?"

"Looking in your front windows. Pushing on the door." He shrugged. "He looked suspicious."

An image painted itself in her mind, of a client trying to assess if she were open or closed. A regular occurrence since she spent so much time out in the field. "Did it ever cross your mind he might be a customer?"

"I didn't recognize him when I saw him from the feed store. I didn't like it and I ran over."

"You ran over? Like some avenging angel hell-bent on saving me?"

The words were at complete odds with the concern he'd shown and the fear that still lingered and pulsed in subtle waves between them. They were unkind at best and terribly ungrateful at worst, but just like always, her heightened emotions around Ace got the better of her.

"I was concerned about you. About your business. The guy looked shady so I ran over to check it out. A fact that became even more clear when he ducked around back and then disappeared. There's no sign of him anywhere."

"I need to get inside."

"Or you can stay right here and explain to me what has you so bothered?"

"I need to handle this."

She tried to escape that penetrating green stare but his hand snaked out and rested just tight enough on her forearm to keep her in place. "Right. By ignoring a threat just to spite me."

"It's not spite."

"Then what is it? Because it sure as hell isn't gratitude."

"I'm grateful you noted. I'm sure it's nothing, but that's what I need to get inside and find out."

His hand dropped away but that deep, haunted stare never broke from hers. "It always ends up here. You and me on opposite sides of a very large line in the sand."

The bold lie—the one that would have told him she had no idea what he was talking about—sprang to her lips, but Veronica held it back.

They did always end up right back in this place, both

of them coated in a layer of willful, stubborn animosity no amount of chemistry or heat or attraction could erase. Only he was wrong about one thing.

The line wasn't sand. It was concrete. Hard. Immovable. Unyielding.

"I know," she finally said.

"Why is that?"

"I wish I knew."

Ace waited in his truck, unwilling to go home, yet equally unwilling to get in the middle of Belle's investigation.

Truth be told he didn't even belong here. But truth or reason or rational thought had long since vanished, along with the clown who'd been peeking inside Veronica's office windows.

He'd given his statement, detailing what he saw and how he'd run around the back, his quarry out of sight by then. After taking it all down Belle had suggested he head back home, but she hadn't pushed when he'd said no.

It was a quality he admired in her.

A willingness to push, and an understanding of when to back off.

The tap on his window pulled him from his thoughts and he turned to see his brother standing outside the truck. Tate's ready grin was in full evidence, but it held none of its usual easygoing warmth.

"What are you doing here?" Ace asked as fresh air blew in through the open window.

"Came to check on you. Belle texted me a little while ago. Said you've been brooding out here for the last hour."

That shine of admiration dimmed a bit.

"She doesn't need to be worried about me. She's got

a lot more going on in there." Ace tilted his head toward Veronica's practice.

"I know my Belle. She can handle it."

"Sure she can."

There was a time that knowledge hadn't set well on Tate's shoulders. His fear for Belle's safety, all while she insisted that she wanted a career in law enforcement, had pushed the two of them apart. So far apart, in fact, that they'd kept to opposite sides of Midnight Pass for over a decade, only crossing paths when absolutely necessary.

There were times when it reminded Ace of his situation with Veronica, but each time he gave the idea free rein, turning it over in his mind, he had to admit the truth.

He and Veronica were nothing like Belle and Tate. His brother had needed to work past the idea that the woman he loved, despite working a dangerous job, needed his support as she followed her dream.

Veronica Torres was an entirely different matter.

On the surface, the two of them were highly compatible. Combustible, even, with the chemistry that flared to life between them. But none of it could make up for the fundamentally opposite way they approached everything. Ace hadn't understood that fully until she'd broken up with him, fled the Pass and married a man less than a year later.

No. They were nothing like Tate and Belle.

Tate shrugged his shoulders and walked around the front of the truck before opening the passenger door and slipping inside. "Want to really tell me what's going on?"

"I already made a statement to the police. Since your soon-to-be wife was so insistent on calling you out here, why don't you make her tell you?"

"It looks like we're serving surly with a side of asshole." Tate rolled his eyes. "This'll be fun."

"Get out of my truck, then."

"If only it were that easy." His younger brother let out a long-suffering sigh. "I'm here to save you from yourself."

"How you going to do that?"

"Common sense doesn't work. And I can't just pound on you like I do Hoyt."

Ace finally smiled. "Because I'll win?"

"Nah. Because it's too much like hitting Dad."

The smile fell so fast he could feel his facial muscles contracting. "Low blow."

"Then quit acting like an old man. You like the woman. Hell, you even loved her once. Don't be as stupid as I was and keep up this lunacy."

It was startling to have Tate strike so close to the very thoughts he'd just had. "We're not like you and Belle."

"Oh, no? Because looking at you both it seems like I'm watching my miserable, clueless self muddle around a little over six months ago."

"It's not the same. Saying it doesn't make it true."

"Denying it doesn't, either."

That pounding Tate spoke of sounded a hell of a lot more comfortable than this conversation, but short of throwing his brother out of his truck, he was trapped. And no matter how good a well-thrown punch might feel in the moment, it was never the answer.

And the resulting bruises never felt good the next day.

"Belle mention any strangers seen around town?"

Whether his brother was ready to end the conversation or not, Tate picked up the new thread. "Nothing specific but I know there's a lot she chalks up to a day's work that she doesn't think to mention. FBI's still here so that's got to mean something."

"I'm starting to wonder if they'll ever leave."

"That makes two of us. Their pop-up field office has become awfully permanent."

The drug trade in Midnight Pass had always flourished through the hidden ravines that ran along the border, but it had become so extreme over the past few years that the FBI had set up shop. Ostensibly to help the local police, Ace well knew they were in town to nab a bigger score. They'd set their sights on some of the largest drug cartels and the feds had little time for the comings and goings of the small town they'd basically invaded.

He'd asked Belle about it once. How it felt to have interlopers with bigger badges and the power of the entire government behind them. She'd hedged a bit, but had finally admitted that the intrusion chafed. A sentiment shared by the entire town, who'd recognized that caliber of law enforcement meant the little problem they'd done their level best to ignore was not only real and present but it had also grown out of control.

And now it had landed at Veronica's door.

The actual door—the one he hadn't looked away from for more than thirty seconds at a stretch—opened, with Julie, Belle and finally Veronica trooping out. He watched her nod at something Belle said, a tight smile pasted firmly on her face. It was a smile that couldn't hide the tension beneath, especially when matched to the tight set of her shoulders.

Ignoring his brother's careful attention, Ace pushed out of the truck, determined to get to her. And caught the tail end of Belle's response.

"Patrol's pretty active around the town square, but we're going to put extra attention on the building. The team'll do sweeps around back, too."

"Sweeps? Won't that draw extra attention?" The demand was out of his mouth before he could stop it and he was rewarded with dark looks from both Veronica and Belle.

Belle responded first, her voice snappish. "So I can do my job."

"And what if it antagonizes the bastard?"

"I think you need to leave Belle to do her job." Veronica interjected. "I appreciate your looking out for me and my practice but the police have this covered. You don't need to ride over here like some avenging hero."

Avenging hero?

Is that what she thought he'd done? That he'd seen this as some sort of glory play for himself?

"Okay, then. I'll get going." Ace lifted his hat to Veronica, Belle and Julie, nodding to each in turn. "I'm glad this is under control."

He didn't wait for a response, but turned on his heel and headed for the truck.

Tate had already jumped out and was standing by the front. Ace saw the slight opening of his brother's mouth, followed by the clear decision to say nothing, Tate's lips slamming closed.

Good.

It was about damn time someone kept their opinions to themselves and left him the hell alone.

Arden Reynolds had always figured God had blessed her with three older brothers because she was gifted in dealing with the often pigheaded nature of the human male. Her petite frame and big eyes had always had an odd, calming effect on men and she'd assumed she was born to the role because, in her mother's immortal words, she could handle anything.

Add on that her great-grandmother had played a similar role in her own family—a woman who she was said to resemble in every way and whom she had been given her surname as her own—and it was fate.

Lately, she'd begun to think she'd had it wrong. Her mother had it wrong. Fate had it wrong. And her sainted, beloved great-grandmother must have been more fool than understanding angel.

She did *not* understand the male of the species. Nor did she have any more patience left in any part of her body for their damn fool antics and idiotic behavior.

With self-righteous anger burning in her breast, Arden let it carry her into the stables, stomping each and every step to Ace's office. When she'd determined she'd made more than enough noise on her approach, she took a deep breath and let it rip.

"Andrew Reynolds! Get your ungrateful ass out of that office and into the kitchen. I do not cook for you because I like it. Nor do I do it because I'm your servant. The least you can do is eat it when it's hot."

Ace glanced up from his desk, never even wincing at the use of his given name. "Why do you do it, then?"

His clear green gaze was as full of misery as she'd ever seen it. Her rant hadn't even managed to light a small spark in those depths. Determined to change that, she pressed on. "Because I decided a long time ago the only way to put anything halfway decent into my mouth was to make it myself. Thank God Reese came along and Tate finally learned to make a burger on the grill without burning it to the consistency of a brick. Belle and Hoyt, however, remain absolutely useless unless I want to subsist on sandwiches."

She leaned in and planted her hands on the edge of his desk. "News flash. I don't."

"I made dinner last Friday."

"Spaghetti and hot dogs are not a meal."

"You ate it," he pointed out.

Despite her frustration and increasing understanding that she still hadn't lit a fuse, Arden pushed on. "Under duress. And you know what else?"

"What?"

"You didn't put any love in it."

Although she didn't spark a fight, she finally got something at that random statement. Ace's gaze narrowed. "What does that mean?"

"When you make that god-awful dish you always cut up the hot dogs in small, even chunks. This time it looked like you'd hacked up a package of hot dogs with a hammer."

"I cut them."

"Whatever." She dropped into the seat opposite his desk. "Why are you hiding out here?"

"I'm doing work."

"No, you're not. You're brooding. Which can be a productive work strategy from time to time, but it's sat on your shoulders for too long and now it's turned into wallowing."

What had been modest concern and lingering frustration morphed into something else entirely. "Ace. Please tell me what's wrong."

He hesitated and it was in the pause that concern moved firmly to worry and fear.

"Her business was invaded today. She's possibly in

danger and maybe even in someone's sights based on what I observed."

Arden didn't need to ask who the "she" was. And while she didn't want to dismiss Ace's concerns, there were other possibilities. "Belle said they're putting a patrol on to watch out for Veronica's business. And whether we like it or not we do get strangers in town. The man might have been looking for a vet to get help."

"I saw him, Arden. He wasn't looking for help. He was looking to make trouble." Ace's head dropped, the burden of pain and worry riding his shoulders before he looked up again. "And I'm the last person she wants help from."

"That's not true."

The husky words floated into the room. Arden turned to see Veronica standing at the doorway, her dark brown gaze as miserable as Ace's.

She'd always seen Veronica Torres as this sort of goddess. The fact that they were several years apart in age had probably helped that image, but they were also physical opposites, the vet all the things Arden wasn't. Tall, with long dark hair that fell down her back in waves. Her deep brown eyes were striking and full of mystery, where Arden's bright blue ones had always told everyone exactly what she was thinking.

It was only in that instant, staring at the woman who so obviously loved her brother, that Arden finally saw the real Veronica. The one who was vulnerable and scared and trying determinedly not to give her heart up to a man.

Arden knew that look. Had lived it herself and knew that she was never going to put herself in that position again. Other hearts might heal but hers never would and she'd long since come to accept that fact.

While she might not risk herself, she had no problem seeing a future for others. And she wholeheartedly wanted to see a different outcome than her own for Ace and Veronica. Standing, she gestured to her seat. "I was just leaving."

Veronica gave a vague hand wave. "I can go. I'm sorry to interrupt."

Arden took the woman's arm and pulled her gently toward the chair. "I really do have to go. You sit."

Once she got Veronica settled, Arden headed for the door and out into the stable. As she walked past the stall doors, far quieter than when she'd come in, she listened. And when she heard her brother's deep voice, full of concern and understanding, she had a moment of victory.

Ace and Veronica just might have a shot at that different outcome.

Chapter 7

She shouldn't have come. Shouldn't involve him in this. Shouldn't be here wanting the safety and comfort those broad shoulders and muscled arms could give.

But try as she might to do otherwise, Veronica had driven right through every one of those shouldn'ts and headed over to Reynolds Station, anyway.

Arden's hasty departure had stunned both of them for a minute but Ace finally picked up the conversation. "You doing okay?"

"Yeah. I'm fine."

Ace's gaze searched her face. "I wasn't trying to scare you earlier."

"I don't think that. At all. It doesn't seem real, but I know that it is."

"I know my family has seen more than its fair share of bad happenings around here and I'm not asking for trouble, but there was something off about that guy. I'm not going to ignore it or pretend my gut isn't blaring like a siren."

Ignore it? Had she been so wrapped up in her frustration that she'd given him that impression?

"Once again, my inability to speak to you with any measure of my normal civility left the absolute wrong impression. I'm grateful to you."

Those sexy green eyes widened, but he said nothing so she continued on.

"You were watching out for me and I couldn't even manage the most basic level of appreciation." She stood, suddenly unable to sit still. "I am grateful. More than you know. I just—"

Before she could say anything—before the awful, terrible words could spill out—Ace was there, those big strong arms wrapped around her.

Just like she'd wanted all along.

"What happened?"

Her face was pressed to his chest but it gave an added layer of protection to say what she needed to say. To let the terrible words spill out. Words she'd sworn to herself she'd never say again after she got through the horror of police statements and endless questions by drug company lawyers and even more endless questions by insurance lawyers.

She'd said them all over and over, even when it seemed as if no one was listening.

Or worse, that they even believed her.

But she'd said them each time she'd been asked. And then swore to bury them all.

His arms tightened, his strength pouring into her. "You can tell me."

"I know." She whispered the words against his chest. With one more deep breath, she allowed her mind to go back to that awful, terrible night.

The one that had nearly ruined her business.

The one that did finally ruin her marriage.

"I had a practice in Houston. After—" She stopped and then thought better of it. Ace knew her and her situation. Pretending that it hadn't happened was an insult to him. "I moved there after I got married."

"I'd assumed so."

"I was out a lot of the time, tending to patients, but I still spent time in the office. Managing invoicing and payments, accepting the drug shipments, managing all the needed tax documents. That sort of thing."

He didn't say anything, just kept those wonderful arms wrapped tight around her as he made slow, soothing circles over her lower back.

"It was a few days after one of the drug shipments. A vet keeps a lot of medicines in stock and a large-animal vet even more so."

"More medicines or higher doses?"

"Both. I see a broad variety of animals and need different types of care options."

He didn't ask anything else but Veronica realized immediately how he'd centered her. With that simple question Ace had channeled her clinical side and had turned this into a professional story instead of a personal one.

"I noticed something off with the door one afternoon after I came back from one of the horse farms out in Katy. Someone had clearly played with the back door to the office, a fact made clear when I barely pushed and it swung open."

The sheer panic that had coated her stomach in that

moment came once again, roiling and sloshing as adrenaline pumped liquid fuel through her veins.

"Shh, now," Ace whispered. "Just get through it."

"The staff had followed protocol. The pharmacy was locked down tight and no one had gotten into anything. The police came and I got new locks and I figured that was the end of it all."

Only it hadn't been. The determination to make the drug score had lit a fuse and it was too late before she realized that she'd set the match.

"They came back?"

His voice never wavered, nor did those large, soothing circles, but she felt his tension all the same. With her retelling, his body seemed to electrify, growing stiffer and more alert with each word.

"Yep. I didn't know until after but I'd become the object of a gang initiation ritual. The missed drugs and my report to the cops incited something and they came back after me. Only now I was the target and the game had ratcheted up beyond just a drug score.

"A few weeks after the initial break-in I was there late doing paperwork. I'd already locked down the pharmacy, but they forced their way in and then held me at gunpoint to open the locks."

The cold fear that had unfurled in her belly spread, solidifying through her veins like ice down a tree branch.

She'd relived that night over and over in her mind and it had only been with intensive therapy, her work with her animals and the return to her family that she'd finally gotten past most of the fear she'd lived with after the attack. Upon returning to Midnight Pass she'd been determined to buy her home and live on her own—a hard-won victory but a victory all the same. And she'd forced herself to go out to her appointments and come back to her practice, day after day, week in and week out.

"How did you get away?"

"For all our mutual flaws as a married couple, Mark was a caring man. He sensed something was wrong when I didn't come home, and when I didn't answer my phone he drove to the practice, calling the cops en route. Luckily, the Houston PD beat him to the back door by about two minutes. Which as it turned out was enough time for them to disarm the thugs and even kill one."

"How did this news not make it down here?"

"This isn't really big news in a city the size of Houston. And I asked my parents to keep it to themselves. It was hard enough to try and get back to a normal life. Telling people about a drug holdup doesn't really scream normal."

"You don't need to bury your pain."

Veronica stepped back from his arms, wiping at the tears that covered her cheeks. "It's in my past and I've developed skills to cope with it. I can manage the anxiety."

"Are you managing it?"

"I think so. I also think I have a right to my upset when something happens to blow that calm sky-high."

A right, Veronica knew, but still a reaction that churned acid low in the belly. She'd worked so hard; had come so far.

For what?

An image of those seemingly endless hours held at gunpoint inside her practice in Houston reared up in her mind's eye.

It had obviously all been for nothing.

Cope and manage?

Veronica's words hung in his mind, the steadier cadence of her breathing evidence of that fact. All the while, Ace wondered how he was keeping it together.

From the moment she'd begun her story he'd barely kept a leash on his emotions. He might have let them go entirely if it wasn't for her marked upset and need for comfort.

He knew this wasn't about him. And knew even more that making it about him would make him a total and raging ass. But the idea of her in the crosshairs of criminals, held against her will, filled him with a level of rage he'd never felt before in his life.

Not when his father betrayed them. Not when Tate found a dead body on their property. Not when a local threat had gone after Reese and burned down their barn.

Nothing felt like this.

Pure, unadulterated rage.

Only now Veronica had backed away again. She'd taken comfort in his arms and then pulled away, as if she didn't belong there.

As if.

Going on nothing but instinct, Ace reached forward and pulled her close once more. He might have expected resistance, but the absolute lack of any was almost scary.

"I can't imagine you having to go through that. But know that you're safe here."

"I have moved past it." She pillowed her head against his chest, her arms settling comfortably around his waist. "It's not something I think about every day. It hasn't stopped me from living my life."

"I can see that."

"But I also can't ignore a possible threat." She lifted her head from his chest and stared up at him, those warm brown eyes wide, her pupils filling the space. "What if they found me?"

"Did you tell Belle all of this?"

"I did. That's what took us so long."

"Then know that she will do everything in her power to figure this out. It could be just as you say, a random person looking in the windows hoping to find you because they need your expertise."

"And if it's not?"

Her words were quiet, but the question hovered between them with all the power of a gunshot.

"If it's not, then we will find him. And we will take care of it."

He'd never considered himself a violent man, but he did protect what was his. His brothers had his back, that he had no doubt. And he put considerable stock in his sister-in-law and in her ability to get things done.

But in the end, it really did come down to one thing. He protected what was his.

And Veronica Torres was his.

Had she ever been anything else?

Of course, who would have known, the way he'd avoided her these past months. His family had made steady work of ignoring the fact that they noticed, but it came up at odd moments. Was he joining Hoyt for a review of one of the horse's X-ray scans? Would he head to Veronica's office with Tate to review a new course of treatment for the next time they dealt with an illness in the herd?

He hadn't accompanied his brothers either of those times, or so many others that had come along that would have put him and Veronica in close proximity. There was always an excuse, always a reason. But deep down, he knew.

It broke his heart to be within one hundred yards of

Veronica Torres. Because of it, he stayed away. He found the right excuses and worked himself to the bone on other things.

Always avoiding her and the truth of what had been between them all those years ago.

Like that had worked.

Not only had his strategy failed miserably, but he'd also missed the opportunity to work with her and see her expertise in person. She was an extraordinary large-animal vet and Midnight Pass was fortunate to have her. Reynolds Station was fortunate to have her.

He was fortunate to have her.

In his life.

And, if he could fix things between them, more permanently than the occasional visit to the ranch.

"Veronica?"

That dark gaze never wavered from his. "Yes?"

"I don't want you to leave. Tonight." *Ever.*

They both stood there, each equally aware they balanced on a precarious ledge. The present, so tempting and real, beckoned them both. But the past hovered behind, clawing with sharp fingers.

"I don't want to leave, either."

Those claws might be sharp, but they fell away as if they had never been. With that satisfying knowledge, Ace reached for the present.

Veronica was an adult and she'd long stopped hiding or feeling embarrassed about real and human needs. But she couldn't hide the thrilling shot of adrenaline that spiked as Ace rushed her through the back door of the ranch and up a back set of stairs to his room.

Or living suite, Veronica thought as she stopped short. Oh, yeah, *suite* would be a *way* better term.

"What's the matter?" Ace was at her back, his arms wrapping around her waist as he bent to nuzzle her neck.

"This is some bedroom. It's more like an apartment." Even with the distraction of his lips hot against her neck, she took a moment to look around at the large living room and the bedroom beyond.

"Do you think I'd be able to stand living with my brothers and my sister if I had just a room?"

"Did you have this…" She nearly stopped herself before continuing. "Before?"

Before.

Even as the fact that they had a *before* was quickly being eclipsed by the fact that were having a *now*.

"When it became obvious we were all determined to stay here on the ranch, we added on to the house. So no, I didn't have this before."

"Okay. I didn't think I'd forgotten that much."

"I don't think I've forgotten anything." His voice was husky, his lips returning to her nape, and Veronica forgot all about bedrooms, suites or house reconstruction.

And all she remembered was Ace.

She turned into his arms willingly, the memories that had haunted her for so long replaced by something she hadn't imagined she'd ever find again.

Ace.

Real and in the flesh. Here. Now.

The tears she'd cried for him at her mother's dining room table—had that only been a few hours?—seemed a lifetime ago. As if she'd become a different person from her afternoon to her evening.

Hadn't she?

The sadness and confusion that had accompanied her to her family's home had vanished upon her return to her practice. Ace was there, determined to protect her. Determined to show he cared.

While sex wouldn't solve anything, it would hopefully go a long way toward assuaging the tension that persisted between them. If they could get that under control, then they might have a shot at finding their way again. If not as a couple, then at least as friends.

Could they get to that place?

Or maybe a better question was, could they really go on as they were?

Sex was an itch, a conflagration of hormones, nothing more. But it was also an itch that, once managed, would give them both a chance to assess the situation between them rationally. It was her last thought as she lifted her arms around his neck and pulled him close for a kiss.

His firm lips met hers and she felt the small, triumphant smile that curved against her mouth before matching it with one of her own. It was that moment—that small moment of connection—that vanished the very last thought of maybe turning tail and running.

She wanted to stay. She'd come up to his room with every intention of staying. But the reality of what they were about to do had lodged somewhere deep, reminding her that making love with Ace wasn't a choice she could undo tomorrow.

It was that smile, though, that made it all come together. That shared moment that was as intimate—and as powerful—as the joining of their bodies.

His mouth moved against hers, his tongue firm yet gentle as he explored her. For all his size, he wasn't a man to overpower a woman. Rather, he knew the exact ways to taste and tease, drawing his partner along on the journey. And, oh, how she went willingly.

Pulling back, she stared up at him. "I'm glad I came over."

Passion hazed the green depths of his gaze, but his voice was clear when he spoke. "Was this what you had in mind?"

"Not exactly. But I'm glad I'm here. And if you'll have me, I really would like to stay."

"I'd like you to stay." He resettled his mouth over hers before exploring a path over her jaw toward her cheek. His whispered words sent shivers racing the length of her spine. "I'd like that very much."

"Me, too."

While he'd always been a damn fine credit to the image of the American cowboy, Veronica marveled by what she found as her hands explored his body. Their years apart had only honed his physique, nearly a decade more of daily labor shaping his muscles into an impressive expanse for her exploration. Her fingers drifted from the width of his shoulders on over his chest and then on to his stomach, that flat panel of flesh shooting a thrill through her midsection until it settled low in her belly.

Goodness, he was solid.

Suddenly impatient with waiting and desperate to see him, she tugged at the buttons that brushed against her fingers, slipping each from their enclosure. The warm T-shirt underneath provided a second barrier and she reached for the hem after her impatient fingers had shoved off the soft flannel of his work shirt.

"Slow down."

"I don't know if I can," she whispered.

"Well, then."

Veronica sensed his movements a nanosecond before she was in motion, pressed hard against that warm chest. He moved them from the sitting room to the bedroom with impressive speed, falling onto the bed with her in a heap. He cushioned them as they fell and it was only when they hit with a delicious *oomph* that she started laughing.

"You don't like my moves?" Ace smiled as he shifted to his side, a hand propped under his head.

"I like all your moves. And I think I'll call that the cowboy special."

"Hmm. I like that." He trailed a hand over her cheek and down over her chin, the gentle strokes enough to have the laughter dying in her throat.

"It's the type of full-body move I expect you use to shove cows into the shoot for branding."

"That paints a sexy image."

"Doesn't it?"

At his subtle frown she reached up and traced her fingers over his jaw, the journey a match for his explorations. "Did I say I didn't like it?"

"I'm not sure cows and sex go in the same conversation."

"Then consider yourself the luckiest of men."

"Based on where I'm at in this moment, I can't think of myself as anything else."

She lifted her head to press her lips to his, murmuring as she went. "I talk about cows and sex all the time. To a large-animal vet you can even consider this foreplay."

Laughter still shook his ribs as Ace sunk into the kiss. Cows? Sex?

Foreplay?

He had a lot of memories of making love with Veronica. He'd learned to bury most of them, the pain of remembering too sharp to bear, but what he had retained was the carefree way they'd made love. Each time together had been a joy, and laughter had threaded through it all. Happy and joyful and, well, *fun*.

He hadn't had a lot of fun in his life since and laughing with her over the cows forced him to consider that maybe there was more to his stoic steadiness than he'd ever realized. Maybe he needed the right channel to bring out his softer side.

Maybe he'd just needed Veronica.

"That's very good to know."

"You know what else I like."

He nipped at her lower lip. "What's that?"

"Not talking about cows having sex and talking about me having sex." She tugged on his shoulder, effectively pulling him so he lay on top of her. "Just me and you."

"I can get down for that conversation."

"Then by all means." Her hands reached for the waistband of his jeans. "Let's."

It was the work of moments for them to finish undressing each other. What he thought of as her workday uniform—blouse and slacks—were easy to remove. Her boots took a bit more time, each dropping to the floor with a thunk when she toed them off.

And then it was just the two of them, naked and wrapped up in each other. Ace fought to stay in the moment, the demands of his body keeping him firmly grounded even as his memories kept tugging him toward the past.

Back to that place where they were young and carefree and in love. To that time when he'd pursued her, the pretty, newly minted vet in town his sole object of affection and interest.

He'd known her, of course. They'd gone through 4-H together and had grown up in the same town. But in the way of teenage boys, her gangly frame and flat chest and seeming easy ability to muck around in horse and cow dung hadn't brought her to his attention.

A mistake he'd done his level best to make up for once he began courting her.

"What are you thinking about?" Her voice was breathless but he saw the clear interest stamped in the dark depths of her eyes.

"What an idiot I am."

Her hand rested against his cheek. "I'd say you're the most brilliant man in the world at this exact moment but do tell."

"I don't know what it is about you. About us. I'm nearly ready to go off like a firecracker and I still can't stop thinking about where it all started. How it all began."

The humor that rode her gaze faded, replaced with something far more serious. Something that looked a lot like understanding.

"I know. And it's there. Whether we want to admit it or not, it will always be there."

"Our connection?"

"That. But more than that."

"What?" he asked, surprisingly afraid of what she'd say.

"The past."

Chapter 8

Veronica wanted to curse herself for breaking the mood. Why the hell was she bringing up the past or anything having to do with what came before.

Hell, why was he?

While she admired and wanted honesty in a man, did the two of them need to rehash everything?

Especially while naked?

"It's always going to be there." He laid his forehead against hers.

"I know." She lay there absorbing the truth of that. Their past. The things they did to each other, both good and bad. The harsh words that had exploded between them, ultimately incinerating their relationship to ash. And the simple reality of all the time that had come since. "But maybe we don't need to make it everything."

"I'm not—"

She pressed a quick kiss to his lips to slow him down, before continuing on. "I think that's what we have been doing. I know I have and I think you have, too. But maybe we can leave that where it belongs for a while. Focus on the here and now?"

"I'd like that."

"I would, too."

More than she could say.

And maybe that was the problem. They both seemed insistent to say it and perhaps it was time to just feel. To push on beyond the past and given themselves both a chance to get to know each other now.

The people they'd become.

Determined to show him that, she ran her hands over his back, her fingertips trailing lightly down his spine. The flesh beneath her fingers sparked to life, electricity arcing between them everywhere she touched. As if that simple touch was enough to convince him to join her on the journey, Ace's lips returned to hers, the magic that always flowed between them returning.

She continued her exploration, shifting her focus from his spine to his hip, then on closer to the heat that throbbed between them. With deft movements, she captured his erection in her hand, rewarded with a heavy intake of breath against her lips.

The past was overrated, Veronica couldn't help thinking, especially as all that heated male flesh pressed against her palm.

Way overrated.

She shifted over him, capturing his groans with her mouth, the past vanishing as if it had never been. But it was the way his hand closed over hers, stilling her movements, that settled somewhere deep in her heart.

"Together this time." He devoured her mouth for another hot, carnal kiss. "You and me."

Before she could blink, his other hand had snaked out, rummaging through the bedside table. In moments he had a condom in hand and had shifted to roll it on.

"Let me." With the same slow, torturous movements she'd used against bare flesh, she rolled on the condom, deeply satisfied with the response.

"Temptress."

"That's the bar I was aiming for."

The laugh started again, low in her belly, sheer joy at being with him. It was only when he shifted once again, his body poised at the opening to hers, that the laughter died, replaced with awe.

Unimaginable awe that she was back in his arms.

As he began to move, that feeling of wonder grew, keeping tempo with the pleasure that built in every cell of her body. They were light and beauty and magic and miracle.

And when the pleasure broke wide open, suffusing them both, Veronica let herself fall into the moment, not even a whisper of the past holding her back.

Veronica knew sex didn't solve anything, but she was hard-pressed to say it didn't go a long way toward putting a spring in her step and a smile on her face. Even a phone call from Belle about twenty minutes after Veronica walked into her practice the next morning couldn't quite diminish the shine.

It did, however, put her feet firmly back on the ground.

The guy Ace saw through the front windows of the feed store had seemingly vanished, as if he'd never been in Midnight Pass. The various businesses on Main Street had been woefully lacking in back-side video security—hers included—and there wasn't anything popping on front-side security feeds. No one looked suspicious or questionable. The conversation did, however, get her on the phone with her security service to make the needed—and necessary—upgrades.

It also reminded her to add a camera to the corner of her building. Ace swore he'd seen someone lurking in the windows, yet a review of her own camera feeds hadn't revealed anyone.

Which meant the lurker had known what to avoid.

When that produced nothing but a lingering chill, Veronica shut down the train of thought. She wasn't a victim and she wasn't sitting idle. The scheduler for her security company had assured her there would be someone out that afternoon. And Julie had already bustled in with lattes and scones.

Veronica knew she was doing all she could to stay safe and avoid any sort of repeat of her experience in Houston.

And she'd had sex with Ace.

Good sex, that had her body humming and nearly every one of her brain cells focused on having it again.

With Ace.

In his house, no less. When she'd seen Belle's number come up on the caller ID she'd had the momentary sensation akin to getting caught as a kid, only this wasn't anything as simple as sneaking a cookie from a jar.

It wasn't simple, either.

So why had it *felt* simple?

She'd lived with the reality for way too long that there wasn't another man on the planet who was like Ace Reynolds.

"You doing okay?"

Veronica looked up from her paperwork to see Julie standing in the door, the box of miniscones she'd purchased held high in one hand. "I'm fine. Why?"

"I had to call your name three times."

"I'm sorry. I'm just distracted, is all."

Julie came fully into the office and set the open box on Veronica's desk. The scent of vanilla icing that coated each miniscone wafted toward her, their siren's call of sugar and carbs too wonderful to resist. Veronica reached for one, reasoning she'd worked off enough calories the night before to enjoy all that sugar, and promptly choked on the first bite at Julie's words.

"Because of the sweet, loving care of the sexiest cowboy this side of the Rio Grande?"

"Julie!"

Julie glanced over her shoulder in a furtive gesture before waving a hand in a come-forward motion. "Come on. Spill. I need to live vicariously through you. Because while I love my husband to distraction and would not trade him for any man anywhere, William Esterson will never, ever look like that in a pair of jeans."

"What do you want me to tell you?" Did Julie actually think she'd share sex stories? And while she had never been the kiss-and-tell type, why was there this manic urge to share just how happy the sexiest cowboy she'd ever seen made her feel?

"He came swooping in to your rescue yesterday and then you gave him the cold shoulder. Rather well done, I might add." Julie reached for her coffee. "But it's easy to see there are sparks between you two."

Understanding dawned. Julie meant the time at the clinic yesterday. Despite the fact that it felt like a night spent with Ace Reynolds was branded on her forehead, it wasn't.

Just like Belle, Julie didn't know anything had happened.

And while the urge to sink into herself was great— she didn't kiss or tell—Veronica couldn't resist sharing a little bit. Especially with a friend.

"Ace and I go back a long way. He was just looking out for me."

"I don't think that's all."

"Sure it is." Veronica had taken a smaller bite of scone this time but even that smaller piece turned to paste in her mouth.

"The two of you are more than friends. Anyone can see it, and the sooner you both do something about it, the better off you'll be."

"It's not like that." Even if it was, her conscience argued.

"What's it like, then?" Julie's smile grew broader, her eyebrows wiggling. "You thinking about using him for sex and then discarding him in a puddle of washed-up man goo?"

She did choke this time and used the cover of a coughing fit to sct her scone down and take a sip of coffee. When she finally could speak again, Veronica asked, "Man goo?"

"It's a metaphor. Go with it."

Veronica glanced down at her scone, happy to have the companionship and silly camaraderie. "What is in these things?"

"Sugar. Which works at times, but not nearly as well as a tall, big man in jeans and boots." Julie waved a hand in front of her face like a fan. "Oh, and that hat. Lord deliver me from heart palpitations from a man in a cowboy hat. Something my Bill does do. Quite well, I might add."

"How long have you been married?"

"We celebrated twenty-seven last year."

"But you're only, like, forty-five."

Julie shrugged. "When you know, you know. We were high school sweethearts and got married two weeks after we graduated. We would have married sooner if we could have convinced our parents."

"Wow." Veronica eyed another scone and decided to save it for lunch. "That's pretty amazing. That you knew so young."

"Some of it's knowing and more of it's feeling and even more of it's a hell of a lot of hard work."

Her mother had said something similar through the years, as had two of her sisters, but for some reason Julie's words stopped her.

She had been married before. And either she and Mark had never gotten to the hard work stage or they'd bypassed it all for a steady, level sort of living. The sort of steady that had left her with the questionable feeling of how she'd gotten into the whole mess in the first place.

"How is it work?" Veronica finally asked. "It's not like going to a job. And it's not like cleaning out exam rooms or doing paperwork."

"Have you ever done taxes with a man?"

"We filed separately when I was married."

"You have no idea what you're missing." Julie snorted. "But that's definitely the paperwork part of marriage. That and mortgages and car loans and school forms. There's definitely paperwork."

Veronica knew those things didn't make up a marriage. Although she was no expert, she had experienced enough to understand shared responsibilities and building a life and the give and take that was required in making that life with another person.

But she hadn't enjoyed it.

She didn't want to dismiss Julie's feelings, but she was curious enough that she finally asked what had been bugging her for far longer than she'd realized. "So how is that fulfilling? How is any of it designed to actually make you happy?"

"Because that's not all it is. It's also laughter and shared secrets and years together. And it's the only family member you actually get to choose."

Memories came flooding back to her in a rush. Waking in Ace's arms. The way he'd held her and taken care of her when she'd come to find him the night before in the stables. Making love throughout the night.

He'd been there for her in every way possible. And while the sex was momentous, the rest of it had been, as well. The way he'd looked out for her. And the way he'd accepted her, without question or censure or demands on what had come before.

It had been wildly fulfilling, and even with all that was left unsaid and unanswered between them, some small part of her understood that Mark hadn't been the reason for her marriage's demise.

She had.

And the love for Ace she'd never really gotten past.

With Walter grazing in the pasture behind him, Ace looked out over Reynolds Station. The calves were growing, their bodies becoming bigger and stronger, shoulders filling out in the readily identifiable frame of a head of cattle.

For over a hundred years, cattle had roamed this land, helmed by his family. It mattered to him. This legacy.

His legacy.

And with the same inexplicable knowledge, he could admit he felt Veronica as deeply in his bones.

The woman was a part of him. As rooted to his soul as the land and as ethereal as the wind that whistled and swirled around him. The night before had been amazing. There had been more than a few tense moments, but the fact that she'd come to him—chosen to come to him—meant a lot.

It meant everything.

He'd dreamed of her so many times, long after it was reasonable to do so. And now that she was back and they'd found what seemed to be a tentative way forward, he had to admit to a rough and raw shot of fear.

They could ignore their past but that didn't mean it wasn't there. And while they'd found a way beyond it last night, the two of them would have to deal with it eventually.

The pain they'd caused each other was nothing to the pain they *would* cause each other if they pressed forward without admitting the gaping chasm that lay between them.

And wasn't he a barrel of fun today for a man who'd had mind-blowing sex last night?

"Careful out here. You'll scare the calves."

He turned to find Tate, mounted high on Tot and staring down at him with a cocky smile painting his face.

"That's funny coming from a man whose ugly mug could scare off a rattler at ten paces."

"Ha ha." Tate swung off his horse, then pointed Tot

in the same direction as Walter, sending him off with a light swat to the rump.

"Belle loves my ugly mug."

"Thank God for that." Ace slapped Tate on the back, his lingering unease fading in the presence of the crazy force that was his younger brother.

"Thank God indeed. And in eight more days, I'm making that woman my wife." Tate looked toward the calves in the distance and Ace took the rare moment to observe his brother. Color rode high on Tate's cheeks, a testament to the cooler temperatures that had blown in with late October and the steady work spent outside under the sun.

They were working men and, despite the near-maniacal regimen of sunscreen and moisturizer their sister pushed on them, small lines fanned out from the green eyes that were a match for Ace's own.

"You excited?"

Tate shifted his gaze off the herd. "Hell, yeah, I'm excited. And scared and crazy in love and ready to do it this moment if we could."

"She means that much to you."

"She means everything."

Tate's gaze never wavered, nor did his broad smile dim a single watt. "Heard you had a visitor last night?"

"And how would you have heard that?"

"Doc Torres's SUV is recognizable around this place. Even more so parked all night in our driveway."

Ace rarely reacted with his fists, but he did have the fleeting thought that today wasn't the day to start. His soon-to-be sister-in-law would have his ass if he marred the singular perfection of Tate's face. And besides, it was rarely fun to punch when the other man was one hundred percent right.

"You going to make a big deal out of this?" Ace asked.

"No."

"Not at all?"

Tate shrugged, apparently unaware of the shiner Ace imagined blooming over one glass-green iris. "Rest of the family has eyes. They could just as easily have scanned the driveway this morning."

"You think any of them did?"

"How would I know?" Tate gave one more nonchalant shrug. One that was completely at odds with the mischief spreading his grin wide. "I'm the one not making a big deal."

Ace considered his brother, all the while wondering who else might have seen Veronica's car. It wasn't exactly a secret. And while he didn't regularly parade women through the house, choosing more neutral territory for dates and what came after, they all had private quarters for a reason. He didn't owe anyone an explanation.

Which made the words spilling out next that much more uncomfortable.

"We spent a bit of time together. If she's willing, we'll spend a bit more. No big deal."

"Wow. What a resounding declaration."

"You were expecting something else?"

The October breeze hummed between them, carrying the light sounds of the cattle as they grazed.

"I guess I was," Tate finally said, breaking the silence. "Something a bit less casual and a bit more along the lines of how much you like the woman and like spending time with her."

"I do like spending time with her."

"She's not a casual fling, Ace. You know that as well as I do."

"Then what is she?"

Tate's gaze momentarily drifted toward the sky before he caught himself. "She's Veronica. The woman you loved. Still do, you stubborn ass. You can act all casual about it, but that doesn't change the facts."

"You're dangerously close to overstepping."

"Fine. Slug me for it. Or turn and walk away. You're better at that, anyway."

The slap firmly hit its mark but Ace remained calm. "What the hell are you even doing out here?"

"My job. And my brotherly duty." Tate stepped closer, any hint of his casual and easygoing nature gone. "I told you the other day what a fool I was to wait so long to find Belle. But I did find her. And I'm never letting go. If you have half an ounce of sense you'll take my advice and do the same."

"And I believe I told you that Veronica and I aren't like you and Belle."

"What are you like, then?"

Mom and Dad.

The idea had nearly flowed straight out of his brain and directly over into words, spilling out of his mouth with all the force of a dam breaking before Ace stopped himself.

Held back what he'd always believed, even if none of it had made a lick of sense until that very instant.

It was Tate and Belle who had been childhood sweethearts. Two people who had found each other young and realized the spark of attraction instantly. They might have danced around the flame for far too long, but there was something inevitable about the two of them. That flame had always been there and Ace, Hoyt and Arden had innately understood it was a simple matter of time before the two of them found each other again.

He and Veronica were different.

Hell, he'd thought it the night before, even in the midst of making love to her. The fact that he'd never really noticed her when they were young, chalking her up to that gangly girl who preferred animals to people. He'd never seen her as an object for his attentions and had barely registered in school that she was alive let alone female.

It had only been when she'd come back after college and vet school that he'd taken notice. That he'd seen an attractive woman behind the love of animals and cool competence. That her confidence at her job had helped transform her overall confidence as a woman.

That was when he'd grown interested.

Maybe his lack of initial recognition of her was the real heart of their heated battles. There might be wild attraction, but there'd always been a distance, too. Like his inability to truly see her until she'd blossomed was a stumbling block to their happiness.

That their attraction came with an asterisk on it.

All his adult life he wondered why they couldn't find their way. Or rather, what stood in their way And maybe he had his answer. Maybe he was doomed to repeat the poor lessons of his parents if he continued to pursue something?

His parents had fought the same way he and Veronica did. Wild passion interspersed with cool detachment and a desperate desire to prove something to the other.

Was that love?

Or worse. Maybe he wasn't made for anything else.

Chapter 9

Veronica pulled down the long driveway of Reynolds Station straight into Bedlam. She'd gotten word that one of the horses needed seeing, and since she and Ace were headed over to her parents' house for one of their last Friday fiestas of the year, she'd decided to kill two birds with one stone.

Staring at the craziness unfolding all around the back side of the ranch house, she had to wonder if the birds should have lived another day.

She climbed out of the car, only to find herself nearly waylaid by the town baker, Wendy Parker, stomping her feet as she swept past in a cloud of anger. At least the cloud smelled pretty, the distinct overtones of sugar and chocolate like a perpetual coat around the woman's shoulders.

"Wendy!" Veronica called after her, but got a waved hand in the air for her troubles.

"I'm off to make a damn groom's cake in the shape of a horse," Wendy hollered over her shoulder. "And if Tate Reynolds argues with me I'm going to make the ugly brown thing look like it's lying on a pillow."

The Godfather reference was easy to understand. The anger—or the idea that Tate Reynolds was some sort of wedding diva—harder to fathom.

She'd almost convinced herself of the idea that Wendy must just be in a bad mood when Arden slipped out of the house, rubbing a hand over her forehead. Veronica caught the distinct words "damn brother" before Arden lifted her head and realized she'd been overheard.

Her friend walked over to greet her. "I will never again make a negative comment about a bridezilla."

"That bad?" Veronica held back a giggle and tried diligently to wipe the smile from her face.

"Bad? Who would have thought my laid-back jokester brother would be such a pain in the ass?"

"What's he doing?"

"You name it, he's doing it." Arden shook her head. "Wendy works with sugar all day. She is the sweetest human being I know. And Tate just managed to drive her off with all the finesse of a rattler in springtime."

"But what did he actually do?"

"The man's been bound and determined to have an armadillo for his groom's cake since he was seven years old and watched Steel Magnolias with my mother."

"Made with red velvet cake and gray icing?"

"You got it."

"What changed?" Veronica asked, narrowly avoiding wrinkling her nose at the image of that ugly cake.

"He suddenly decided after a middle-of-the-night vision that he needed to memorialize Tot as part of the wedding."

"Isn't that sorta gross?"

Arden waved a hand. "That's what I told him. That's what Wendy told him. And that's what Belle told him. Man won't listen."

"She sounded upset, but I think Wendy will do it."

"She'll do it. And she's still getting paid for the armadillo that she made last weekend and put in the freezer."

Arden shook her head and offered up one more platitude about the patience of a saint and pigheaded brothers before gesturing vaguely behind her. "I'd better get to it. The florist is coming next and Belle texted me an SOS to get over to the barn to help mitigate any last-minute changes."

"See you later."

Veronica watched Arden stomp off and wished good vibes on her friend. She then headed for the stables and the waiting Mabel, who needed to have her foreleg looked at. She navigated the swirling mass of contractors who were bringing in tents and a surprisingly large number of chairs. A few more carried what appeared to be wood panels for a dance floor.

She'd nearly reached the stables when she was intercepted once more, this time by Hoyt.

"This is what a church and a reception hall are for," the man muttered before catching sight of her, his embarrassment at being seen talking to himself a match for Arden's.

"No need to explain." Veronica held up a hand. "I just saw Arden and Wendy the baker. Sounds like things are getting a little stressful as you all count down to the wire."

"You have no idea."

If Tate was the jokester of the family, Hoyt was its

Steady Eddie. The fact that the man looked haggard, worn and ready to chew on a nail was indicative of the madness that had obviously descended.

"It will be beautiful when it's all done." She tried to find common ground or, if not common, at least a way to settle the situation.

Hoyt looked around, before shaking his head. "It had better be."

She waved him on, making a quick comment that she needed to see to Mabel, and watched him stomp toward the house, another smile creasing her face.

"It's not funny, you know."

Veronica whirled to find Ace behind her, his own smile firmly in place.

"It sort of is."

"I know it is. Who knew Tate would be the crazy one? He's normally so levelheaded."

"Momentary lapse in judgment?" she asked, inordinately happy to see him again. Late-afternoon sun haloed him in a silhouette and all that golden paint had her blood jumping in her veins.

Oh, my, did she want this man. He'd come to her place the night before so it had only been a matter of hours since she'd last seen him, but it felt like an eternity. Without giving him a chance to respond to her question, she leaned into him, lifting up on her toes so their lips met. Her hands settled on his sun-warmed shoulders and she drank her fill like a woman drowning in the desert.

He responded immediately, his lazy smile transferring to more interesting activities with his lips. He maintained that steady, lazy charm even as the pressure of his tongue turned her bones to liquid, need racing through her like a thoroughbred at top speed.

"That's quite a welcome," Ace said when he finally lifted his head. He wrapped an arm around her waist and drew her toward the stables. The greeting was spectacular, but even it couldn't quite compete with the easy, gentle way he'd taken hold of her. It was comfortable. Familiar. And oh-so-welcome.

"So Tate's been a bit of a groomzilla."

"Either that or he's had a complete personality transplant. All I know he was out in the pasture with me yesterday giving me a hard time and today he turns into the demon of the county."

"Weddings can do that to people."

"It didn't do that to Hoyt and Reese," Ace pointed out.

"They're different people. And they didn't have quite as much time to build things up in their mind as Tate has."

Ace stopped alongside Mabel's stall, turning to face her. "Maybe."

"He and Belle have been in love for a long time. And then when things happened with Russ Grantham—" Veronica broke off, shaken to realize how close Tate and Belle had come to losing what was between them.

Or worse, never making it to their wedding day at all.

Grasping for a new topic, she landed on Ace's last comment. "What was Tate razzing you about?"

"Nothing important."

The response was stilted, and as evasions went it was a poor one. She nearly pressed the point but a soft whicker from Mabel echoed out of the stall and Veronica focused on her patient.

She wanted to be disappointed when Ace backed away, claiming something he needed to see to in his office. More than that, she wanted to be surprised or shocked at how the two of them were still able to put up walls when a subject grew sensitive.

Only she wasn't.

Instead, she was forced to admit the truth. The past she'd been so desperate to put behind them had just paid her a call.

Ace finished parking and walked down the long street that led to Veronica's parents' house. He'd dropped her off at the driveway, her arms full of two casserole dishes filled with a dip she'd made for the dinner. It had been a convenient—even courteous—choice, but the drop-off had served another purpose.

The truth was, he needed a few minutes to himself.

How could he have slipped so easily in the stables?

Tate had them all confused, his behavior so at odds with his usual demeanor, but Ace could hardly claim that as the reason. He'd grown comfortable with Veronica. In a matter of days she'd gone from being important to being necessary and it didn't rest well on his shoulders.

The street was full, the cars of her family and their friends parked on both shoulders, and he'd finally found a spot about two hundred yards from the driveway. He loved these gatherings and had missed attending them. Marcelita and Esteban Torres opened their home nearly every Friday from May to October to their friends and family, hosting a large dinner full of food and laughter and dancing. Everyone attending brought some contribution to the dinner and each week the Torres backyard provided the backdrop for the celebration.

He'd been wide-eyed and naive the first time he'd attended, having no idea families actually met up with each other like this. He'd stood at the fringes until one of Veronica's older aunts had drawn him into conversation, gesturing him to a seat at the table. He had a functional handle on Spanish and had been able to communicate with most everyone. Using a mix of the Spanish he knew and the English they knew, he'd made it through the dinner.

By the end of that first night he'd been invited fishing and by the end of that first summer he was as comfortable at those dinners as he was in his own home.

A happy chorus of *hola*'s rang out as he walked around the house and in through the backyard. The space was decorated much as he remembered, but things had been updated. White lights were strung up on poles, crisscrossing the entire backyard and lighting up the area full of picnic tables and seats. A chimenea still sat at the edge of the patio pavers, emitting heat in the cool evening air. Her father had added a large smoker, visible at the back of the property. They had also upgraded the large fence that surrounded the backyard, the dark wood gleaming in the fading light.

"Ace!"

He turned to find Veronica's father, the man's hand extended in greeting. Before he could check the impulse, Ace pulled Esteban Torres close in a warm hug. "It's good to see you."

Although he'd seen the man through the years, in and around the Pass, there was something different about being in his home once again. Just like the ease with which Veronica had come back into his life, walking into this backyard felt exactly the same.

Why had he walked away from it all?

"It's good to see you, Ace. And I know Marcie is excited to see you." Esteban pointed a finger toward the kitchen. "Go ahead on in."

Although he knew Veronica's family would be kind, Ace hadn't anticipated the warm welcome. Especially from her father. "It's okay that I'm here?"

"It's always okay that you're here, my son." Esteban gave him a solid pat on the shoulder. "You are always welcome in my home."

The promise humbled him and reminded Ace that breaking up with Veronica hadn't simply been about two of them. He and his family had missed Belle during the years when she and Tate had been broken up. Why would he have assumed the same didn't apply to him and Veronica?

Well aware the mention of Veronica's mother wasn't a casual one, Ace headed for the kitchen. And found himself enfolded in the warm embrace of Marcelita Torres.

"Andrew. Andrew." She hugged him, her grip as tight as he remembered. "Oh, I have missed you."

"I've missed you, too, Mrs. Torres." He hugged her back, and for the second time in two days thought of his own mother.

For all the drama that played out daily with his father, Betsy Reynolds was a loving woman. She loved her children to distraction and made sure each and every day all of them knew it. He still missed her and felt her absence daily, but in that moment, wrapped in that tight hug, it was as sharp as the day he lost her.

He hadn't started dating Veronica until after his mother died, and it always bothered him the two women had never met. They'd likely known of each other, broad acquaintances in a town where no one was technically a stranger, but they hadn't truly known each other.

His mother had never seen the way Veronica's eyes lit up when she spoke of animals or had the opportunity to watch her competence when she worked for the health of stock. Nor had Betsy Reynolds ever had the chance to see her son's face as he stared at the woman he loved.

He'd always felt cheated that his mother had died before seeing so much of her children's future, but it wasn't until that instant, his arms still wrapped around Marcelita, that he realized just how much she would never see.

The health and restoration of the ranch.

Tate's and Hoyt's wives.

And come the spring, her first grandchild.

Those images assailed him, one after the other in a barrage of pain he had no idea he'd been holding.

"I made extra tamales for you." Marcie's voice was gentle, as if she understood the direction of his thoughts, as she pulled back from the hug. "You share them with your brothers and those pretty sisters of yours and bring all of them next time we get together."

Coughing around the thickness in his throat, he latched on to the easy softball she'd managed to tee up. "I thought this was the last party of the season?"

"Bah." Marcie waved a hand. "I think we have one more in us. And I want to see that pretty Reese and her baby bump."

"She's getting bigger every day. There's a real baby in there."

Marcie swatted him on the shoulder, but it had little power behind it. "You never say that to a pregnant woman."

"What? She looks as gorgeous as always."

"Doesn't matter." Veronica's mother wagged a finger at him. "As far as you're concerned she's as skinny as ever and you can't even see evidence of a baby unless she brings it up."

"I'll remember that."

She winked at him. "Now pick up that tray and take a pass out there with the tamales. Our happy party-goers will be clamoring if they don't get out there soon."

"Aye-aye, Captain."

Veronica caught his eye from across the room, smiling at him as he hefted the large ceramic serving tray. She winked at him, much the same way her mother had, and Ace was shocked at how different the effect.

He hadn't imagined the tension in his truck on the drive over. He also knew full well he was the one to blame, blabbing about Tate and then not following through on explaining why. It felt as if the storm had passed, but in the end it wouldn't have mattered if it hadn't.

He owed Veronica an explanation. He *wasn't* his father and he wasn't going to repeat the mistakes he'd grown up watching.

The two of them might not have a future. They needed far more time together to determine if that was in the cards for them or not. But he was determined to play things different this time.

Their future seemed hazy but the present was sharp and clear. And if he had any hope they might find their way forward, it was time to make the required changes to get them there.

"Again! Again!" Veronica's nephew, Matteo, shrieked his enjoyment as Ace lifted him high before swooping him low toward the ground.

"Someone's going to sleep well for me tonight." Veronica's sister Valerie had a big smile on her face as she watched Ace with her son. The two of them, along with their other sister Maria, had found chairs in front of the chimenea and were out of earshot of the broader crowd. "Please tell me I can go kiss him for that."

"No way!" Veronica said.

"Ooh. Territorial already?" Maria asked.

"I'm not territorial." Veronica heard the prim tones in her voice but couldn't quite shut them down. "I simply think Valerie's lips need to stay firmly on her husband's."

"Right. Sure." Valerie's smile never faded. "It's for the health of my marriage."

"Exactly."

"Is he taking you to the wedding?"

Veronica couldn't hide the shot of excitement that leaped under her breastbone. The morning before, as Ace was kissing her goodbye after their night of lovemaking, he'd asked her to join him at Tate and Belle's wedding. It has been a simple request—no frills—but it had been equally clear that it meant a lot to him.

"Yes." A small giggle floated from her throat, loud enough to share but still far enough away from Ace and Matteo not to be heard. "He invited me to go as his date."

"Hot damn." Valerie smiled. "That's going to be quite the shindig."

"What's going on with you two?" Maria asked. Her sisters might want details, but they were all tight enough to keep it between the three of them.

But did she dare say anything? It was still all so new. And it wasn't like they'd made a raging success of dating the last time they got together.

"Nothing is going on." Veronica nearly let the lie stand, only she'd never been particularly good at keeping things from her sisters. Nor did she really want to in this case. "We appear to be seeing each other again. Which you had to suspect since I brought him tonight."

"I knew it." Valerie made the slightest grimace at the "appear to be" reference before lifting her hand and high-fiving Maria. "Pay up, big sister."

"You're betting on me?"

"We're always betting on you." Valerie smiled. "In the very best sense of that statement. So are Mom and Dad. But in this case actual money will be changing hands."

"I don't believe it," Veronica said. "To think the two of you are well-respected, upstanding mothers in this community."

"You have been to one of Valerie's cutthroat bunco parties, haven't you?" Maria asked. "It's vicious and there's as much gambling there as in a Vegas casino."

Veronica couldn't argue with her sister's assessment, but she did laugh at the remembered evening with Valerie and her friends. She'd only recently returned from Houston and was surprised to realize that a home party, supposedly playing a dice game, was actually a front for a lot of laughing, drinking and blowing off steam on the part of Valerie and her friends.

She hadn't made many more bunco evenings, but now sitting there with her sisters, Veronica wondered why. She'd embraced her return to the Pass and had believed that she'd settled in. But had she, really?

Yes, she had her job and she'd thrown herself in there, working hard to make it a success. But what else had she really done?

"All I know is it's good to see a smile on your face." Maria reached out, taking Veronica's hand. "We haven't seen one, a real one, in much too long."

"Has it been that obvious?"

"No. Not too obvious. Just—" Valerie broke off. "Well, just there. Like you were going through the motions."

"Ace makes you happy. He always has."

"Let's not go too fast, Maria. We haven't been seeing each other that long. And, well—"

Her nephew's screams of laughter still echoed around them, his tireless enjoyment of Ace's game evident in the continued shrieks. The music her parents played still spilled out of the speakers that sat at each corner of the lawn. And the chimenea still crackled and popped with the burning wood inside.

It was all normal and comfortable, happy and carefree.

Until three loud shots rang out, shattering through the air as the backyard fence splintered under the assault.

Chapter 10

Ace covered Matteo's body with his own and charged toward the house. The happy shrieks and screams that so recently filled his ears faded, replaced with loud, heavy sobs that racked the small body in his arms as laughter morphed quickly into scared confusion.

"Hang on, buddy. Almost there."

Ace had no idea if the house was under siege, as well, but figured it was a better choice than being out in the open in the backyard. He saw Matteo's father and handed off the boy before turning and racing back out to the yard.

He had to get to Veronica.

The heavy popping sound came again, as more wood splintered under the assault, and Ace stopped. His gaze flashed around the yard, assessing and cataloging, until he saw Veronica. She and her sisters had been sitting in a small circle of chairs, but now all three women lay on the ground.

Shouts and screams echoed around them, several of Veronica's family members hollering through the melee. It was only when he saw movement, all three of them covering their heads as they tried to see what was happening, that he let out the breath he'd been holding.

They were still okay.

He moved carefully, picking his way through racing family members, unwilling to slow anyone down or get their way. But his sole focus was getting to Veronica and her sisters. They were the closest to the fence and, despite their prone positions, if anyone came through the battered fence they'd be the first in the line of fire.

Ace refused to think about that possibility.

Instead, he looked for something to protect them as he moved steadily across the yard. The picnic tables were too heavy, but somebody had set out a small card table to hold bottles of soda and water. He raced for the table, knocking over what was left of the bottles. Turning the table on its side and using it as a shield, he moved as fast as he could toward the women.

"Veronica!" He positioned himself on the other side of the women. "Get behind me. All of you. Now!"

The three scrambled behind him as another series of shots hit the fence. Ace held the table by its legs, instructing them as they moved in unison. Veronica laid her hands at his waist before shouting out orders. "Maria! Valerie! Make a chain. We're moving in single file toward the house."

Inch by inch, they crept as a unit, a phalanx of survivors determined to get to the house. As if by unspoken agreement, everyone knew what to do, and after an eternity, Ace felt the hard edge of paving stones beneath his feet. With the table still held up as a shield, he waited until they'd cleared the threshold into the living room before he tossed the table aside and charged off toward the side fence, following the direction some of the other men had taken.

He'd seen Valerie race toward her son the moment she'd cleared the living room. Maria immediately went to their mother. Only Veronica still stood there, exposed at the window. If the situation weren't so urgent he'd go back, pushing her to the ground himself and covering her with his body.

But the others needed help.

And he hoped like hell they could stop whomever had decided to make the Torres family a target.

The Torres property was set back off a two-lane road in the eastern reaches of Midnight Pass. Not farmland and not quite residentially zoned, the property was large enough to have privacy and small enough to still be part of a neighborhood. But Esteban's two acres gave the shooter plenty of room to hide.

Several of Veronica's uncles had pulled shotguns from their trucks and were even now sweeping the ground, searching for their quarry. It still bothered him to leave Veronica and her family back in the house, alone and unprotected, but the threat seemed determinedly outside. External.

Other.

No matter how he turned it over in his mind, from the moment he'd seen the man lurking around Veronica's practice, he could only visualize and identify the threat as outside of all of them. A stranger visiting some sort of perceived justice or mindless revenge on Veronica. It made no sense and she had little reason to have enemies, but Ace was unable to shake the brutally clear image from his mind.

Although Tate had borne the brunt of the investigation the prior spring, a murder on Reynolds property had affected them all. For as horrifying as it had been, the murder had carried marked overtones of the personal. Like some indefinable signature, they'd all sensed the intimacy of the threat.

This was different.

The strange man lurking. The indeterminate gunshots. Even the facelessness of it carried a strange measure of the cold and the calculated.

"Here!" A loud shout went up from one of Veronica's brothers-in-law and Ace followed the pack of men toward the spot. A depression was visible in the grass, marked with two clear footprints. The shooter had obviously stood there for a while, the October ground, already soaked by rain, capturing his impression in the dirt.

Watching them?

Waiting for the right moment?

A chill ran through him. He and Matteo had played their game of lift and drop mere feet from the backyard fence. The child had been in imminent danger and Ace had been unaware of it.

Ace stared at the ground as several flashlights swept the ground. This far outside the main city limits, there were few streetlights and the night sky had provided ample cover to the shooter. But it had also done them a favor.

"Wait!" Ace shouted, waving for a flashlight to swing back around. "There. By Antonio's foot."

The lights illuminated the ground and Ace watched for that telltale flash of metal. It was a matter of moments for them to alight on the shell casing he'd seen in the merest flash of light.

"Bastard left a clue," Esteban muttered, bending to pick up the shell.

"Looks like he got most of them." Antonio hadn't moved from his spot, but he swung his own flashlight over the ground, back and forth in slow arcs of light. "But all we need is one."

Several more men with guns fanned out in pairs toward the woods that abutted the property, but the ones without weapons pointed toward the house and voiced the desire to get back inside.

"We should go back, too." Esteban laid a hand on Ace's forearm, pointing toward the house.

Ace sensed there was more to the request and within a few feet his instincts were proven correct.

"What do you think this is about?" Esteban asked as soon as they were out of earshot of his family.

"I'm not a hundred percent sure," Ace said.

"The man at the practice. The one from the other day."

Although Ace wasn't going to hold back the possibilities that the man was responsible, he was glad to know Veronica had told her parents what was happening.

"Veronica played it off like it was nothing, but I know." Esteban tapped his chest. "A father knows. She's in danger."

"If tonight is any indication, I'd say you're all in danger." The thought was grim but there was no help for it. "And I don't think this is the last we'll see of the shooter."

"No." Esteban stopped and stared at the back of his home. "Violence like that. A strike without warning or provocation. It's only the beginning."

"We can set you up at the ranch. We're no strangers

to violence and we've made considerable improvements to our security over the past six months."

"I won't be driven from my home."

Ace understood the sentiment, but it didn't keep him from pushing. "Just for a little while."

"No. But I would like Veronica to stay with you. She'll be safer there. More people and more advance warning. And a cop right on the property."

His thoughts had already veered along the same lines, but Ace wasn't about to share that. An invitation was far better than a demand and he'd take the moment as a silent victory.

Now to convince Veronica.

"Of course."

They walked in silence to the house when Esteban stopped once more, turning toward Ace. The night was still dark, but the lights from the house lit up the side of the man's face, agony painting itself in the careworn lines there. "You know what happened in Houston?"

"Yes."

"All but one of the bastards got away." Esteban let loose with a string of curses in Spanish before gathering himself. "Cowards, each and every one. Sick cowards, looking for a drug score and a point of valor in their gang politics."

"Not quite my definition of valor."

"Or mine." Veronica's father spit on the ground. "They scared her and could have hurt her if not for the quick thinking of Mark and the Houston police. I'm grateful to both every day."

Although he'd never expected to say the same, Ace had to give her ex-husband his due. The man had recognized something was wrong and had alerted help as soon as possible. Veronica was possibly still here because of her ex and Ace knew a shot of gratitude that was wholly unexpected.

And ran far deeper than he had ever imagined.

What would he do if he lost her again?

Things had moved so fast between them and he was still trying to sort it out and make sense of it all. But there was nothing to sort about wanting her in his life, happy, healthy and whole.

A piece of him had been broken and lost since she left. He'd buried it deep—had known he had no choice, especially after she'd married—but it had been there all the same.

But if he lost her again? Especially to violence that could be stopped.

Ace knew, with certainty, the outcome.

The broken pieces would be all that was left of him.

Veronica stared out the back window of her parents' home, unable to believe the destruction that had descended in a matter of moments. The bright white lights still hung across the backyard, but several strands were now drooping because of the broken fence. It had been the work of seconds to take the backyard from haven to war zone.

And had taken even fewer seconds for Ace to race off into the night.

The high-pitched keening coming from her mother tore Veronica's gaze off the window. Although they had no idea if another assault would come from the front, for the time being they were all inside. They were all seemingly safe.

She moved next to Maria and wrapped both her sister and her mother in her arms.

"Who would do this?" her mother wailed. "What is this evil?"

The remembered fear from those endless hours in her clinic in Houston returned on viciously swift feet. How had it found her again?

Was it the same man who had been looking in her office windows? The one Ace had seen and chased after?

Could it be anyone else?

Veronica tightened her grip on her mother and Maria and prayed for the safety of the men outside. They *had* to be okay. Her father. Her brothers-in-law. Family and friends. And Ace.

What would she do if she lost him? And so soon after they found each other again.

They all kept their eyes on the backyard, but no further shots rang out. After endless minutes of waiting, the tense grip on the room faded a bit. The heavy crying had turned to silent weeping. And the quiet chatter of her nephew could be heard across the room.

"Is Matteo okay?" she called out to Valerie.

Her sister held her little boy in her arms, seated cross-legged on the floor, her back pressed to the couch. "He's okay." She continued to press kisses to his forehead, that small body nestled against hers as he continued to chatter softly. "No small thanks to Ace."

"Where's Ace?" Matteo asked. "Where's Daddy?"

"Shh, baby," her sister said, pressing more kisses to his head. "They'll be back soon."

The room grew quiet, everyone lost in their own thoughts. Her mother's questions had subsided, but she still cried quiet tears, Maria still held her tight in her arms.

Veronica watched them all with a steady vigilance.

She'd brought this here. It was because of her. She

knew it with a blinding sense of certainty. Someone had targeted her again and she was going to find out why.

Was there something they'd overlooked in Houston? Several years had passed, but a person with a vendetta and a plan could wait endlessly for the perfect opportunity.

For the perfect time.

Had that time come?

Goose bumps covered her flesh and Veronica rubbed at her arms, suddenly impatient. She wasn't a victim. She'd moved past what happened in Houston and she was never going back to that dark and terrible place. The one that had shut her off from the ones she loved. The one that still haunted her, several years after she'd sold her practice and moved away.

It was the reason she'd thrown herself into her work and little else. It was the reason she'd missed bunco games and nights out and a normal dating life. And it was the reason her family hadn't seen a smile—a real one—on her face in more than two years.

But no more.

The steady tromp of feet could be heard through the windows just before the front door was thrown open and the back door filled by members of her family. Her father moved immediately to her mother and her brothers-in-law did the same with her sisters. Uncles and aunts and cousins all hugged, everyone talking at once.

She stared at them all, grateful they were back and determined they'd never face a threat like that again.

It was only as she took stock, counting off each and every family member, that she came up one short. She nearly raced out to the yard when Ace walked through the back door.

Had she ever seen a more welcome sight?

* * *

Ace stood at the corner of the living room and watched while the Midnight Pass PD swarmed the Torres house. Four cops were visible through the windows, roaming over the backyard with high-powered flashlights. Three more sat in the living room, questioning family members one after the next. And then there was Belle.

His sister in every way that counted, so recently wrapped up in the discussion over a new groom's cake and fresh flowers, was in full cop mode.

"Did you see anyone outside, Mr. Torres? Anyone who could have been the shooter?"

"No. By the time we rounded the fence the damn coward was gone." Esteban Torres practically spit the words, his disdain for the shooter a living, writhing beast.

Sort of like his own, Ace thought.

He'd tried to steel his emotions, but every time he got to a point where he might be able to think rationally, the sound of gunshots filled his mind. That small, laughing, wriggling child in his arms was in danger once again. And Veronica lay on the ground with her sisters, in easy range of the faceless shooter.

Damn coward was right.

He'd believed that he and Esteban had said what they needed to say outside. That they'd purged that initial anger and had come back to the house more rational and focused.

How odd, then, to find his anger had no limits and his frustration at the insensibility of it all only grew harder and darker and more raw.

He'd catch Belle's eye every so often, her flat gaze all cop. He knew she was thinking the same thing he was.

The man who had scouted Veronica's practice had somehow found her here with her family.

It was the only explanation.

Add on that it was cold, calculated and deliberate and it meant they had a far bigger problem on their hands than a peeping Tom searching a local business.

Someone floated by—Veronica's aunt Lucy?—with a cup of coffee, pressing it into his hand. "Take it, sweetie."

He didn't want the coffee, but he wouldn't refuse the kindness. Besides, maybe the hot liquid would go a long way toward thawing the ice in his midsection.

Belle wrapped up with Esteban and stood, taking one of Lucy's passed coffee cups. She strolled over to him, her movements casual as her gaze continued to roam around the room. "Quite a night."

"You could say that."

She cocked her head. "What would you say?"

"I'd say we were all witness to a targeted attack."

"I'd like to say you're wrong." Belle took a sip of her coffee, whether for something to do or fortification Ace wasn't sure. "But I don't think I can."

"He came here. He came here after her." The words were so bitter against his tongue Ace wasn't entirely sure how he was able to speak them.

"We've had patrols and we've all been watching. Anybody who sees anyone they don't recognize has been given orders to discreetly follow and assess."

"Clearly it wasn't enough."

She looked about ready to argue with him, but sipped her coffee instead. Only he saw the frustration riding her cornflower-blue eyes all the same.

Good.

If the police were on high alert they'd be more careful. More diligent.

And they wouldn't be stupid enough to let a madman roam around Midnight Pass, shooting at innocent people.

Unable to stand still any longer and unwilling to politely drink the damn coffee, he stomped outside. The night was calm once again, and other than the visible destruction in the backyard, the violence that had been so palpable had vanished.

What if she'd been hurt? What if one of her family members were hurt? Veronica would've been devastated.

He'd seen her face. He'd watched her the other night when she told him about what had happened in Houston. He felt the raw fury turning in his gut and had no idea what to do with it then.

How ridiculous of him to think that was fear. That a story in the past—one that had procured a safe outcome— was somehow the same as facing it down in person.

Not even close.

Real fear. Churning, gut-wrenching horror was what roiled through his stomach now.

And with it, a cold fury that he'd never felt in his life.

He eyed the lawn chairs that had scattered when Veronica and her sisters had pushed them away and kicked at one. It was mindless and stupid, the chairs overturned but not broken, but it felt good to kick something.

To punish something even if it was useless against the unremitting terror coursing through his body.

"Why are you out here by yourself?"

Veronica's voice stilled him and Ace stopped midkick to a second chair. He didn't turn around, instead standing still in the grass, his attention focused on the destroyed back fence. "You should be inside."

"So should you. The police have it taken care of out here. You can go home if you'd like."

Ace whirled at that. "Without you?"

"Well, sure. I think I should stay here with my parents and…" She took a deep breath, her eyes flat and empty as she looked past him to the destruction beyond. "I don't think I should leave them alone."

"None of you should be alone. We should bundle all of you up and bring you back to the ranch. More of us to keep eyes out there. I can get the ranch hands to take rotations."

Veronica shook her head. "Daddy will never leave his house."

A fact Esteban had already made perfectly clear. And a challenge Ace was determined to find a way around. "Then maybe we should make him. Or Belle can. I'll get Belle to make him."

"Ace. You can't make him do anything. He's a grown man and a prideful one at that. This is his home. He won't be driven from it." She moved closer, laying a hand on his chest. "I'm sure you can understand that."

The hell of it was, he *could* understand it. There had been roughly ten seconds of discussion about leaving Reynolds Station when they'd faced their own threat the prior spring and they'd all agreed they weren't leaving.

Why would Esteban Torres be any different?

"Please don't pull away from me." She moved closer, settling her other hand over his heart.

"I'm not pulling away."

"Could've fooled me. Your mind is a million miles away."

"Veronica—" He stopped, not sure what to say. Unable to put into words what burned through him.

So he opted to show her instead.

Laying his hands over her small, slender ones, he leaned down, pressing his lips to hers. Part reverence and part prayer, he murmured the desperate need for her to stay safe against her lips, even as he sunk into her.

The reality of her. The warm and the physical and the *real*.

She was here and she was whole and he had to focus on that. He had to keep reminding himself that fear of what might have happened wasn't a replacement for the celebration of life that was right here. They were all scared, but they were all whole and unharmed.

Ace deepened the kiss, his lips pressed to hers, his tongue seeking entrance to the warmth of her mouth. The gentle merging of bodies, breath shared between them, went a long way toward soothing that writhing beast and he took comfort in the kiss.

This wasn't about arousal or sexual need. It was about comfort. And gratitude.

And life.

She was unharmed.

He'd tell himself that over and over. And maybe, once this was all behind them—once the faceless bastard who hunted her was disposed of—he'd take his first normal breath.

Chapter 11

The lights of the Reynolds kitchen burned bright as Veronica, Ace and Belle trooped in around three in the morning. Hoyt and Tate were already at the table, matched mugs of coffee in hand, and Arden bustled in fastening her robe within moments of their arrival.

Belle went to Tate immediately. He had her in his arms, whispering words against her ear in a quiet world that belonged to the two of them.

Although Ace hadn't understood his brother's unwillingness to accept Belle's job for so many years, after the events of the evening he had a better grasp on how scary and torturous it was to be the one watching another in danger. Belle lived with the reality of that every day and, as her spouse, Tate would, as well.

It was humbling to realize that his judgment of his brother was not only misplaced but that Tate bore a much bigger burden than they'd given him credit for. It was hard enough to love someone. But to love someone who walked out of the house each and every day, not guaranteed a return because of their profession, was an unexpected thought.

"You want a cup?" Veronica asked, pointing toward the coffeepot.

"Your aunt Lucy made enough to keep me awake for a week. So yeah." He shrugged. "What's one more cup?"

The mention of her aunt's coffee had its desired effect and Veronica gave him a small smile before busying herself with mugs and coffee. She got head nods from Belle and Arden and set about pulling down four cups from the cabinet.

He watched her, the simple ritual of fixing coffee an easy and quiet way to keep busy. To do something—anything—but stand still and think.

"What happened tonight?" Arden began, taking a seat at the table.

"We went to the Torres Friday fiesta."

"Were there tamales?" Tate's question interrupted the flow, and while Ace knew the question was misplaced, he couldn't fault his brother for the desire to make light.

"In the car." Ace tilted his head toward the door. "In a cooler."

"You're all invited to the next one, too. My mother insists." Veronica distributed the mugs all around before turning to Hoyt. "And she's wildly determined to rub Reese's baby bump, so my apologies in advance."

"No apology needed." Hoyt took a sip of his coffee.

Ace started in again, determined to get through the events of the evening. They weren't sitting there to talk about tamales or babies or parties.

Someone had shot at them.

Hoyt asked several questions, his military training taking over as Ace talked about the shooter. "Where was he positioned?"

"Behind the fence."

"You sure?" Hoyt probed. "Was it possible he was above? Positioned in the trees?"

Belle chimed in. "No. Preliminary ballistics indicate the shooter was beyond the fence."

Ace sat back in his chair, frustrated by the constant interruption.

What was wrong with all of them? Could he get through his damn story? Could he tell it and get some damn freaking attention for once?

When had he become the one they all talked over? And worse, when had he lost control of every person in his life? He was the big brother. The protector.

And obviously he was doing a piss poor job of it if the chatter and the questions around the table were any indication.

Slamming back, he caught his chair just before it hit the ground, and stomped into the living room. He wanted to go to his room but he was too keyed up to sleep and he didn't care for his own damn company, anyway.

But hell, he didn't care for his family's very much, either.

Could he tell his story? Could he get it out, in a dry, clinical retelling, so maybe—freaking *maybe*—he could find some way to make sense of it?

"Ace?"

Reese stood on the stairs, her hair mussed from sleep even as her brown eyes were clear and alert. "You okay?"

"Sure. I'm fine. I'm sorry if I woke you up."

"Nothing to be sorry about." Reese came fully into the room. "What's the matter? You look upset."

Without knowing how or why, the events of the evening spilled out, pouring from him in a steady stream of words and curses. He jumped around, a mix of telling what had happened at the Torres house and the strange impressions of what he *felt* was happening.

And she listened to it all.

Quietly, her big eyes solemn, she let him spill every word.

It was only when he was done, exhaustion racking his body, that Ace realized what a gift he'd been given. "I'm sorry to burden you with all that."

"We're family. That's what you do with family."

"Isn't it bad for the baby? Upsetting topics, I mean."

"If that were the bellwether for a successful pregnancy I don't think I'd be having one. Fortunately, my doctor continues to tell me that baby is doing well and I'm progressing just fine." Reese laid a hand over her stomach. "We have a very healthy child kicking around in here."

Then she reached out, capturing his hand with both of hers. "It's okay to be upset. And it's okay to talk about it."

Ace caught the flicker in her eyes and turned to see his family and Veronica standing in the entryway to the living room. "Eavesdropping?"

"Nah," Tate said. "We just thought you might like a bit of support."

"Everything will be okay." The determination in Belle's voice was unmistakable. "We're going to catch who was responsible for tonight. We won't let anything happen to Veronica or her family."

"I wouldn't bet against my Belle," Tate added. "Besides, she has extra incentive to get this case closed."

Arden turned to look at her brother, curiosity riding high in her gaze. "And why's that?"

"She's got a honeymoon to get to full of wild, unbridled beach sex."

Belle shook her head, exhaling Tate's name on an embarrassed sigh.

But it was Ace's quick "Ewww"—echoed around the room by his two other siblings not getting married the following Saturday—that finally broke the tension in the room.

The laughter died away as Ace took in Veronica's still shell-shocked face. "I'm sorry if my brother's honeymoon plans left you with a mental image you can't quite shake."

Veronica didn't smile. The joke didn't seem to even penetrate the bleak expression that covered her face. "This is all my fault. I'm so sorry to bring this to your door."

Immediately, words of support rose up from his family.

"You have nothing to be sorry about—"

"Don't say that—"

"We're here to help—"

But it was Reese who found the words. Reese, who so recently had dealt with her own personal hell. She stood up from the couch and crossed the room to Veronica, taking the woman into her arms. "Please don't say that. You are welcome here. Just as you are, with nothing expected of you. You're exactly where you need to be."

As she'd known the exact right words to help Ace through the resulting emotional crash from the evening's events, Reese seemingly knew how to help Veronica, as well. With a soft cry, Veronica huddled in her arms and hung on.

As he sat in the comfort of his home, the danger at bay, Ace couldn't help but wonder what would come next.

Even as he knew that with this room of people behind him, he could face it.

He could face anything.

Ray took the phone call, his hands shaking at the news Rocky shared. She was so close.

He was so close to his goal.

And Rocky hadn't let him down.

"No one has seen you?"

"I've been a ghost man. I've done just like you said. I stayed away from the cameras on buildings and laid low till I needed to do my business. Rest of the time I've stayed out of town. The stupid morons don't even know I'm here and that includes the dumb hick cops."

"Good. Very good."

Rocky finished recounting the last few days. What he learned from nosing around Veronica's vet practice to the stakeout he'd made of her parents' home.

It was a new angle and one Ray hadn't considered yet. *Go after the family.*

"I had an idea, too. I know how we need to do this."

Ray frowned at the eagerness in Rocky's voice. He had a plan, and while he appreciated Rocky's focus and attention, he knew what he wanted done. "It's going down like last time. We capture her at her business, get the drugs and then deal with her."

Victory filled his veins, the idea that she would finally be his. He lost a good man to the cops who'd swarmed her place in Houston, and while Rocky was coming along, he wasn't Jack.

"Yeah, yeah, I know. But hear me out."

Ray didn't say anything and in Rocky's excitement he didn't seem to notice. "I heard 'em tonight. When I

Loyal Readers
FREE BOOKS Voucher

We're giving away THOUSANDS of FREE BOOKS

Suspense

Suspenseful Romance

Don't Miss Out! Send for Your Free Books Today!

Get up to 4
FREE FABULOUS BOOKS
You Love!

To thank you for being a loyal reader we'd like to send you up to 4 FREE BOOKS, absolutely free.

Just write "YES" on the Loyal Reader Voucher and we'll send you up to 4 Free Books and Free Mystery Gifts, altogether worth over $20, as a way of saying thank you for being a loyal reader.

Try **Harlequin® Romantic Suspense** books featuring heart-racing page-turners with unexpected plot twists and irresistible chemistry that will keep you guessing to the very end.

Try **Harlequin Intrigue® Larger-Print** books featuring action-packed stories that will keep you on the edge of your seat. Solve the crime and deliver justice at all costs.

Or **TRY BOTH!**

We are so glad you love the books as much as we do and can't wait to send you great new books.

So don't miss out, return your Loyal Reader Voucher Today!

Pam Powers

LOYAL READER
FREE BOOKS VOUCHER

YES! I Love Reading, please send me up to 4 FREE BOOKS and Free Mystery Gifts from the series I select.

Just write in "YES" on the dotted line below then return this card today and we'll send your free books & gifts asap!

➡ ___ YES ___ ⬅

Which do you prefer?

☐ **Harlequin® Romantic Suspense**
240/340 HDL GRHP

☐ **Harlequin Intrigue® Larger-Print**
199/399 HDL GRHP

☐ **BOTH**
240/340 & 199/399
HDL GRHZ

FIRST NAME	LAST NAME

ADDRESS

APT.#	CITY

STATE/PROV.	ZIP/POSTAL CODE

EMAIL ☐ Please check this box if you would like to receive newsletters and promotional emails from Harlequin Enterprises ULC and its affiliates. You can unsubscribe anytime.

HI/HRS-520-LR21

was waiting to fire at the fence. There's a big wedding over at the ranch of this guy she's been dating. I heard her going on about it all. She was all cool about it, like the guy doesn't matter, but you could tell he does. She's all giggly and girlie about him."

Ray considered, a new idea taking root. "Tell me a bit more."

"Same bastard I was telling you about. The one who chased me down at her vet place. I think it's his brother getting married or something."

Although Veronica was his full focus, Ray didn't mind improvising. And if this guy was causing trouble for Rocky *and* was important to Veronica, just like her family, he could be useful to the endgame.

"It's at one of those ranches here in this Podunk town, next Saturday. They're having a big wedding, lots people coming and going so it'll be easy to slip in. She should be an easy mark and we can make a statement. Let her know we never forgot."

Ray didn't want to admit it, but he liked it. He liked it a lot. And it had a sort of poetic justice to it. He'd bided his time, now this was the big strike.

He was the Rat King, after all. He knew how to take care of his family, knew how to take care of his business.

And no one—no one ever—would take him down.

Veronica woke with a start, her head pillowed on Ace's shoulder. They'd finally moved up to his room around four that morning. Based on the sun now streaming through the window, she had to assume it was at least eight or maybe even nine.

She'd already damned the late hour and sent Julie a text message the night before, not to come into the office today. Belle had asked to spend some time at the practice, looking around, and Veronica had acquiesced. She'd already planned to close for a few days as they figured out what was going on and she took stock of the contents of her practice.

Did she need to carry such a large supply of drugs? Were there some more potent offerings she could keep off-site or work with suppliers to get quickly on an as-needed basis? She kept many things on hand simply because Midnight Pass was so far out of range of any big towns, but she had large vet contacts in El Paso as well as several key drug reps. She could likely get what she needed and not have to wait more than half a day for it.

While she had a tight lockdown on her pharmacy room, she'd also decided it was worth another review by her security company. She'd make that call this morning and see what improvements they might have made in the past two years since she set up and upgraded Doc Talente's practice upon her return to town.

So it might not be in-the-office time, but she had quite a few things to handle, all of which could be done remotely. She'd take a few days of focus and some time away from the practice and get it all done.

And then she'd figure out her next move.

The hand that rested on her stomach shifted, moving in a lazy arc over her bare skin.

"You awake?" Ace's words were sleepy, at direct odds with the deft strokes of his fingers as they swept lower in their explorations. She caught her breath when he hit a particularly sensitive spot, barely suppressing a small moan.

"I am now."

"Good." He added a trail of kisses to her neck. "Because I am, too."

"Well, isn't that convenient?" She murmured the words as he took control, his fingers seeking entrance to her body. Although they'd both stripped the night before with the intention of making love, both had dropped off in exhaustion from the events of the evening and the late hour.

And both of them were wide awake now.

Unlike the urgent needs that had pushed them their first two nights together, the years apart creating a sort of fever to couple, the quiet morning gave them both room to relax and rediscover.

To savor.

Ace explored her body, tracing and retracing her skin. He'd added deliciously sleepy kisses to the mix and she felt any remnants of fatigue fading away. This was real. All-consuming.

It was life.

He slipped two fingers inside her and with more of those long, lazy strokes made love to her. Only there was nothing lazy about her body's response. Her orgasm hit her with shocking immediacy, the swift response at odds with the quiet morning.

"Come for me." He whispered it against her ear, taking the moment of vulnerability and pressing his advantage. "Just for me, baby."

She complied, the wild storm racking her body all for him.

Only for him.

Wave after wave of pleasure filled her and she gave it room, riding the maelstrom. She'd spent so long without this—how had she survived? she wondered abstractly before mentally drifting once more, even as one thought lingered.

These feelings, so lush and all-consuming, were only for one man.

Ace.

And as he continued to murmur against her ear, her satiated body drew out every last bit of pleasure. A sense of completion so deep and comfortable took hold, and with it, the desire to give Ace what he'd given her.

Everything.

The condom they'd slipped from the drawer still sat on his end table, unused because of their deep drop into sleep, and she reached for it blindly. As her fingers closed over the foil, she knew a moment of victory before shifting their bodies so that she straddled him.

"So that's how we're playing this morning?" His smile was lazy as he stared up at her.

"I'd give you some pithy response about how turnabout is fair play but I have a much better answer."

"You do?" His voice still held those lazy overtones but she heard the quiver beneath them as she sheathed him in the condom.

"I do."

"Lay it on me." He lifted his hips so that his body pressed closer to her, the hard length of him rubbing against her core.

She giggled at the suggestive double entendre but pressed on, wiggling her hips as she spoke. "I think I already am."

He groaned and laughed at the same time as she positioned herself, taking him in hand to guide him into her body. The deep satiation of her first orgasm vanished as Veronica responded to the needs of her own body, even as she took determined care for his. Wild need gripped her hips and she set a harsh rhythm for both of them, their bodies straining and bucking toward the sweet promise of oblivion.

The hard pleasure that had gripped her at the work of his hands took over once more, her body clenching around him. And as he let out a shout, she matched it with one of her own.

And let the world fall away so that it was simply the two of them, lost in each other.

"Let me just say again how lovely it is you have a small wing of this amazing house all to yourself."

Ace couldn't stop the smile at her words and pulled Veronica tighter against his chest. Was there anything better on this earth than morning sex? "Thank you."

"No one can overhear us."

"A small perk but one I'll remember next time Hoyt, Tate and I reminisce about the beastly hot summer we put on the addition."

The lazy exploration she made over his chest with her fingers stilled. "You did this yourself?"

"A lot of it. We contracted out the interior stuff like plumbing and electricity but we did the framing and the drywall. A lot of the trim work, too."

"All by yourselves?"

"Sure."

"Wow." She scrambled up to a sitting position and looked around the room. "I have to say it again. Amazing."

He took in the slim curve of her back, his gaze tracing the line of her spine where it peeked out beneath the long fall of dark hair before he reached out with a fingertip to trace the same path with his touch.

She was amazing.

And not just because he was naked, although the raging desire that couldn't get enough of her was certainly appreciative of that fact.

But it was so much more.

He loved her.

His finger stilled over the center of her back, midtrace of her spine. Love?

But he knew the truth.

He'd always loved her. With a madness that bordered on desperation and a fierceness that scared him even as it lifted him up.

And there was no freaking way he was going to admit any of it.

She turned, questions riding her dark gaze. "You okay?"

"I'm good." He forced a lazy smile he didn't feel. "Better than good. That was quite a wake-up call and a very welcome good-morning."

He scrambled up and leaned into her, pressing a kiss to her lips before she could ask any more questions. He might be right back in love with her, as besotted as the first time, but he needed some time and space to figure out what to do with it.

All of it. The fierce emotions and the abject terror. Because he might want her to distraction, but a few rounds of sex hadn't gotten them any closer to solving anything. She still left Midnight Pass, marrying someone else in the process.

And he still was convinced they had more in common with his parents' relationship than his siblings.

And… Well…

She might not love him back.

He kept kissing her, even as the thought soured his tongue. They were enjoying each other's company, but that didn't mean she was in love with him.

It didn't mean that at all.

Chapter 12

Veronica unfolded the large sheet, spreading it high and smiling in wonder when the slow, steady breeze caught the ends, flying them high like a kite.

"Here. Let me help you with that." Ace set down a huge basket before reaching for the other end of the sheet. "It's not too windy today but there's enough breeze to keep things interesting."

The twin scents of laundry detergent and grass hit her at once and Veronica breathed deep, simply happy for the day.

Although they'd woken with a lazy morning of loving and talking, the suggestion to take out a picnic lunch felt like the height of decadence. After calling her parents and then her sisters to check on them and confirm everyone was okay, she knew the relaxed day was just what she needed.

She hadn't had a lot of carefree and easy of late and she wasn't going to miss the chance to take a bit of both. "It feels endless out here."

"That's what twenty thousand acres will do." She didn't miss the pride in his voice or the broad smile that painted his face.

Nor could she stop the feeling of safety, despite all the recent evidence to the contrary. The wide open space, the seemingly endless vista with no one but them.

And Ace.

Wearing that beautiful smile, his eyes crinkling at the corners.

It was fun to see. That clear excitement. And the pride that ensured he would be there, year in and year out, taking care of what was his.

"You love the land, don't you?"

"With everything that I am. It's part of me. Part of my heritage. My present." He stopped, and she sensed that there was something else he wanted to say.

"And?"

"Nothing. It's silly." He reached for the picnic basket, busying himself with settling it on the sheet.

"No, it's not. Your love of this place is evident. It's easy to see." She waited another few beats, but when he didn't say anything, she pressed on. "Please. Tell me."

"It's my future, too. And my children's. I want them. I want the name Reynolds to carry on." Ace scratched at a small spot over his ear, considering. "Well, now with Hoyt, the name will carry on."

"But you want it to carry on from you, too."

"Yeah, I guess I do."

Although the two of them had talked easily about any number of topics when they were dating, they avoided specifics about what was between them. Because of it, the future had always seemed a bit hazy. Not unwelcome, but just…distant.

The subject of children had felt distant, too.

The future—her future—had continued to seem hazy and unfocused, dim even, when she married Mark. Things had happened quickly between the two of them, but they did have the requisite conversation about having a family. And both of them had said it was something for the future.

Only when the future came, neither of them ever seemed ready. And slowly, over time, talk of having children faded away. That probably should have been one of her clues. Yet one more reason why she never should've married Mark in the first place.

"What about you?"

Veronica knew what Ace asked, but wasn't sure what to say. The only person she'd ever really considered having a family with had been him. The picture might have been unfocused, but she had imagined it. She hadn't wanted to think about it too much, but she had considered it, in her quiet moments she kept to herself. But like a dream, she'd buried those thoughts way down deep after they'd broken up.

And while the past three days had been amazing, it wasn't like a few days of invigorating sex gave her permission to bring it up. Goodness, the man would run for the fence line as fast as his legs would carry him. But he deserved an answer, too.

"I do think about it. I guess I always thought it was something that would happen someday. Only it hasn't. Life has happened instead."

"It certainly has a way of doing that."

As if he sensed the conversation had turned heavy, he pointed toward the picnic basket. "You hungry?"

"Yes. And if there's fried chicken in there like I thought I saw your sister pack, then I'm definitely hungry."

"There is. She snuck some from the caterers' visit the other night. Belle and Tate are serving it as one of the dishes at their wedding."

"Oh, wow. Lucky me. Fried chicken twice in one week."

"Lucky us." In addition to the fried chicken, he pulled out a container of coleslaw, an even bigger one of fruit salad and what looked to be fresh, yeasty rolls.

"Your sister is amazing."

"She is. Arden loves to tell us the cooking is a burden, but the woman can do it like a champ. I think she secretly loves to feed us."

Veronica reached for a roll. "Sure she does. She's a caregiver. And food is one of the ways she gives love."

He stared at her, his mouth drooping. "She does?"

"Sure. That's her role in the family. She keeps you all together."

"But she's the baby."

"No, she's not. She's your matriarch."

If Veronica had told him she had scales under her skin Ace would have been less shocked.

"Arden? Our matriarch?"

Wasn't that supposed to be his mother's role? Wasn't it somehow supposed to stay with her, sort of like her name, even so many years after she was gone?

Only things didn't work that way. They'd grieved the loss of both their parents—whether their father had deserved it or not was still in question—but they had grieved. And then they'd moved on.

"Well, yeah." Veronica pressed on. "Everyone plays a role and that's hers. She assumed it after your mom passed and you all obviously let her."

"How do you know this?"

Even as he asked the question, he couldn't deny her point. And with startling clarity, Veronica's comments forced Ace to see Arden in a new way. Had she taken them all under her care by choice? By fate? Or just by circumstance?

"Because I can see it when I watch all of you." Her response was so simple—so matter-of-fact—and it shook him to his core.

"What else can you see?"

"Hoyt is the serious one, but because of it, you all take him seriously. It's obvious Reese is good for him. She lightens him. Keeps him from the dark."

It was an accurate assessment of his youngest brother, and again showed just how perceptive Veronica was. "I think that's true. I'd never put it in those terms before, but I can see it since Reese has come into his life. His time in the service, while important and while I respect it, left scars."

"I'm sure that it did." Her voice was soft. "It's a sacrifice. A noble one, but a sacrifice all the same."

"And Tate?"

"He's the jokester." Veronica smiled and pulled off another piece of her roll. "And he's good at it. It's not put on, but he uses it to hide the more serious side of his nature."

"Again, rather perceptive of you."

"We all handle stress differently. Even in animals, we see different responses to different situations. They can't speak, but they communicate. We're more like them than we give ourselves credit for."

The breeze thickened, blowing the edges of her hair over her shoulder. Ace reached out to curl the end over his finger, mesmerized by the soft strands. "I think Belle is a solid match for him, too."

Her dark gaze softened as she stared at him, their bodies so close their shoulders met. "Was there ever any question? One look at the two of them and you can see it."

"Do you think people say that about us?" He wasn't sure why he asked the question, but now that it was out he wasn't sorry.

"I don't know. My sisters sure noticed."

"When the three of you were cackling around the firepit last night?"

It was his turn to deliver a surprise and he definitely got the result he was aiming for. Her dropped mouth and wide eyes his proof. "How'd you know?"

Those soft strands slipped from his fingers as he enjoyed the rare moment of taking the upper hand. "The three of you kept shooting me furtive glances and whispering."

"We weren't cackling. We might have been whispering," she added.

"You did both."

"How would you know? You were playing with Matteo."

"I was listening, too."

"That's eavesdropping."

"It isn't when you're already in earshot."

She stayed silent for a moment before her question seemed to get the better of her. "What did you happen to listen to, then?"

"Nope." He wagged a finger. "Not telling."

Although it wasn't a match for the light, convivial air, Ace found himself asking his next question, anyway. "What do your sisters think about the two of us?"

"Why do I feel like this is a trick question?"

"No tricks. But I am curious to hear you say it." And he *was* curious. It was one thing to know their relationship was the subject of sisterly gossip. It was another to get the details directly from Veronica. To know what she was actually thinking and feeling.

"Well, of course they're interested. But I knew that going in. You don't exactly bring a date to a family party and not expect some questions. Especially someone you had a history with."

"Is that what we have? History?"

Her eyebrows lifted nearly to her hairline. "You'd call it something else?"

Would he?

For the longest time he'd considered their year together a period in his life to forget. A way to question his sanity from time to time but not much more. The past few weeks had shown him another side.

Had he blown his memories out of proportion? Or more to the point, had the pain of their breakup and her seeming rapid ability to move on left him with a skewed perspective?

Ace wasn't sure but he did know that the more time he spent with Veronica, the more time he wanted to spend with her. Each hour in her company made those lingering memories fade further into the past.

"I guess you could call it history." He finally said. "Or maybe we can look at these past few weeks as a reboot."

"Computer terms from a cowboy?"

"Hey. I'm a cutting-edge cowboy. We use technology

on the ranch." He pretended to wince. "Some damn expensive technology, as a matter of fact."

She laughed at that. "I know you do. In fact, I've been really impressed with your feed management and your herd rotation. I'd love to do an article with you about the ways you blended technology into the running of the business. Several vet journals are always looking for broader articles on evolving husbandry practices."

And just like that, they sunk into that comfortable place they somehow always managed to find. A common ground. Things to talk about. And a camaraderie that went well beyond the physical.

Ace reached for the picnic basket and pulled out the plate of fried chicken Arden had packed. Extending the platter, he offered Veronica first pick, then selected a few pieces for himself. As they settled into the blanket, Ace gave her a few ideas for the article.

It was nearly an hour later before they even thought to get up and move from their perch on the blanket.

"Right there. That's him, isn't it?" Veronica pointed through Ace's windshield at the herd grazing in the distance. "The little guy who isn't quite so little any longer."

"That's him." Ace nodded, putting the truck into Park. "The one you checked out a few weeks ago. He still likes to keep close to his mama, but he's growing."

"I had a feeling he was a tough little guy."

"We've been lucky this year. The herd's doing well overall and I'm pleased with the stock."

"You should do well this season. Reynolds stands for quality beef. It's easy to see why."

"It wasn't always that way."

"Maybe not." She shifted in her seat to look at him,

her gaze direct. "But it was for a long time. And now it is again."

"Yeah, I suppose."

Her gaze never wavered, those fathomless depths searching his face.

"What?" he asked. "I can see you're curious about something."

"I am. I'm interested to know why, after complimenting you on all your hard work with your stock, you felt the need to talk about a darker time."

"I was just stating a fact." A small itch settled between his shoulder blades. It was the same twitch that struck whenever he thought about the embarrassment of his father's actions.

"No, I don't think you are."

"What was I doing?" He heard the tense edge to his words but left the question hang.

"I would've thought you would be past this by now."

"Past what?"

"Feeling like you're responsible for the sins of your father."

The barb landed just as he suspected she meant it to. "Care to explain yourself?"

"Nothing to explain. You were singing this song almost a decade ago and you don't seem to have come up with a new one."

Ace had no idea how it happened. Twenty minutes ago, they were wrapping up their picnic and laughing in easy conversation. And now here they were, both on the edge of an argument.

"We had a pretty deep and dark pit to claw our way out of." Memories of those endlessly long days nearly choked him. Days when nothing he did seemed to be right and he was balancing the business, the health of the books and their relationship with their buyers on the most delicate tightrope.

Even his family didn't know just how touch and go it had been for a while. He'd wanted to shield them— wanted to protect their image of Andrew Reynolds Sr.— but in the process he had discovered just how badly their father was in debt.

"Well, you did it. Go you."

"I did it with the help of my family."

"And they did it with you. You. Ace Reynolds, cowboy, rancher and very bitter son."

Any ability to remain calm had vanished. "You think I'm wrong?"

"I think you've somehow convinced yourself that you're responsible for the sins of your father. It was Andrew Reynolds who tried to run this place into the ground. He would've done so, most likely, if he hadn't gotten caught."

"I know who and what my father was."

"Yet you continue to feel as if you need to apologize for him. Make yourself less than, for reasons that make sense to no one but you."

"What the hell is that supposed to mean?"

"You're damn near obsessed with this. The choices he made. The reputation issues that came with that. You didn't commit the crime but you continue to feel as if you need to pay for it."

Obsessed? Is that how she saw him?

The thought hung above his head like a weight about to drop off a frayed cord, until another one struck. This one brighter—and far darker—than the first.

What right did she have? It wasn't like she'd stuck around.

"It's easy to judge from a distance, isn't it?" Bitterness left an unpleasant, smoky taste on his tongue. "To run away when things get hard and take up with someone else so you can forget this life. Hell, so you can escape from it."

He overstepped.

Ace knew it the moment he chose to mention her marriage. Knew it even more when anger tightened her lips and something painful rose up to fill her gaze.

"I didn't escape."

The argument had turned dirty in a matter of moments, further proof of what he'd already worried about. Their relationship really was no different from his parents'. How many times had he seen the way the air changed between them, practically instantaneously? How quickly one of them could grasp the hottest poker in their relationship and use it as a weapon.

He was no different.

The reality of her marriage had bothered him for years, and now that he had a chance to let that ire free, he'd leaped at it.

"I didn't, Ace." Veronica repeated the words. "I knew our relationship was over and I needed to move on."

"By getting married less than a year after we broke up?"

"By moving on with my life."

He still remembered the day he'd finally understood that. Arden had caught the news in town after seeing Veronica's sister Maria at the market. Maria had broken the news, leaving Arden with the responsibility to come home and do the same.

It stung to realize Veronica's light comments about Arden being the family matriarch had been spot-on, re-shaping that memory in his mind. Arden had been as kind as she could, but she broke the news in a rush.

"She got married, Ace."

"Who?" He was distracted and he had no idea who Arden spoke of as he snagged a water out of the fridge, wishing it were a beer. He'd spent another hard day out on the property and had gone a round with one of their distributors to cap off his day.

"Veronica." Arden rubbed at a small spot on the table before bringing her gaze back to him. *"Some guy she met in Houston. They got married last weekend."*

He fumbled the bottle in his hands, water dribbling out the top, but it was the only outward sign that Arden had tripped him up. "Good for her."

"Come on, Ace," she said, her voice quiet. *"You cared about her."*

Cared?

Hell, he'd loved her. Despite their endless volatility, he'd loved everything about her. And she'd left. Just up and gone after their last fight. She refused to give up nagging at him about the business, convinced the storm of their father's feed practices would abate.

Hell, she was a vet. Didn't she understand the problem? Rendering was not only illegal but it put the herd at serious risk. His father hadn't cared, choosing to save a few bucks in the worst way as if that would make up for the deluge of his debts. Yes, feed was expensive, but the debts Andrew Reynolds had racked up were mind-numbing.

And he'd known nothing. Had blithely rode the ranch

day in and day out and had no freaking clue the business was on the verge of collapse.

"Ace? Are you okay?"

He wasn't but he'd be damned if he was going to stand in the kitchen and rehash a relationship that had obviously meant little to Veronica Torres. In fact, he realized as he drained the water bottle, it must have meant nothing if she was already married to someone else. He'd been nothing more than a way to spend the time until she could escape Midnight Pass.

"You're right, Arden. I did care." He crumpled the bottle in his hand before tossing it in the small bin she kept in the kitchen for recycling. "But I don't anymore."

"You don't mean that."

"Actually, I do. And I'd better get used to it because she has a new life now. She chose someone else."

"Ace..." Arden's voice faded out behind him as he walked out of the kitchen, the door slamming in his wake.

He'd go back to his desk and his paperwork and the mound of payments Reynolds Station still owed.

And he'd forget the woman he loved had bound her life to someone else.

The memory faded as he mentally returned to the cab of his truck. "Exactly. You moved on."

"Are you going to make me keep paying for that choice? You've ignored me for nearly all of the two years I've been back in the Pass."

"There's nothing to pay for. It's a fact. You did move on."

"Didn't you?"

Had he?

If anyone had asked him even a month before he'd have said a resounding yes, he had. He'd believed himself healed from his disastrous relationship and from the volatile feelings that always swamped him when he thought of his time with Veronica. But maybe he'd deluded himself.

The fact that the first chance he got to shove her marriage back at her was a pretty sizable clue he'd never gotten over it.

Over her.

"I had a life. I had no choice."

"There's always a choice, Ace."

"Not in this case. Not really."

She tilted her head, clearly about to say something before she pulled back.

When she didn't respond, Ace shifted his gaze to the herd, the calves roaming before him the visible proof that life did go on. The business had gone on. And despite his lingering anger at his father, along with his brothers and sister and a slew of hardworking hands, he had saved the ranch and their reputation.

He hadn't needed Veronica Torres in his life. He'd moved on, done what needed to be done and restored his family name in the process.

That meant something.

Up until this afternoon, he'd have said it meant everything.

Yet as he stared out at the wide-open land stretching as far as he could see, Ace couldn't help but wonder if it was enough.

Chapter 13

Veronica drove out of the Crown Ranch, her SUV bumping over the uneven ground at the edge of the property before she hit the main road. The call for help from their ranch foreman had come at the perfect time—one of their cattle had been cut up pretty badly along a damaged line of fence and needed attention—and Veronica had jumped at the chance to be useful.

And away from Ace.

How had their afternoon gone so wrong?

The lazy picnic had been wonderful. More than wonderful, in fact. The two of them had continued the work of getting reacquainted, their conversation warm and friendly and fun. And it had proven, once again, that they had as much in common out of bed as in.

The ride out to see the calf she'd treated several weeks ago had been her idea, as well. It was both a way to prolong the time together and to see to a patient, and things had been going just as well there.

Until she ruined it.

Why had she insisted on poking Ace about his father? It had been a sore spot before and the passage of time hadn't helped the matter.

It might not have been a complete surprise he was still sore on the subject, but what had been unexpected was how fast he glommed on to her marriage as a sticking point between them.

She'd spent so much of her own time regretful for the end of her marriage that she actually had very little understanding what that choice had meant to him.

But it was now clear that her marriage to Mark had cut Ace deeply. How had she missed that? Or worse, what did it say about her that she never even considered how that choice had made him feel?

Maybe it was the talk of his father, but suddenly the memory of why she'd chosen to leave filled her mind's eye. A bitter memory, but one that was a part of their history all the same.

They'd had one of their raging fights. She'd finally had enough and decided to leave. After she broke up with him he didn't do anything to come after her.

They'd established the pattern early and their fights had only grown more and more intense as they spent more time together. In retrospect, it was hard to remember the things that would set them off, but just like today, it usually had something to do with a comment that could just as easily lie unspoken.

Comments they bore equal burden for.

Sometimes it was her, callously poking at something having to do with the ranch or his stress in managing through his father's crimes. At other times it was him, questioning a medical decision she'd made or a treatment suggestion.

They were volatile. It was how she'd always thought of their relationship and for the longest time she'd ignored that aspect, content to be with him.

Until the day she wasn't.

Every time the passion between them led to a fight, they'd battle through it. The conversation never turned truly ugly—neither of them fought dirty or spoke disrespectfully—but they were a lot like a lit fuse. Once turned on, nearly impossible to turn off until it had burned out.

Although she'd regretted the decision almost immediately, a comment from a girlfriend had planted a seed of doubt.

Was Ace the only one for her? Shouldn't relationships be easier? Why wasn't her relationship with Ace more like the one shared between her parents or her sisters and their boyfriends at the time?

So that last time they fought, she'd run. And in some misguided attempt to run from that volatility she'd run straight to Mark.

Sweet, simple, steady Mark.

Was it any wonder their marriage died? It hadn't been built on much to begin with. A truth she knew—and had lived—but which seemed even more callous and cold in the light of Ace's assessment.

Snatches of their conversation in his truck floated through her thoughts, as sharp and pointed as if they still hovered in the air.

It's easy to judge from a distance, isn't it?

To run away when things get hard and take up with someone else so you can forget this life.

There's nothing to pay for. It's a fact. You did move on.

At the time, she had truly believed that she'd moved on, but had she really? The home she'd built in Houston had been with a man who was good and decent in his own right, but a poor comparison to someone so big and vibrant and *real* as Ace Reynolds.

The vet practice she'd built in Houston had slowly become more home than her actual one and, in the end, had contributed to her attack. There was no reason to be there late at night, managing paperwork, except for the reason that she'd had no desire to go home. And with that decision, she'd made herself an easy target and had paid the price.

Her cell rang through her Bluetooth speakers and she hit the answer button on the steering wheel, not even bothering to look at the caller ID.

And realized her mistake as the first words filled the car.

"Why, hello, Dr. Torres." The voice was deep and pointed, with a manic sort of perfection underlying the enunciation of each word.

"Who is this?"

"You know who it is."

She nearly hung up. Was so close to hitting the off button on the steering wheel even as some idiotic sense had her frozen, stuck listening to whatever it was he had to say. "Why don't you refresh my memory, anyway."

He let out a quick, ugly curse before pressing on. "The Rat King doesn't announce himself."

"The Rat King doesn't exist."

Another round of curses rumbled through the phone and she sensed that her taunting wasn't going to help her situation. But it did reinforce the crazy that sat on the other end of the phone.

"How'd you get this number?"

"You're not hard to find, *Dr.* Torres." He again enunciated the word *doctor*, as if mocking her. "You give out that number freely. To your patients. To your friends. To your new boyfriend, I bet, too."

At the mention of a boyfriend, all the sorrow and anger and guilt that had haunted her as she drove away from the Crown Ranch changed. Galvanized, really, into a mix of mind-numbing fear and calm, cool control.

Ray Barnett, regardless of whatever the hell he wanted to call himself, was never going to touch the people she cared about. She'd see to that.

Forcing bravado into her tone, Veronica fought to keep her voice even and level. "I don't know what you're talking about."

"Oh, no? You sure did move on after that sad-sack husband of yours. Got yourself a big bad cowboy now. I've heard all about him. How he tried to protect you at your mama and papa's house. The big guy thinks he's tough against a gun."

"Let me guess. Were you the coward hiding in the dark with the gun?"

Another round of curses, triggered by the word *coward*. When he finally settled once more, she heard the barely controlled fury in his voice. "My soldiers are loyal to me."

"Soldiers? Is that what you call them? I call them cowards who hide in the dark."

The words came winging back through the speakers in the ceiling, swift and immediate, anger rising with each word. "They. Are. Soldiers."

"They're criminals. And so are you."

"You're just as clueless as before. So believe me when I say this. I'm going to win this round. And you're going to be sorry you never gave me what I came for in the first place."

The connection winked off, the radio that had been playing softly before the call coming back up on the speakers. The sugary '80s pop tune was at odds with the menacing call and the threat that still swirled in the air.

Even worse was the way that menace had lodged beneath her breastbone, battling the raging beats of her heart she couldn't get under control.

Veronica pulled the SUV to a stop, unable to control her shaking hands. She was okay at the moment, no matter how dark his threats. So were her parents. So was Ace and his family. No one had been harmed.

Yet.

She had to focus on that. She might have no idea where Ray was or when he would strike again, but for the moment, they were safe. Now she needed things to stay that way.

Her fingers still shook, but a firm resolve settled low and deep, pushing against that sense of dread. She needed to fight this, and unlike the last time, she wasn't clueless. Nor was she unaware of what her enemy meant to do.

She wanted to call her parents and warn them but she needed backup first. Her father would never agree to the plan brewing in her mind if she wasn't secure in the help she needed. On a deep breath, Veronica put the car back into gear and bumped the last few yards to the main road. Only instead of turning toward town and her practice, she swung around the way she'd come.

Back to Reynolds Station.

And straight back to Ace.

Their relationship might be volatile and after that afternoon they might not even have one to speak of, but he'd help her. She knew he'd help her.

Now she just had to hope like hell the idea she'd cooked up would be the very thing to keep them all safe.

Arden slung her yoga mat over her shoulder and headed for the small convenience store on the corner. The quiet Saturday afternoon practice had done a world of good for the tension in her shoulders and she used the renewed sense of calm to focus on the problem at hand.

Namely her stubborn brother.

What was wrong with the man? She'd done her level best to play Cupid that morning, and while she'd stopped short of aiming arrows at her brother or the love of his life, she'd done the next best thing. Added fried chicken— her mother's secret recipe—into a picnic basket and sent the two lovebirds on their way.

No one could resist Betsy Reynolds's fried chicken. It was a family secret that had been entrusted to her and Arden used it with great care.

And Ace had *still* managed to blow it all.

He'd stomped back into the house, sans Veronica, and dropped the picnic basket in the laundry room. He'd hollered strict orders that she not clean it up, then headed straight for his room with barely a backward glance.

Since her mothering instinct stopped short of cleaning up after anyone but herself, she wasn't going to touch the basket, anyway, but she did take a quick peek, delighted to see the food she'd packed had been eaten.

What had gone wrong, then?

It was the one idea that had nagged her through her practice, keeping her from sinking totally into the Zen zone her yoga usually provided. She'd diligently pushed it down, deepening her Warrior One pose, but hadn't managed to fully erase the confusion.

Or the irritation that things weren't falling into line.

Ace and Veronica weren't like Belle and Tate. A fact Tate struggled to understand but which was as clear to her as the feel of the sidewalk beneath her feet. In one of their late-night chats earlier that week, Tate had questioned how Ace could keep fighting the inevitable. He loved the woman, so what was their big brother waiting for, Tate had asked.

She'd been tempted to ask Tate how he'd done the same for so long, but kept it to herself. And instead enumerated all the hurdles Ace and Veronica had to conquer. Hurdles that were quite different from the fear for Belle's safety that had kept Tate from her.

No. For Ace and Veronica it was something else entirely.

The crazy fights that seemed to sweep up out of nowhere. Ace's lingering insensibility over their father and some near-mythological need he had to restore the ranch to a standard that was inhuman. And most of all, their brother's lingering hurt pride that Veronica had married someone else.

If Ace didn't learn to put the past firmly in the past— on all counts—he wasn't going to have a future.

The short bark caught her first and Arden looked up to find a pretty chocolate-colored Lab tied to a bike rack, staring at her and blocking her path on the sidewalk. The sweet baby couldn't be more than a year old and sat pretty as a picture where he—Arden did a quick check—was tied up.

"All by yourself out here?"

A large brown tail thumped hard on the pavement but that was the only sign of response she got.

"It's a pretty day, isn't it, baby?"

A bit more thumping greeted her but the dog remained seated, exhibiting extraordinary control for such a young dog. Realistically, Arden knew the owner would be back soon. It wasn't animal abandonment to run a quick errand into the small coffee shop that rose up beside her, but something about the dog out there all by himself bothered her.

Why was he so still? Was it good training or a sort of punishment to see how long the dog would wait?

Which was heaping a whole lot of judgment on a dog waiting for its master who'd only stopped off to get a quick caffeine hit.

Maybe an hour of yoga hadn't done the trick.

She'd nearly convinced herself to walk on, bending over to give the dog a quick pat on the head, when a sharp command echoed behind her.

"Murphy. Down."

The dog dropped immediately, head pillowed on his front paws, and Arden's hand met only air. She swung around, affronted by the swift command, and came face-to-face with six feet of broad shoulders, lean muscle and a glint in the eye that had forever set her off attractive men.

Too-attractive men, she amended to herself as those deep brown eyes did a quick assessment of her figure. It wasn't a leer—she had to give credit—but it was a solid sweep of appreciation before his gaze lifted firmly to meet hers.

What was unexpected was how it stayed there.

"He's a working dog. Unsolicited petting confuses him."

"Then maybe you shouldn't leave him out on the street alone." And just like that, the judgment she hadn't quite tamped down on spilled out in full force.

His smile never wavered. In fact, if she weren't mistaken, it had upped in wattage. "Maybe it's part of his training."

"So you can take a coffee break? I don't think so. Leave him home, then, if you feel the need to take breaks."

"You work with dogs?"

Arden knew a challenge when she saw one. It also didn't sit well that his amusement continued to ratchet up instead of matching any of the sudden ire she was feeling.

Shouldn't he feel insulted by her assessment?

"No, I don't," she finally said.

"Who do you work with, then?"

"I'm a yoga teacher."

"Oh, obviously." He waved at her outfit and the mat still strapped to her back. "It clearly chills you out, too."

"I beg your pardon?"

"Isn't yoga supposed to help? You know, dealing with life and stress and all?"

"I deal with stress just fine. And besides, it's a daily practice. Some days are harder than others."

He moved a step closer, still well within a suitable distance, but something in Arden fired at the nearness. The sandy brown of his hair was a match for the eyebrows that quirked over those dark eyes. Eyes, she couldn't help but noticing, that were a match for Murphy's coat. Warm and oddly comforting, despite the humor that still rode there. He had an impressive set of shoulders, broad and rounded at the ends. A perfect place to settle her hands.

Which she would *not* be doing, she belatedly admonished herself, even as her assessment moved on to the dark gray T-shirt that covered an equally impressive chest. The sleeves weren't too tight, but she could still see the muscles that lined his arms, especially that delicious ridge of triceps that ran down the back sides.

"I'm sorry for your bad practice, then."

"What?" His comment finally made it through the haze of awareness that had distracted her. "Who said I had a bad practice?"

He gestured vaguely toward her with his coffee cup.

"You're looking awfully grumpy for someone who should be feeling pretty calm right now."

"I'm not—" She stopped, unwilling to be ridiculed. "I need to get going."

"Don't you want to pet my dog?"

The question was so absurd she nearly laughed. Who was this guy? She hadn't seen him around town and while she knew she needed to be on her guard—Veronica's break-in was proof of that—she didn't get a dangerous vibe.

No, she amended to herself. Mr. Broad-and-Lean-and-Way-Too-Sexy had plenty of dangerous vibe about him, but not the criminal sort.

But the dog was pure magic.

It wasn't much but it also went a long way toward managing her attitude toward the attractive stranger.

Besides, she'd never been one to resist an animal and, at the invitation, Arden dropped to her haunches to pet Murphy. The tail thumping continued, but it was the quiet command—"Relax"—that had Murphy moving forward to preen beneath her touch. The dog was beautiful, his coat soft and lush beneath her hands. She felt his muscles bunch and flex as she pet him, running over the strong ridge at his shoulders before returning to his bony head.

"You're a sweet guy." She looked up at Murphy's owner. "What does your dog work at?"

"He's K-9."

"I didn't think we had any K-9 units here in the Pass."

That humor flashed again. "You keep up with local police protection?"

Suddenly aware he physically had the conversational upper hand, she stood up, reluctantly ending contact with

Murphy. "My sister-in-law is an MPPD detective. It's dinner conversation."

He didn't ask any other questions, just gave a small head nod. "Okay."

Okay? That's all she got?

Based on the quiet way he sipped his coffee, Arden suspected the answer to that was a hard yes.

Irritated at the nerves that buzzed and jumped in her belly—heck, irritated with the entire conversation—she laid a hand on Murphy's head for one final pat. "Good to meet you, Murphy." With a dark glance, she added to Murphy's master, "See you around."

She turned on her heel and continued to her car. But she didn't miss the quiet words that floated in her wake.

"I certainly hope so."

Ace didn't feel any better about his day with Veronica than he had upon returning to the house, but he was on kitchen duty and he had five other adults in the house who were depending on him for dinner. Besides, the walls of his room had begun to close in, anyway, and a rare afternoon watching sports news hadn't done anything to assuage the conversation that continued to play over and over in his mind.

When had he gotten so prickly?

He banged against a few cookie sheets as he dragged a cutting board from a long skinny cabinet beside the stove, the heavy clanging noise unable to hide the answer that winged back, loud and clear, in his mind.

Forever.

He'd always been prickly. Not in the stoic way of Hoyt, but in the superior, big-brother, prissy-first-child way that he'd lived with always. He wanted things done right. He wanted everyone to be happy. And he felt determinedly and doggedly responsible for both of those things.

In minutes he had several packages of chicken out of the fridge, cutting them up to make the chicken potpie that was one of his regular dinner staples. He'd add on a large salad and a side of steamed broccoli and dinner was done.

The work soothed, the easiness and his own familiarity with the dish allowing him to go on autopilot. Step by step, he worked his way through the recipe. By the time he was at the roué, just adding in the flour, a knock came on the kitchen door.

"Come in!" He hollered out the greeting, instantly alert when a breathless voice whispered behind him.

"I'm sorry. I didn't know where to go."

The delicate steps of the sauce had his concentration and it took a few seconds for the words to sink in. As soon as they did—and the woman who spoke them—Ace turned from the stove, dinner be damned.

Veronica.

"I am sor—"

He cut her off midsentence, enfolding her in his arms. "I'm the sorry one. I shouldn't have been such a jerk. Shouldn't have—"

It was her turn to stop him and she lifted her head from his chest, replacing her cheek with her palm. "I know. And we will talk about all of it. But I need to talk to you." She glanced over at the stove. "As soon as we make sure that doesn't burn."

Veronica slipped from his arms and had the sauce stirred, all while shutting off the burner. "I've had your potpie before. It'd be a shame to ruin it."

She continued to stir, nodding her head toward the

chicken now cooked and cooling in a separate pan. "Dump that in. We'll get this finished and in the oven. Then I need to talk to you."

With the same deft, economic movements she used when handling the animals, Veronica had the meal poured into the waiting pie shell. He capped off the top with a second piecrust and put it in the oven. It was only when he turned back to her that her initial greeting came back to him.

I'm sorry. I didn't know where to go.

"What's going on?"

He stared at her, her back now against the counter and her normally tanned skin pale. "I'm sorry to bring this to your door."

His first thought—hope, really—was that she'd come back to make up. But at the ready signs of fear filling the delicate lines of her face, Ace knew the truth.

"What happened?"

"He's back." She wrapped her arms around her, as if the motion could ward off the evil of what she was about to say. "The man who kidnapped me in Houston. The one who invaded my business and was going to hurt me until the police came. He's back."

"How do you know?"

"Because he called me. He's not going to miss this time. He's going to hurt me the first chance he gets."

Chapter 14

How was it even possible she felt better, saying the words? Giving them free rein to take shape and form. She'd buried the last attack so deep. She'd tried to forget about it, using the excuse that therapy had been a huge help. Further justification had come by moving away and moving on from Houston so that—voilà!—new life and new Veronica.

But she knew the truth.

That last year in Houston had been her own personal nightmare and it had only been the past month that she'd begun to find herself again.

Because of Ace.

The past wasn't something she could change. The choices she'd made—solely her own—had to be owned and dealt with. But she'd rather deal with those choices and find a way to move forward with him than continue to bury them and live without him.

They *would* figure this out. Together.

The confusion and pain that had accompanied her earlier as she drove over to the Crown Ranch had faded away. What had they even been fighting about? Ray's call and series of threats were far more upsetting than whatever ephemeral issue had set them off earlier.

Ace pulled out one of the kitchen chairs. "Tell me everything he said."

Veronica took the seat and the bottle of water he plied on her from the fridge, considering her words. She wouldn't hold anything back, but she also needed to focus on what to say. And how to bring him along with her plan.

Ray needed to be stopped and the Houston police hadn't been successful in doing that. Although she'd never gotten mastermind vibes off him, he was a lethal snake who knew the exact opportune moments to strike. He'd found a niche for himself in a major city's criminal underworld and was going to do everything he possibly could to stay in power.

Which made coming after her that much more personal.

Why leave the confines of his home base to torment her? Had the fact she'd gotten away put a dent in his power? Was she a loose end he needed to clean up or did he look weak to his opponents?

She had no idea how gang warfare or criminal hierarchies worked but she did know animals. She understood pack and the dominance that came because of a show of strength. If her ultimate escape in Houston put a mark against that strength, enough time had passed that Ray would likely be near-manic to get it back.

"Veronica?"

"I'm sorry." She took a sip of the water. "I was just considering another way in."

His green eyes grew darker at the mention of a "way in" but Ace seemingly caught himself before saying anything rash. "Before you go there, tell me what happened."

She walked through the call she'd taken as she'd driven off the Crown property. The threat and the clear admittance that the man who'd shot at her parents' home wasn't Ray but someone working for him.

"And he called them soldiers?" Ace asked when she finished recounting the conversation.

"Yes. And he didn't take it well when I suggested they were cowards."

The first smile she'd seen since arriving at the Reynolds ranch house tipped the corners of Ace's mouth. "Imagine that."

"He also said he's going to win the round. That I will be sorry."

"Sorry for what? You were a drug break-in gone bad."

"It was part of an initiation ritual. I stood in the way of that."

"So now he's hunted you to Midnight Pass as some sort of revenge for all that?"

"I guess so."

"But why? What's his endgame?"

And with those words, the entire situation became all too real once more. She'd driven herself to Reynolds Station under the power of positive thinking that everyone she loved was still safe.

But what if Ray really was as crazy and messed up and as determined as he seemed?

"His endgame is me, Ace."

Ace fought the chill that raced down his spine and focused on the conversation at hand. He knew Veronica was scared—hell, he was out of his mind—but he also sensed there was something they were missing. More than a puzzle piece, it was something hovering just out of view.

"But why?"

"Because I got away. Because I was responsible for getting one of his minions killed when the police raided my practice. Because he's crazy." She threw up her hands. "Who knows?"

On some level he knew she was right. Trying to figure out a psychopath's reason for anything was likely a futile exercise, but...

Madness didn't answer the question of *Why Veronica?*

Nor did it give any reason to why she'd been targeted well after she'd left Houston. Wasn't there enough in his day-to-day life to keep this so-called "Rat King" busy? Why try to manage on two fronts, essentially?

If he really did manage soldiers, the man's battleground was Houston and all the ill-gotten opportunity that remained there. It wasn't chasing after one woman who got away, two years later.

"What does it matter why? He knows about you, Ace. He referred to you as my boyfriend. He knows about my family and my practice and what I do each day."

"Have you called your parents yet?"

"They're next on my list. I'm not sure how to get them to leave town for a while, though."

"They're welcome here. You know that. But as you said yesterday, getting your father out of your home is likely a difficult exercise. I'd suggest you take the opposite approach."

"Which is?"

"Put your whole family on lockdown. Your uncles appeared to have more than adequate firepower and can be soldiers for the Torres side of this battle. Get the entire family over there and keep things safe."

"They'd do that." She nodded, the first sign of comfort settling in her gaze. "And it would keep them all together and in one place."

Whatever nagged at him—and most everything about this situation did—was still elusive at the moment. "Go call them. You'll feel better and we can work through what comes next."

She stood, hesitated. "Thank you."

"You don't need to thank me."

She moved a few steps closer and laid a hand on his arm. "Yes, I do. I know we still have things to say. Today was proof of that. But I appreciate the help, anyway."

"Those things. They were the heat of the moment. They don't matter."

"They do matter. A lot. But your support. Here. Now. Without any question, just a willingness to help. That matters more than I can say."

He'd spent his afternoon replaying their argument over and over in his mind. Each word and nuance, every feeling and moment of frustration. He'd cursed himself for his quick fuse and the feelings of lingering hurt over her marriage he couldn't quite erase. They were feelings that had to be dealt with.

But as she'd told him of what happened on the call, he knew he had to figure a way past it. Her own mention of burying hurt deep instead of dealing with it was as much a confession as a reflection of all he knew about himself. The things that bothered him burrowed deep, clawing and scratching until they left scars.

But if he acknowledged them, then he could also find a way forward.

"Go call your parents. You'll feel better once you do."

She nodded before bending to press a light kiss to his lips. It was different from the heated ones they'd shared earlier that day on a blanket over a picnic lunch or that morning, waking up and making love in his bed. But layered with the simplicity of gratitude and comfort, Ace saw the kiss had as much power as the others that had come before.

A different facet to the same bond between them.

And yet one more thing for him to puzzle over in his mind.

He waited until she was gone to cross back to the oven and check on dinner. Her pragmatism had ensured they'd gotten the pot pie done and in the oven and even now the crust rose, growing golden brown in the heat.

Just like it was supposed to.

Heat applied to flour and butter cooked it. Time and energy and effort applied to the land and his stock created a working ranch. Plans and focus and vision even brought a wedding to life, as evidenced by the tent sitting in his backyard.

Yet nothing about Veronica Torres worked like it was supposed to.

Wasn't that the heart of the matter? Or maybe a better question, Ace acknowledged to himself as he snatched a fresh water from the fridge, was why it all bothered him so much? Change was part of life and you were never guaranteed things would go as planned. Not even from the people you loved the most.

Growing up with volatile parents had proven that. It wasn't as bad when he was small, but by the time he was in high school it was as easy to believe he'd come home to one of them moved out as it was to assume they'd resumed their great love affair.

His father's betrayal of the business had also taught the lesson. A lifetime spent working hard—working toward his birthright—had nearly been ruined by his father's choices.

And then Veronica had gotten married so quickly after they'd broken up.

He'd believed the issue was that they were too much like his parents, but maybe the problem was deeper.

Maybe he was afraid of being betrayed again.

And that scared the ever-loving hell out of him. Because Veronica Torres was the only woman he wanted. The only woman he loved.

Hopelessly so.

What had to be thousands of twinkle lights winked above her as Veronica walked through the wedding reception tent with Belle, Arden and Reese. The caterers had been busy, the tent she'd observed midconstruction that morning now transformed into a wedding oasis, smack in the middle of Reynolds Station.

"It's gorgeous," she breathed out for at least the tenth time.

"Isn't it?" Belle practically twirled in a circle, her blue eyes alight with happiness and an anticipation that was palpable.

The ballet twirl was in stark contrast to the stoic cop Veronica had seen the night before as well as earlier in the week at her vet practice and it was wonderful to see. It gave some normalcy to a day that had been anything but and also gave credence to the idea that a real, fear-free future possibly did await her.

It also reinforced the fact that she was sick of talking about the call earlier that day from Ray Barnett. Belle had taken her statement, writing it up after dinner, but once that was done, Veronica had insisted talk turn to the wedding. She'd brought enough danger and dour thoughts into this home—one filled with the joys of an upcoming wedding and an upcoming baby—and she wanted some moments to be happy.

Moments not about talk of gangs or drugs or threats and, instead, full of hope for the future.

Even if Belle had snuck in the reassurance that the wedding would be crawling with cops, several of whom would remain sober, because they'd be on duty.

The thought comforted, even as Veronica was forced to admit, "once a cop, always a cop."

A very happy cop, Veronica smiled, as she watched Belle move through the tent.

The bride-to-be pointed out the area where the caterers would set up and then on along the back wall of the tent where the band would play and Veronica followed it all, her imagination filling in the players. She could nearly hear the music and already imagined dancing in Ace's arms when a small tap came on her hand.

"Come over here," Reese said. "I want to show you the wine bar. I'm going to pick out what I want you to drink for me since I can't have any."

Belle and Arden smiled and waved them on, the two already wrapped up in a discussion of the linens and centerpieces on the head table, and Veronica followed Reese to the bar area.

"That's quite a selection." Veronica's gaze traveled over the large wooden boxes, stacked behind the serving station, and saw the various labels Tate had brought in for the wedding.

"It's going to be quite a party," Reese said, her gaze shooting toward Belle and Arden. Seemingly satisfied by whatever she'd seen, Reese then leaned forward. "I want to know what happened today. Ace filled Hoyt and me in, but I want to hear it from you."

"Aww, Reese, I appreciate it but I don't want to ruin this moment. Belle already took my statement. This time is for her."

"It is for her and she's oblivious to us talking because she's so wrapped up in the height of the roses for the centerpieces." Reese shot her soon-to-be sister-in-law a fond smile. "As she should be. So come on. Spill."

Since Reese already knew the high points, Veronica focused on the outcomes instead. "I talked to my parents before dinner. They're on their guard and are going to batten down the hatches for a few days."

"That's good." Reese nodded, her gaze knowing. "I had the same worry for my mother a few months ago."

"I think they'll be safe."

"The urge to protect them is strong, but they need knowledge to fight the unknown."

"They do. I know they do." It was the singular thought that had accompanied her through the conversation with her parents and it was the same idea she pushed back at them when they tried to insist she come to stay at the house.

Knowledge was an armament. And while it wasn't as powerful as a loaded gun, she was at the epicenter of this and needed to find a way to stand on her own. More than that, she needed to find a way to not only survive but to emerge victorious.

Hiding out with Mom and Dad was not the pathway to victory.

So she would assume they were as safe as they could be, had given them her vow to keep them informed, and now here they were. "I don't like any better that I've brought this to your door."

"It's the only way unless you want Ace camped out on your front lawn."

Before she could say anything, Reese pressed on. "He's horrible at showing his real emotions, but they're there and there are a lot of them. He's so convinced he has to be strong for everyone else he forgets we're all here to be strong for him, too."

"He does do that, doesn't he?"

"They all do." Reese leaned in closer. "A more stubborn set of humans you're not likely to meet. It's like it's stamped in their DNA and Arden is as bad as the boys."

"They're a bit big to be boys, aren't they?"

Reese smiled at that, a broad grin that spoke of knowledge and, underneath it all, a truly deep affection. "When they get all territorial and edgy it's what they get. I love my man but I never forget, especially when dealing with his family, that somewhere inside is a ten-year-old boy who comes out in times of family politics, drama and discourse."

"I have the same with my own family." Veronica thought of how she and her sisters communicated. Thick as thieves and as quick to anger now as when they fought over dolls and tag and who would lead as they rode their bikes in summer.

"I never really got the joy of those relationships, losing my brother so young. Certainly not as an adult." Reese's smile dimmed as she ran an abstract hand over her belly.

"But it's an unbreakable bond and trying to find reason or rational thought in it doesn't really work."

Although she'd been in Reese's company a limited number of times, the reference to her late brother wasn't lost on Veronica. But it was an entirely different perspective to look at adult sibling warfare as something to be joyful about. Yet as she thought about her own sisters and the times they drove each other nuts, she could only conjure up one emotion.

Gratitude.

"The Reynolds family doesn't do calm and quiet very well," Reese said, her gaze firmly focused on the two women standing on the other side of the tent. "But they do love like champs."

Reese's declaration still echoed in Veronica's mind, long after everyone had gone to bed. Long after she and Ace had come to some sort of unspoken truce, falling into each other's arms and making love with a ferocity that only contributed to—or perhaps was the culmination of—the emotion of the day.

Sleep eluded her as she lay in the circle of his arms, but she took comfort from the warmth she found there. Which was something.

More than something.

"He lied to me."

The words, groggy with sleep, whispered into the darkened room with all the finesse of a gunshot.

She knew with absolute certainty who Ace spoke of. But it was a different matter entirely to take the monolith that had stood smack in the center of their relationship and have it find its way into the light.

Not sure how to play it but desperate to get him talking, Veronica shifted in Ace's arms. "I wasn't as still as I thought I was?"

"You were plenty still. It's my thoughts that wouldn't settle."

"Want to talk about them?"

"Not talking about them hasn't gotten me anywhere." Ace shifted to a sitting position, pulling her close as he settled against the headboard. "Maybe it's time to take a different tack."

"That's one way."

"I think it might be the only way."

He's so convinced he has to be strong for everyone else he forgets we're all here to be strong for him, too.

With Reese's observations still fresh in her mind, Veronica laid a hand over Ace's chest. "I'm here when you're ready."

His heart beat strong beneath her palm, his voice rumbling low when he finally spoke. "The ranch has been in my family for five generations. William 'Wild Horse' Reynolds staked his claim on the land after a winning hand of poker and started with a hundred head of cattle in 1895."

Veronica knew the story. Just as she knew the history of the Vasquez and Crown ranches, the roots of Reynolds Station ran deep in Midnight Pass.

"He realized pretty quick he had a love for it all and never gambled again."

"Why not?"

"According to my grandfather, Wild Horse claimed it was because he'd finally found the meaning of life and he didn't need the artificial high of gambling when he got one each and every day riding his horse beneath a vast Texas sky."

After all she'd experienced on the ranch, including

her own personal tour yesterday, Veronica could see that. How a man who had spent his life searching for something would—and could—finally find fulfillment in a place like Reynolds Station.

"And the name?"

"He'd spent a few years in Australia as a young man, helping run cattle on a ranch there. He'd always loved the idea of calling a farm a station, and when he finally got his own, he adopted the moniker. Felt it threw people off a bit. Made them ask questions."

"As I understand it, the ranch's name still does."

"That it does. *Texas Agriculture* magazine even did a small write-up on it." She felt the spread of his smile against the crown of her head. "In modern parlance, Arden keeps telling me that's what we call marketing."

"Whatever works."

Ace laid his free hand over hers, tightening the hold of his other arm. "Much as I love stories about my great-great-grandfather, he's not the liar. But maybe his gambler's blood ran too strong in my father."

"You think it's that simple?"

"Nothing about my father's choices were simple. But he made them all the same. Somewhere I feel I've found peace with that. Working past it, restoring the ranch. Seeing the respect light in people's eyes again. It's proof to me that those choices could be overcome."

The resentment that had accompanied that work for so long had faded, replaced with the obvious pride of what he and his family rebuilt. Veronica heard that pride, happy that he could finally recognize what had come of struggle and toil and flat-out hard work.

Yet even as she saw growth, the hurt still lingered. It had taken on new form, but it was there all the same.

"You should feel that way," she said. "So why do I sense a 'but' somewhere underneath?"

"It's the lies that hurt. Any way I twist and turn the situation, that's the piece that lingers. No matter how much time passes, it never goes away."

"Lies have power."

"They still have the power to hurt, I guess."

Veronica knew of Andrew Reynolds's choices. Even if she hadn't heard the gossip around town or the more professional strains of chatter that had circulated once the news came out, Ace had told her himself. Had confessed over a round of beers in a quiet corner of the Border Line one night early in their relationship.

He'd claimed at the time she deserved to know the truth. Only in his telling, Veronica had heard something different. Even now, after so many years had passed, she heard the same, filling Ace's voice with each syllable.

The pain of betrayal.

"He hurt you terribly."

"Yes. Do you know how humbling it is to learn the person you looked up to most in the world was a liar and a cheat?"

She didn't know, but she had a sense of how terrible that would be. An understanding that somewhere, way down deep, the hurt a human heart would bear from the betrayal of a parent.

She shifted her position to stare up at him, waiting to speak until their gazes met in the dim moonlight filling the room. "I'm sorry. I wish something you loved so much wasn't tainted by such sadness."

"How do you know that?"

"Know what?"

"That I feel that way."

Sadness still clouded the green of his eyes, but with it a determined beam of comfort. And—Veronica desperately hoped—the slightest measure of acceptance and self-forgiveness.

"I don't know what you lived through. I can't say I've experienced the same and it would be disingenuous to even suggest anything I've lived through was a match. But I do have empathy. And I care about you. I know you're a good man and I understand how much you love this small square patch of Texas.

"I also know how much you love your family. You can run from it or be angry or stubbornly refuse to acknowledge it, but you loved your father, too. A big part of you still does and that's not only a bitter pill to swallow but it's damned hard to reconcile."

"I go over and over it in my mind. What was he possibly thinking? How could the man I believed I knew do the things he did?" The anguish was back, lining his face in the muted light.

"That's the mystery inside all of us. The face we show to the world and the face that stays hidden, buried deep. For some, the faces are the same. But for many, the scars from living change that inner face into something unrecognizable."

"Reese can tell you all about that." Ace let out a rueful snort. "But Russ Grantham was the exception. He hid the face of a monster. All my father needed to do was tell us. We'd have stood by him. Would have helped. Hell, as much as I love this place, I'd have sold it in a heartbeat if it was something he needed."

"Maybe he was ashamed."

"To talk to his own family?"

"Yes." She nodded and willed him to understand. The

shortcoming wasn't Ace's or his siblings'. It hadn't been his mother's, either. It had belonged to Andrew Reynolds and his inability to lean on the people who loved him in the moment he needed them most.

"But we were here for him."

Memories of their afternoon argument came back and she tried desperately to find the right way to put her feelings to words in a way that helped him find acceptance. "How much do you lean on your siblings?"

"It's my job to look out for them."

"That's not what I asked." She reached up and laid a hand against his cheek. "How often do you actually let them know you're sad or hurting? How many times have you tried to have the conversation we're having right this minute?"

He hesitated, clearly struggling to speak, before emitting a soft sigh. "Never."

"They love you the same way."

"I don't lie to them about it."

"I'm not suggesting you do. But you're not forthcoming with them, either. Maybe your father got so in over his head he didn't know how to make it right. And then it was too late."

Veronica wasn't sure if she'd gotten through to him, but she did sense a calming in him. The bunched muscles that had tensed beside her had relaxed, as if the very act of speaking the words had given a bit of healing.

But it was when he pressed his forehead to hers that Veronica knew Ace had taken at least a few steps forward.

"It should have been different," he whispered.

"I know."

"But maybe it is time to start accepting it never can be."

Chapter 15

The hard, body-tiring work required of a rancher had ensured Ace had spent relatively few sleepless nights in his life. Even at some of the worst moments he'd ever experienced, discovering and uncovering his father's crimes, Ace had at least found escape in sleep.

He had spent more than a few restless nights in the months after Veronica left, but even those had carried a mix of anger and a weird, nearly vengeful need to move on.

This morning, he was just damned tired and had found little worked in his attempts to deal with his exhaustion.

"You look like hell." Hoyt muttered the words as he passed over the large thermos they kept in the truck. The two were trying to get a few things done before the end of the weekend in order to prep for their time out for the wedding. Hoyt had roused him early and the two were out assessing the next pasture rotation for the herd. Even with the bracing morning air that had finally arrived in late October, Ace felt his body dragging.

"Thanks." He took the heavy thermos, surprised when it bobbled in his grip.

"Whoa there." Hoyt steadied him and Ace nearly snatched his hand back before Veronica's question from the night before seared his brain.

How much do you lean on your siblings?

Was he that big a bastard he couldn't accept help over a thermos of coffee? Or maybe a better question, when had help from the people he loved become something he not only avoided but outright feared?

"Didn't sleep much."

"Unless you've taken up driving hot pokers in your eyes, I figured as much."

"Nice image."

"I'm the one looking at you." Hoyt took the thermos and added some to his own travel mug. He added a mock shudder as he screwed the cap back on. "It's scary."

"Bite me."

"I thought that was Veronica's job."

The response was more Tate than Hoyt and it caught Ace off guard just enough to snag a laugh. "You're an ass."

"Yes, but for reasons that never fail to amaze me, Reese loves me, anyway."

"She sure does."

"And I'm the luckiest of men for it."

Damn, but it was good to see his youngest brother so happy. Aside from his natural reticence, Hoyt had never set easy with emotions and feelings and relationships. He loved fiercely—his family never doubted that—but he didn't love easy. Which had made Reese's arrival in his life that much more awesome to watch.

She'd undermined every defense he had and, with it, brought a joy Ace had never seen before.

And now there would be a baby.

"You ever think about him?"

"Think about who?"

"Dad," Ace offered. "Now that you're going to be a father?"

Hoyt looked up from the top of his mug. "All the time."

"Does he make you as angry as he makes me?"

"He didn't betray me the same way he did you."

If he hadn't been holding his mug so carefully from lack of sleep, Ace would have dropped it in sheer surprise. "Run that by me again."

"Come on, you know it's true. Dad betrayed us all, but he really stuck it to you. You have his name and this place is your birthright as if it were tattooed onto your foot the day you were born."

"It's yours, too. Tate and Arden, as well."

"Yeah, but none of us are you. The firstborn son, carrying the weight of the Reynolds name. Besides..." Hoyt looked out over the land. "I had my time in the military. Special ops teaches you there's a hell of a lot of bad crap going on in the world. It made me grateful for this place but it also left me with an inability to own it the same way."

Although his brother had shared the basics of his time in the military, it was exceptionally rare to get a glimpse like this.

"Why?" Ace asked.

"My soul is scattered all over the world. Different jobs I did, different people I met. I left a bit of me behind. But all of you is here. It's always been that way." Hoyt slapped him on the back. "It's the way it should be."

"And that doesn't bother you?"

Hoyt turned the full focus of his gaze on Ace. "Why should it bother me? That you have a place you belong to?"

"No. That you don't."

Those green eyes, so like his own, went flinty. "First, you're my brother. Why wouldn't I want that for you?"

"I don't mean—"

"But even if we put that aside, and I don't, that's where you're wrong, anyway. I never belonged anywhere. Here included. It was only when I met Reese that it all changed."

Although they didn't often talk deeply about the things of the heart, he'd lived with his brothers for pretty much his entire damn life. As oldest, he'd watched them grow, had understood the things that mattered to them. That drove them.

How was it he never understood something so fundamental about his brother? "How couldn't I realize you never felt like you belonged here?"

"You weren't ready to understand it. You chalked up my joining the service as a military duty I felt I had to do and I wasn't going to try and change your mind."

He might be fuzzy-headed from a sleepless night, but the pain welling behind his eyes was more than clear. And it was all for his brother. "I'm sorry I didn't understand."

Hoyt waved a hand. "That's not what I meant. I needed to go out and find my way. That wasn't on anyone but me."

"And now?"

"I'm damn glad I found my way home." Hoyt smiled, that same sense of joy that had ridden his shoulders since finding Reese in full effect. "And found a woman who wants to make one with me."

Ace took it in, but just like his conversation with Veronica that had left him staring at the ceiling until dawn, he was shocked to realize how much others saw.

And how clueless he'd been all along.

He'd believed himself a protector, keeping everyone from dealing with pain and unhappiness, and they were the ones who were actually teaching him.

Ace blinked back the wash of tears, even as the hard lump remained in his throat. It was only when he trusted himself to speak again that he pressed Hoyt. "What have you been thinking about Dad for, then? You know, if you're not on the 'he's a lying bastard' train like me."

"I'm going to be a father. A man thinks about his own when that happens."

"You come up with any answers?"

Hoyt reached for the thermos again, refreshing his mug. "I'm not sure there are any answers."

"What is there, then?"

"Hope."

He wasn't going to pretend to understand, but something in his brother's attitude rang true. Maybe there wasn't getting over the past. Maybe the best you could do was still look toward the future with anticipation.

"Fatherhood is on me. How I treat my child. What I teach him. What she chooses to be because of the lessons I provide.

"But I'm hopeful because the baby and all the babies that come after are going to shape me, too. I'm lucky enough to get to watch."

He knew his baby brother was a man. He'd known that for a long time, unbearably proud of the human Hoyt had become. He'd worried about him in all the years he was away from the Pass on missions and had worried even more when he'd come home, ghosts riding his gaze. But it wasn't until now that Ace realized how much he'd learned from Hoyt, too.

"He loved you, Ace. He was proud of you every day of your life. Don't hold the bad choices he made against yourself."

Hoyt had taught him lessons every day. Maybe it was time he let a few of them stick.

The call came at midnight.

Veronica sat straight up in bed, her side cooling quickly without Ace's warmth. She fumbled for her phone on the bedside table, the cool air and the heavy ringing dragging her from sleep.

"This is Veronica."

"Hello, Dr. Torres." The singsongy voice came ripping through the receiver. "How are you tonight? Enjoying time with your cowboy?"

The dread that iced her veins at Ray's voice grew even colder, as if that were possible.

How did he know she was with Ace?

"What's the matter, Dr. Torres? Afraid of waking him?"

She swung out of bed and moved toward the sitting room, trying desperately not to wake Ace as her mind rushed through how to play this.

Was Ray guessing?

Did he see her drive into Reynolds Station yesterday?

Or worse, was he here, on the property?

And how had things escalated so quickly? She knew he was crazy and had believed he'd make good on his threats, but somehow she'd believed she would have a bit more time before he came. That the minion he'd sent to fire at her parents' house was just that. An advance shot over the bough to scare her.

Which was stupid and shortsighted in the extreme.

Worse, in her carelessness she'd brought him right to Ace's front door.

"Give me the phone." The words held zero warmth, only command.

Veronica whirled to see Ace standing there, in full control despite his naked form.

She wanted to argue with him. Wanted desperately to show him how strong and capable she was. She could handle this. She *could*.

But when he took the phone from her trembling fingers she didn't protest. Even as Ace spoke into it, barking out demands for Ray to show himself, she forced herself to take deep breaths to calm her racing heart.

In and out.

In and—

Ace let out a raging curse and tossed the phone across the room where it landed on the couch. "Bastard."

"Where is he?"

"No clue." Ace rubbed a hand over his face, the scratch of stubble audible in the otherwise quiet room.

"He's escalating." She whispered the words, afraid of what they meant. More afraid that if she was unable to take a phone call she'd freeze when she came face-to-face with the enemy.

"He is. Let's go get Belle." Ace turned back to the bedroom and snagged his shirt and jeans from the foot of the bed. Although she knew she needed to go, too, something kept her rooted in place.

She watched Ace drag on the jeans, then the shirt. Watched him drop to his knees and dig around on the floor for his boots. Her gaze even drifted to the second boot, shoved far enough under the bed Ace had to lean in to reach it.

And through it all she was paralyzed.

Her bravado and determination to handle this had been nothing but folly. Her past had caught up with her in the worst way.

Over and over, the night in Houston played back at her. The duct tape wrapped around her wrists as Ray and his buddy waved their guns at her. Their determination to get into her locked pharmacy room, pacing and brandishing their guns so they were shoved in her face, at her head and a few times against her spine. Even the gunshots that had gone off as the two men fired at the police and the officers fired in return rose up in her ears as if they were happening in this very room.

It was all going to happen again.

"Veronica!" Ace's voice and the strong grip on her shoulders dragged her from the memory, the sound of gunfire fading as his gentle words replaced them. "You're here. You're safe."

"He came back."

"Shh. We're going to find him." He continued to run his hands over her arms. The up and down movements were vigorous, but still gentle, and she should have felt some warmth enter back into her skin.

Shouldn't she?

Only instead of warmth, a cold that had nothing to do with the temperature of the room settled deep in her bones. She had no idea fear could be so frigid. So hopeless. So raw she practically burned from the cold.

"What if he finds us?"

Ace had never seen her like this. It was all he could register as his continued attempts to warm her seemed to produce no effect. The phone call had been bad enough, that taunting voice agitated and vengeful and determined.

But to see her so upset had a terrible sense of helplessness curdling in his gut.

He had no idea how he'd known who it was on the phone. Veronica had been quiet, barely uttering a word, and he'd been in a deep sleep, his exhaustion from the sleepless night before causing him to crash hard. All he knew was one moment he was in a still, dreamless sleep and the next he was awake and watching her walk out of the room like a wraith.

And he'd known who was on the other end.

Bastard.

He pulled her close, hoping to find another way to calm her. Shivers racked her spine and he kept a large hand over at the top of her back while the other one pressed her head against his chest. "It's okay. We're going to figure this out."

"He found you. He knows I'm with you. He knows who you are."

"Let him know. It only adds to the odds against him."

She lifted her head, her dark eyes wide with fear. "He'll hurt you. He'll hurt your family."

"We're made of sterner stuff."

"But there's risk. There's a chance something will happen." Her eyes went wide as the fear that had numbed her shifted gears, now rushing through her. "The wedding. All those people coming and going. Or Reese. The baby. What if he hurts her and the baby?"

"Veronica." Her eyes remained wide and a little wild and he said her name again, putting a bit more force behind it. "Veronica!"

The wild didn't fade but she did stop talking. "We're

going to figure this out. The Reynolds family isn't a bunch of pushovers. Hoyt was special ops and has faced a host of nameless, faceless threats. Hell—" Ace tightened his hold "—he *was* a nameless, faceless threat to his enemies. He can take care of his wife and his child."

"They'll be okay?" she asked, hope quavering at the fringes of her question.

"I'm counting on it."

"That's good." The force of his words and the reality of Hoyt's training seemed to give her some measure of relaxation and she nodded. "It still doesn't change the wedding. Caterers, tent people, bartenders. All are coming and going. He could slide in with one of them."

"And Belle is an MPPD officer. The wedding will be crawling with cops and a few feds she's become friendly with. I'm not worried on that front, either. But we'll arm everyone and if he tries it we'll shut him down."

While he couldn't say she relaxed, a bit of the mania faded, her pupils returning to normal size.

"We're going to take care of you. *I'm* going to take care of you," he added for good measure.

"And what if something happens to you?"

"I'm made of sterner stuff."

"You can't outrun a gun."

He couldn't and neither could she. But he'd be damned if he'd let it get to that point. Tightening his hold, determined to take a few last moments with her before he roused his family from their beds, he pressed his lips to her forehead, then rested his there. "No, but I can be prepared for an attack."

With everyone roused, the kitchen became their home base. Tate had already put in a call to the bunkhouse, putting everyone on high alert for any strangers or anything suspicious and Belle had coffee going while she called in to the precinct and the officer on duty. Everyone had agreed Reese should stay in bed asleep but she'd vetoed that the moment Hoyt dragged on a pair of sweatpants and was even now putting the finishing touches on a few packs of cinnamon rolls.

"Woman, you're going to make me fat." Hoyt nuzzled her neck.

"Unlikely." Reese lifted her head and pressed her lips to his. "But it'll be fun to try."

Ace watched it all from his perch against the counter and marveled at his family.

"Where's Veronica?" Arden crossed the room and handed over one of the mugs in her hands to him.

"She's still upstairs. She wants to call her parents one more time. Try to convince them to leave."

"You think they'll do that?"

"I hope so. I know they're uncomfortable enough with her here instead of with them, but they finally gave in to her request to separate. I don't know if they'll leave the Pass, even if she is safer here."

Arden nodded, her gaze thoughtful. "Do you think this Rat King will go through them to get to her?"

Memories of that manic voice filtered through his mind once more. "There's no telling. But getting them out of town will go a long way toward easing her mind. A family hunting lodge near Big Bend is her aim."

Arden stared into her mug. She kept her tone low but her words packed a punch regardless. "If he's determined, he'll find them, anyway."

"Not if we find him first."

"We haven't seen 4:00 a.m. this regularly in a long

time." Tate stood from the table with his and Belle's mugs in hand, crossing to get more coffee. "I don't like what's going on but I do like us. How we come together. The Reynolds family against the world."

Ace supposed it was true—an indication of how much they all cared for each other—and even greater testament to how determined they were to protect one another.

"Patrols have been increased downtown and two uniforms already checked out her office." Belle took her refreshed coffee. "No signs of anyone."

"I suspect he's laying low," Ace said.

"He's lying in wait for whatever it is he's got planned. And all of you are at unnecessary risk." Veronica hovered in the doorway, that same bleak expression he'd seen earlier in his room still covering her features. Damn, but it twisted him up inside to see her this way. Her face was pale, nearly sallow with lack of sleep and the constant stress of fear.

"We're here for you."

"I never should have come."

Ace had believed she'd worked past the shock from earlier, but her wide eyes once again indicated her upset and how the fear ate at her. He set down his mug to cross to her but his sister beat him to the punch. She wrapped an arm around Veronica and led her to the table. "You belong here. You've always belonged here and it's time you started to remember that."

"You're all in danger."

"We're all fine. You're the one we're worried about. A madman has targeted you and we're going to see you through this. Every step of the way until it's done."

Just like earlier that afternoon in his conversation with Hoyt, Ace saw a new facet to his sister. And just as with

Hoyt, he'd never questioned she was a woman. A grown adult, able to care for herself and the people around her.

What awed him was to see how naturally it came. And how easy the responsibility set on her shoulders.

Matriarch.

Veronica had referred to Arden that way, but until that moment he hadn't fully registered what that meant. Humbled, he watched his baby sister offer help and support, care and comfort, to the woman he loved.

Everyone in his family played a role. Whether born to them or simply accepting of what had been thrust upon them, Ace didn't know. He'd embraced his role a long time ago: oldest brother, caretaker and protector. How awesome to see Tate, Hoyt and Arden do the same.

Ace moved in, taking the seat beside Veronica. Arden caught his gaze over the top of Veronica's dark hair, knowing in those blue depths. It was that same knowing that had her standing and herding everyone out of the kitchen a few minutes later.

And it was with an equal sense of knowing that Ace laid a hand over Veronica's. There was still so much to say and so much to work through, but one fact had remained unchanged through it all.

He loved her.

And it was essential that she knew.

"There's something I need to say to you."

Veronica felt the warmth of Ace's hand over hers. She heard the soft edge to his voice and tried desperately to keep things straight. She didn't fully understand it, but ever since Ray's call, something seemed stuck inside her. Like every normal ability to process the world around her had vanished.

She'd kept it together through the conversation with her parents, even if only as a ruse to get them to leave town. She'd forced every ounce of a strength she was nowhere near feeling to project a fierce calm that they might believe her.

It had seemed to work.

By the end of the call her father had reluctantly agreed to take her mother and go to their hunting lodge for several days. She had several aunts and uncles going along with them and her sisters had agreed to get out of town with their families, as well.

Everyone would be safe.

They had to be.

"Veronica. I know this isn't the ideal time, but there doesn't seem to be a better one."

The slow movement of her thoughts seemed to fade away as the urgency in Ace's words finally sunk in. "What is it?"

"I love you. I know I haven't been good about showing it and we still have a lot to work through, but I love you. Nothing will change that, no matter how stubborn I am or how much of an ass I insist on being."

He loved her?

She stared at him, unable to look away. Something raw had settled over him and he seemed to snap with electricity, like a live wire sparking with excitement. "I don't expect you to say it back. I know there's a lot we still have to work through and after my behavior the other day you may have reservations. But—"

She turned her hand over beneath his, linking their fingers. "You love me?"

"Yes."

The idea seemed so foreign as to be impossible. Yes,

they were attracted to each other. And their time together over the past month had proven they had as much chemistry as ever. But after their fight earlier in the week she'd convinced herself they didn't have what it took for the long haul.

They didn't have the easy companionship of Tate and Belle. Neither did they have the ready collaboration of Hoyt and Reese. Instead, they had volatility and quick fuses and a history that had scarred them both.

She knew all that. Realistically, she knew it should be a block to their future. And yet...

He loved her.

Hardly daring to believe it, she pressed him. "Even with all that has happened? With our fights. And with Mark?"

"Yes to all that. I love you."

"But we haven't really dealt with those things."

"We will. We'll deal with all of it and we'll find a way past it or around it or over it. But we will find our way to a future."

Veronica hardly dared to believe it, but staring into that earnest gaze, she swore she saw her future. Not the specific details, but something better and even more important.

She saw Ace.

Her partner in the future, no matter what it brought them.

"I love you, too."

He settled a hand behind her head, drawing her close for a kiss. As their lips met, a loud cheer went up from the other side of the kitchen doorway.

"It's good to know they approve." She smiled and whispered the words against his lips before he took her into the deepest, sweetest kiss she'd ever had.

Chapter 16

Veronica dug into her travel medical bag, searching for the syringe she needed. One of the smaller farms in town had a horse dealing with an injured foreleg and she'd already done a full exam and was now looking to administer an antibiotic to help manage the healing and avoid infection.

It was routine work and she should have felt okay about that. But try as she might, the two cowboys who stood sentinel at the opposite end of the barn made that difficult.

The creepy late-night call from Ray had riled them all up, without any violent follow-up. Realistically she was grateful for that fact, but the lack of action meant they were all on pins and needles and eggshells and whatever the hell else they could manage to come up with.

Tension gripped them all, vying with the stress of Belle and Tate's wedding, now three days away.

The work at Reynolds Station had slunk to a crawl. Everyone was doing the barest minimum to keep the ranch running while spending the rest of their time planning the event of a lifetime all while keeping an eye out for a deranged gang-leader-slash-psychopath.

Just like now.

Ace had accompanied her to Windmill Farms along with one of their ranch hands, Travis. The two men made a formidable obstacle, flanking her sides as she moved around town managing her job. Most who saw her would have only seen two large men at her side, but Veronica knew better. Both were connected by a wireless earpiece Belle had set them up with. Both also carried guns. Lethal-looking pieces strapped to their sides beneath oversize work shirts.

"That's all he needs?" Ace pointed to the horse as she wrapped up the used syringe in a small medical waste disposal bag.

"That should do it," she said, not sure why he was even asking.

"Did you check him for any other problems?"

"It's good. I've got him."

"But what if you have to come back?"

She stilled, hands dropping to her hips. The horse's owner had already walked back to his office and was waiting for her to provide a final diagnosis, so they were alone.

Except for Travis, who beat a hasty retreat when she shot him a pointed look. Once the ranch hand was out of earshot, she whirled on Ace. "What's this about?"

"I don't want you to have to come back here. It's that simple."

"I'd like to avoid the same, but I'm not overmedicating that horse in the hope of avoiding it, either."

"It's a few antibiotics. What's the big deal?"

"The big deal is that he doesn't need it." She gave the horse one last look before stepping out of his stall and closing the door. "The bigger deal is I'm not going to change how I do my job."

"We're all changing how we do things for the time being."

"Not this." She remained stubbornly determined not to budge on this aspect of her life. The administration of medical treatment was her life's work. She'd be damned if she'd skimp on that—even to nonhuman patients—because of fear. Ray Barnett had taken enough from her. He wasn't taking this, too.

"I'll see you outside after I've discussed the rest of Willow's treatment with Mr. Taylor."

Ace disappeared in the same direction as Travis and Veronica headed for the office. She didn't spend much time out here, but Burt Taylor was a good client. His pets were generally healthy and well cared for and he paid his bills on time. His farm didn't provide the sort of volume as Reynolds, Crown or Vasquez, but he was a valued client.

And Ace wanted her to cut corners.

Was this what her life had come to? Slap-dash work so she could stay hidden away, protected from the world?

Pasting a smile on her face, she took the last few steps to Burt's door and waved herself in. She wasn't going to let anyone stand in the way of her work, but what sort of future did she really have? It wasn't like she could drag two bodyguards around for a living. And she'd already

skimped on the work happening at the office because she
didn't want Julie there alone.

Life had already changed because of fear and Ray's
threats.

Would it ever go back to normal?

She gave Burt a quick write-up of Willow's injury, the
treatments she performed and the required management
of the wound over the next few days.

"Call me if anything changes but she should be back
to normal in a few days."

"Thanks, Doc Torres." Burt nodded toward the door.
"It was good to see Ace. Haven't seen him in a few years."

"He's helping me out."

"Sure thing." Burt nodded, his bulldog face and normally serious features growing even more severe. "Heard
you've had a bit of trouble lately. Know I've got my eyes
open for anything out of the ordinary."

"I appreciate that."

"People take care of their own here. You're one of
ours. I hope you know that." Burt nodded as if satisfied
he'd said his piece.

"Thank you. Well. Um. I guess I'd better be going."

"Stay safe."

"I will."

She walked out of the barn, still puzzling through the
conversation. The uncompromising support from Ace
and his family had been humbling and gratifying. But
to also get it from her clients?

"You ready to go?" Ace hovered a few feet from the
barn, his back to the paddock.

"Sure." She glanced around. "Where's Travis?"

"I sent him on ahead. We had about thirty head get out
of the eastern pasture and he's needed back at the ranch."

"Of course."

Burt's support still sat warmly on her shoulders as she climbed into Ace's truck. It carried her down the long lane of driveway and it was only as they neared the end that she turned to Ace. "Burt said something to me. I didn't realize my situation had made the rounds here in the Pass but he seemed to know what's going on."

"The police are all aware of what's happening. Julie knows. My ranch hands know. I can't see that there's much need for secrecy." Ace turned onto the farm-to-market road that led back into town. "More eyes, the better, as a matter of fact."

"I agree. It was more the support he gave me that was the surprise."

"You didn't expect it?"

"Of course not. I barely know Burt. He's a client and I know him to say hi around town. But he was—" She stopped, trying to come up with an accurate way to describe how she felt. Before she could identify the emotion, Ace interrupted her.

"Why does it continue to take you off guard that people care about you and want to help you? You're a good person, Veronica. You're a member of this community and as a large-animal vet you're integral to the success of several of the region's largest businesses. You matter to people."

"But I left." The sentiments spilled out before she barely realized she had them. "I walked away from Midnight Pass, shaking the dust off my shoes as I went."

"I don't recall you kicking ponies as you left town."

"No, but—"

"But what? It bothers you that people care. That

they've embraced you as their own and want to look out for you?"

"I don't deserve it."

His jaw hardened but that was the only sign of his agitation as she stared at him in profile. His focus was on the road but she knew he was only working up to an argument. It was familiar ground, the two of them suddenly on opposite sides of a given situation. Only this time, unlike prior fights, she sensed something different. A frustration in him she hadn't seen before.

Was she misguided in thinking the town had little regard for her? Or worse, had she allowed her own misery at needing to start over somehow color how she saw her place in Midnight Pass?

Her entire family had closed ranks the moment there was a whiff of a threat. Ace's family had, as well. But now to know the town felt the same way? It was overwhelming.

It was—

The slam into the back passenger side tire sent them into a fishtail spin and knocked her against the door.

Out of nowhere, a car they hadn't even seen in their rearview mirrors bore down, clearly increasing speed.

"Son of a—" Ace's curse cut off midstream as another hit came to their rear just as he righted them back to a forward direction. The truck fishtailed against the ridged edges of the road, the heavy weight bumping at odds with the echoing crunch of metal that still trembled through the cab.

Veronica twisted in her seat, trying to make out the driver of the other car but the tinted windows made that nearly impossible. The driver had also placed some sort of film over the front window, shading just enough that she couldn't see into the large black SUV.

"Call 911! We need help." Ace kept accelerating forward but the shaking and bumping of the truck confirmed that they'd been severely damaged by the two hits.

She fumbled for her phone, digging in the front pocket of her medical bag at her feet. Her fingers closed around the cool glass face when Ace barked out more orders. "Brace yourself!"

She'd barely had enough time to pull out of her crouch and position her feet against the floorboard when another hit slammed into their rear, sending the truck into another fishtail. The seat belt tightened across her chest and Veronica fought to keep her focus on the phone and off the determined driver behind them.

Her phone face lit up as she dialed in the call, immediately connected to a dispatcher. "Nine-one-one, what's your emergency?"

"We're on the FM road leading into Midnight Pass. A crazed driver is hitting us repeatedly from behind."

The dispatcher kept her voice calm and controlled, asking details while confirming all the while that she was calling for help. Veronica swallowed back the scream that crawled up her throat when they were hit once more and then heard another string of Ace's curses. He muttered a few more before taking a hard left off the road, bumping over the grassy area that ran alongside the road.

"This is the only way," Ace said through gritted teeth. "We have to hope they don't know the area as well as we do."

The dispatcher continued asking questions to keep her talking and Veronica fed back where they were and Ace's efforts to outrun and escape their pursuer.

Veronica glanced into her side mirror, monitoring how far they'd managed to escape. The big black SUV had fallen behind and she took her first easy breath since the hit that caught them after leaving Burt's place. They might have gotten away. Or at least gotten far enough for the police to catch up and dispose of the threat.

She'd nearly convinced herself when the first shot rang out, shattering the back window.

Ace pressed the pedal to the floor, desperate to outrun the bastards behind them. The initial hit had come as a surprise, the SUV coming out of nowhere, and had taken more out of the truck than he'd initially understood. The subsequent hits hadn't helped but it was that first one that had done the real damage. He felt it in the way the truck grinded beneath him, sputtering even when he gave it all he had.

In a truck made for hard work and the heavy wear and tear that came from bumping over uneven land, the strategic hit to the rear was a death knell.

And now that he had taken them off the road and into a wide-open field, he'd made them sitting ducks.

A second shot hit the truck. It missed the back window but made a solid connection with the back of the truck. The quick pop had him slamming on his brakes as hard as he could.

"Out! Now!"

His fingers fumbled urgently on his seat belt, then scrambled for Veronica's, willing her to understand the urgency.

"We have to get out. Zigzag when you start running."

She nodded, her hands already in motion and reaching for her door handle. "I'm good. Go, Ace! Get out!"

The truck shuddered beneath him from another hit and Ace knew they were in as much danger outside the truck as in, but if the gas tank blew as he believed it would, a bullet would be the least of their problems. He cleared the truck, racing around the front to intercept Veronica.

The phone was clutched tight in her hand and she held it in the air, still shouting orders to the dispatcher as she ran. Ace fumbled for the gun at his hip and tried to keep pace behind her as the two of them zigzagged through the wide-open field.

They had made it about twenty feet when the truck gave one last rumble, then exploded in a fiery ball. The blast winded past them, heat enveloping them both before the force of the explosion tossed them to the ground. Ace fell over her, his attempt at cradling her missing the mark as he fell hard on his side instead. His footing lost, he did the best he could and tucked his shoulder as he tried to keep a tight hold on the gun.

The fall was extra hard as the uneven ground did little to cushion his body, but it did offer a slight benefit. As he slowly came back to himself, smoke filling the air and hazing the space between them and the driver, Ace was able to find a small dip in the ground. It wasn't much, but the grading was low enough they could both hide in the natural depression of earth and have some cover as he fired on their pursuer.

And he couldn't miss.

Ace positioned himself, setting his elbows so he could balance the gun with both hands, lining up his shot. Smoke still filled the air but was dissipating swiftly with the light breezes that perpetually blew in South Texas in October. Pain cramped in his side and he estimated he'd cracked at least one rib if not two. Channeling the pain to focus, he kept his eyes on the land that spread out before him and waited.

"I can't see anything," Veronica whispered.

"He's out there."

"The dispatcher said the police are on their way."

As if she'd conjured them up, the whirl of police sirens echoed in the distance. The land was wide open and Ace knew even with the police in sounding range, there was every chance they wouldn't make it in time to help. The SUV driver was a determined son of a bitch.

A rain of bullets shot in the air, the sound deafening as the shooter laid down a round of fire. Hoyt had talked a few times of the sound of battle, and in that moment, Ace understood it on a level he never had before.

There was no time to think. There was only action. Determined, focused action.

For the briefest moment he thought he had a shot. The smoke shifted on a breeze and the covering the bastard had used to shield himself from view dipped in the front windshield, revealing his wiry form and dirty blond hair.

Ace lined up his shot but the wind shifted once more, again obscuring their shooter.

Another round of wild fire ripped through the air but Ace refused to return the gesture. Instead, he kept his sights directed toward the field, beyond the haze of his still-burning truck.

The hail of bullets stopped abruptly.

And then there was nothing save the continued wailing of the police sirens and the burning, licking flames that consumed the truck.

"I think he's leaving." Veronica struggled to sit up and Ace turned to grab her arm.

"Get down. I think I broke ribs and I can't move fast enough to cover you."

"Don't move if you can help it. But I think he's gone." She moved carefully, but got to her feet all the same to assess the lay of the land. "I can see him driving off."

Ace struggled to get up, his side burning. Pain shot through him in waves, rippling up and down his side as if a demon played his ribs like a xylophone. "Tell the dispatcher we're alone. Armed, but alone."

Veronica relayed the commands before turning toward Ace. "Drop the gun. I've already told her you can't put your arms up."

"They're here?"

She moved up behind him, wrapping an arm around his waist. Her grip was firm but she seemed to know where to hold him because the pain didn't lesson but it didn't fire up at her touch, either.

"They're here."

He stayed conscious just long enough to see two Midnight Pass police officers spill out of their vehicles and rush toward them.

"I'm fine," Ace grumbled.

"You can keep saying it but it won't make it true." Tate shot the words back at his brother before moving around Ace's bed to stand near the window. "Just consider yourself lucky you got out of a hospital stay. Cracked ribs are a bitch no matter how you slice it."

Veronica had lingered back, allowing Ace's family to hover around him after their return from the emergency room. The police had already come and gone to take their statements while they were still at the hospital and Belle had run interference to keep the number of rounds of questions to a minimum. Even with that behind them, Ace refused to take any painkillers beyond ibuprofen.

Exhaustion rode her shoulders but she fought to show even the tiniest yawn. That could wait until everyone left. Right now, they all needed to be here, confirming their brother was okay instead of laid out dead in the morgue.

Which is where they both could have been if the situation had played out differently.

A few more seconds inside the truck before it exploded.

MPPD officers who weren't close enough to race over to help in time to scare Ray off.

Even that initial hit to the back of Ace's truck as they left Burt's could have gone differently. The road was elevated near Windmill Farms and if the hit had come at a different angle they could just as easily have slammed into the ditch.

If.

The near-misses were frightening and further proof of how lucky they were.

Belle slipped into the room, standing near the bedroom door. She waved at Tate, blowing him a quick kiss before gesturing him to stay put near his brother. Veronica was amused by the byplay, her first smile since the whole ordeal making its way across her face, when Belle shifted her attention, gesturing her over. She went, following Belle into the sitting room.

And then followed her again when Belle gestured toward the hallway.

"I need to talk to you," Belle said after they were out of earshot.

"Okay." Something sunk low in her belly. Had Ray hurt someone else? Gone after someone she loved?

"Who's hurt?"

"That's not why I've pulled you out here."

"My parents? My family? They're okay?"

"Shh. Yes." Belle wrapped an arm around her shoulders. "They're all fine. I just want to talk to you. You deserve the news privately."

The adrenaline—and how was it even possible she had any left?—that spiked through her system keyed her up, the exhaustion that had her drooping in Ace's room vanishing. "What is it?"

"Ray Barnett is dead."

"What?"

Belle stepped back, but held tight to one of Veronica's hands. "Your call to dispatch sent out multiple teams of officers. The team that helped you and Ace stayed, but the others moved on and one of them intercepted the SUV. There was a shoot-out."

"Was anyone hurt?"

"No. One of the officers took a hit to his torso but his vest mitigated the damage. He'll be sore for a few days but other than a bit of tenderness he's fine. And he has the dubious honor of taking Ray down."

Veronica took in the rest of Belle's words, shock and disbelief merging with the deepest sense of relief she'd ever known. The pain and confusion and upset she'd carried since that night in Houston cracked, disintegrating to dust under the professional description of the shoot-out.

The Rat King was dead.

And with it the fear and pain and overwhelming sense of vulnerability died with him.

Was it possible?

Even as she asked herself the question, the relief coursing through her veins reinforced the answer.

Yes.

It was not only possible, it had happened. She was—finally—free of the fear. For herself and her family and her future.

Tears she hadn't even realized she was crying coursed down her face, hot and wet. "It's really over?"

"He's been handled. It's over."

Belle opened her arms and pulled her close. Words of comfort murmured over her ears, but in the end, Veronica realized it wasn't the words that mattered.

It was the feeling.

She was safe.

And for the first time in more than two years, she looked toward her future with excitement and hope.

Chapter 17

Ace winced as he struggled to sit up. The pain of lying flat on his back had grown too tiresome and he hoped a shift in position would alleviate some of the unrelenting discomfort. His family had given him a hard time about the cracked ribs, but he didn't miss the relief that emanated off each of them like summer heat off asphalt.

And if he were honest, he knew the pain was a sign he was alive to fight another day.

But where was Veronica?

She had slipped from the room with Belle and he hadn't seen her since. Tate had kept up a steady stream of bad jokes to distract him, but Ace had finally given a verbal shove to get everyone out of the room, claiming a need to sleep.

And now he wanted Veronica.

He might not be able to hold her but just having her nearby was something. Hearing her voice. Holding her hand.

Knowing she was still alive after what they'd survived.

He'd denied the strong drugs to manage the pain and it wasn't because he didn't want them. His body hurt like hell. But he wanted to remember every second of every minute of what they'd survived and the pain would ensure he couldn't forget even if his memories tried to shut down. They'd gotten lucky and now they needed to stay even more vigilant than they had been.

The enemy had not only come to the front door, it had slammed right through and stormed the threshold.

"Ace?" His name filtered into the room, low and quiet. "Are you awake?"

"I'm up."

She came through the doorway from the sitting room, practically electrified with energy. Her presence calmed him, the pain fading as his body lost some of its tension. "How are you feeling?"

Before he could come up with some manly answer to hide how he really felt she held up a hand. "Forget I asked. You feel like crap. But I have the one thing that might make you feel better."

"I know you're a good doctor, but I don't think there's anything in your medical knowledge that's going to heal these ribs any faster."

She settled on the side of the bed, wrapping his hand in hers. "He's dead. The police caught him. It's over, Ace."

The haunted look she'd worn since returning to the Pass had vanished. In its place was a carefree warmth that reminded him of earlier times. Younger days, when they were happy-go-lucky and ready to take on the world.

It had all come back, ease and comfort now filling the depths of her rich brown eyes.

Oh, how he'd missed it.

"That's what Belle wanted to tell me. Another pair of officers intercepted Ray after he shot at us. They got him, Ace." A small line grooved between her eyebrows. "I wish there was another way, but I'm not sorry he's gone."

He ran a hand down her forearm, happy to simply touch her. The soft skin beneath his fingertips was warm and *alive*. "He made his choices. He lived a life on the edge no matter what way you twist and turn it. His decision to come after you was on him. You can't take on any of that as your own."

"No." She settled a hand over his. Again, it struck him how warm and vibrant she felt, the direct opposite to the near wraith he'd observed since the first contact made at her practice. "I can't and I won't. But I can still be sorry about it."

Wasn't that the heart of it all? For all she'd survived, there was still a good, decent woman who wanted to do right by others. He'd seen it earlier at Burt Taylor's farm as she watched over his horse. It had been evident with her family and her determined insistence on their protection. And he'd seen it over and over in her concern for his own family and the risks they all took to house her.

"You're amazing."

"It's funny, you know." She leaned in and pressed a kiss to his lips. "I was just thinking the exact same thing about you."

He kissed her, the steady, throbbing pain in his side fading at the tender moment. Yet again, another facet of their relationship spun out, this one as gentle as it was arousing.

"You shouldn't start things you can't finish," he whispered against her lips.

"Someone has more confidence in his abilities than

he should." She kissed him once more before lifting her head and settling back at his side. "It's time to heal."

"I'm sure that will make me feel better." He snaked a finger out to trace her collarbone through the chambray work shirt she'd worn earlier to go out on calls. The material was thick but he could still trace the lines of her body before palming a full breast.

"Way too much confidence in your abilities." She swatted him away before reaching for the small white pharmacy package she'd set on his end table earlier. "And it's also time for the good drugs."

"I don't need—"

Although he'd have gladly kissed her all day, pushing the limits of his injury, the competent form he thought of as "Dr. Torres" took over. "You do need these. And then you need sleep. Those ribs aren't going to heal on their own."

Ace took the pills from her hand and downed them with a full glass of water. He wanted to fight her on the stronger medicine but he'd suffered enough injuries as a rancher that he knew she was right. The sooner he took care of himself, the sooner he'd be back to work.

And back to her.

"You're a good doctor." He wiggled his eyebrows, even as the movement felt heavy and groggy, his eyes struggling to focus on her face. Undeterred he pressed on. "I think I'm going to need a very thorough exam."

She laughed at that and he felt soft fingers tracing the line of his brow. "You go ahead and fall asleep dreaming about that one, my sexy cowboy."

"I'll be a good patient. Promise." The words seemed to stick to his tongue and he tried once more. "Prom...sie."

"Right."

Those fingers hypnotized with their soft strokes over his skin and he let his eyelids droop closed. Images of her with her medical bag floated behind his eyelids, followed by thoughts of her practice. She could go back to work now.

Could see…to the…animals now. Horses. Cows. Maybe a few pigs.

Windows.

Ace frowned, his forehead bunching against that tender touch. Why was there someone peeking in her window?

Who peeked?

Why…?

Ace fought the dragging weight of sleep, desperate to tell her about the man peeking in the windows. Why was he there? Who was he? He wasn't the dead guy.

Who was he?

Words formed at his lips but his tongue seemed stuck because no words came out. He felt that gentle touch once more as he sunk into the softness.

And the world went black.

Although she knew he hated every minute of it, Veronica kept Ace in bed as much as she was able over the next few days. She wouldn't stoop to hiding medicine in his food, but she did plenty of wheedling and cajoling to get him to take the stronger stuff. He needed sleep and the time for his body to heal—an argument she'd begun to make on autopilot. She'd even sunk to doing a subtle striptease the night before to get him to take the meds, inordinately pleased to see the fire sparking in his gaze, overtaking the pain.

Pain she assumed was a lot sharper than he wanted to

let on when he started mumbling about seeing someone in the rearview mirror when they were shot at. She puzzled at it for a few moments, but ultimately let it go. The Rat King was dead and Ace was on a lot of pain medicine. Mumbling about the shootout was likely a side effect of the overall shock wearing off.

Shock or not, his focus needed to be on healing. And while it would still be a few weeks before they'd attempt to make love again, that didn't mean a bit of foreplay wouldn't be a useful tool to incentivize healing.

With that idea foremost in her thoughts, she shimmied into a fitted A-line dress in vibrant swaths of red and gold. She'd bought the dress several months ago and hadn't had any place to wear it.

It made her happy to know that now she did.

"You look amazing."

Ace stood in the doorway of his en-suite bathroom, a towel wrapped around slim hips. The bruises over his ribs had turned an ugly blackish-purple, but even with the evidence of his injury it didn't detract from the firm lines of his torso and the thick muscle that corded his stomach.

Goodness, the man looked good enough to eat.

Before she could check her thoughts, her mind was already calculating the minimum two-week moratorium she'd put on sex. It was only when her gaze flashed once more over those bruises that she resigned herself to looking only.

A point he reinforced with a hard wince as he sat down heavily on the edge of the bed. She was already headed his way to fuss when he waved her off.

"I'm okay."

The two of them might never have been particularly good at tempering their more fiery natures, but even she knew well enough to leave that one alone. He wasn't fine but saying anything was akin to flagging down a bull.

A wild, raging, hungry one.

She turned back to the mirror and kept an eye on him in the glass. The wedding was in a few hours and she already knew he'd pushed himself too hard standing up as best man. It would be easier to save her chips now and use all that goodwill to convince him on a sedative later.

For all her concern about his injuries, their quiet preparations for the wedding were oddly domestic.

"My little brother is getting married."

Veronica turned from the mirror and finished popping on an earring post. "He's not so little anymore."

"I know. But in my mind he's still somewhere around ten years old. I'm twelve and we can't wait to ride our own horses, free on the ranch."

"You weren't allowed to?"

"We were but it was a hard-won battle. The ranch is large and despite our rather skimpy claims to know every inch of it our parents knew better. We had to wear watches and there was hell to pay if we didn't use them. No matter where we roamed to, the rule was we had to keep an eye on the time and be back at least an hour before supper."

"But they let you go?"

"Yeah. At first it came with a lot of fussing and admonishing, but after a few months it was natural."

"And dinner? You always made it home in time?"

"Nearly."

Ace pulled a tie from the edge of the bed and lifted his arms to wrap it around his neck. Veronica saw how much it cost him, his terse breaths an indication of just how badly the motions hurt, but he got the tie around his neck. Although she respected his independence, she had her limits.

"What are you doing?"

She stood between his knees, reaching for the ends of the tie. "Doing this for you. If you don't want to think of it as help, consider it a prewedding ritual as old as time. And my good fortune to get to tie one on to a very sexy cowboy."

He stared up at her, grinning through the pain. "Would you think less of me if I take you up on that?"

"I'll think less of you if you don't."

"Deal."

She went to work on the tie, measuring the ends. "What was the time you nearly didn't make it back?"

"Tate and I were checking a line of fence. After proving we could go out and ride alone, our old man put us to work. He reasoned if we could go out and run around we could just as soon put our eyes and hands to good use. If we spotted things that needed attention we reported back and if it was something we could handle on our own we did it."

"I suppose there's some logic in there but hopefully it wasn't all hard work."

"That contributed to the nearly."

Veronica stilled, one end of the tie in midwrap over the other. "What happened?"

"We found a downed fence line but didn't realize a few of the longhorns had, too. Our ranch foreman had deliberately separated a couple of bulls who were causing trouble, giving them some needed space. A fact we didn't find out until too late. One charged Tate for getting too close."

Although the longhorns were relatively docile, they were still animals. "Too close to mating season?"

"Yep. And to almost two thousand pounds of cow we looked like the ones standing in the way of his good-time Saturday night."

"What did you do?"

"The bull charged Tate, and that was where the downed fence line worked in our favor. Tate was able to slip through the gap and then race down to an area that was still firmly staked."

"The cow followed him, right? Ignored the downed fence and moved along the interior fence line."

"Yeah." He smiled. "Nobody said they were that bright."

"Only now Tate's on one side of the fence and you're on the other."

"Exactly."

By Ace's smile, and the fact that Tate appeared healthy and whole, Veronica anticipated a happy ending. But she was still curious as to the outcome. "What did the two of you do?"

"We were far out on the property, so I couldn't just leave him there."

"No." She imagined that even with their preteen bravado, both were rather scared at that point, as well.

"But I did recall seeing a few acres back where the ranch hands had brought in fresh materials to fix another fence spot."

All ranching was hard work, but the image of a twelve-year-old boy attempting to drag a line of fence and posts was something else. "You were able to get all of it?"

"Fair amount. I also realized if we could just find a way to get the bull distracted we might also fix a part of our problem."

"The riled-up, looking-for-sex bull?"

"Funny enough, Tate had managed to calm him a little bit. He talked to him, used a lot of soothing words. I swear that man's damn near an animal whisperer when he wants to be."

As someone who made animals her business, Veronica maintained a healthy respect for their boundaries. And while she would never dismiss the need for calm actions and respectful behavior, the image of a ten-year-old boy facing down all that cow still gave her a chill.

With his index finger he tipped her chin. "The story really does have a happy ending. I promise."

She hadn't realized that her thoughts had transmitted quite so easily. "Both of you are still here. And I have seen you naked and haven't noticed any lingering longhorn scars. I haven't seen your brother naked, though."

His smile dropped. "See that you don't."

She pulled the last bit of his tie, deliberately tugging the knot. "Territorial much?"

He settled a hand low over her butt, pulling her close to snuggle. "Always."

The moment was sweet and, she well knew, not guaranteed. Just like with their longhorn story, the danger she and Ace had faced earlier in the week had proven that. Life changed on a dime and you had to be grateful for the time you got.

That still didn't mean he was off the hook to finish the story.

"What happened? In the end? All I still see in my mind is Tate on one side of a fence, you on the other and a big longhorn standing in between."

He lifted his head, memory flashing in the clear green of his eyes. "Those same ranch hands that had laid down the fence materials came along to fix it. We got lucky—they might not have come out that late in the afternoon but one of 'em had a date that bailed on him and he was in a bad mood and wanted to work off a head of steam."

"I bet he was surprised to find you both there."

"Understatement."

"Did you tell your parents?"

"Hell, no." Ace looked shocked that she'd even suggest it.

"Did the ranch hand?"

"Binky? We swore him to secrecy."

Veronica thought about how an enterprising ranch hand could parlay saving the boss's sons into a raise. "He kept quiet? Even though he saved you both?"

"He did." Ace frowned. "And besides, we were a good ways toward saving ourselves."

"Yeah, right." She ignored the male pride that still spiked, more than twenty years after the incident. "What else did you promise?"

His frown shifted, the slightest hint of embarrassment rosing his cheeks. "Tate knew the younger sister of the girl Binky was dating. Or trying to date. He promised he'd pass on what a hero Binky was to save us and not tell our folks."

"And?"

"Last I heard, Binky and Summer were living the good life on a small farm out near El Paso."

Veronica practically floated, happily loopy on the love that filled the day. Belle was a gorgeous bride and she'd leaped into Tate's arms when the minister said they could kiss. The two had satisfied everyone all the way back to the cheap seats with their passionate kiss and happy jaunt back down the aisle, their hands firmly joined. Even Ace's silly story about Binky and Summer had her smiling, the idea that he and his brother had helped make a love match all those years ago special somehow.

So yeah, she thought to herself as she threaded her way out the back door after grabbing a first aid kit in the house. *I'm a little woozy on love.* It was high time she began to feel *something*. A special something that was mushy and fun and gloriously happy.

The first aid kit was a bit of a deterrent, but there was no help for it. Belle's cousin's son had a scraped knee and the caterer had accidentally left the kit in the house after one of the chefs sustained a burn. They'd fix him up and continue the dancing that was already in high gear.

The path to the tent was blocked by a group of people and she momentarily considered trying to work through the throng when she remembered the caterer's entrance. It was just a little farther and would get Zachary's knee fixed a bit quicker.

Delicious scents led the way and she could already imagine the pulled pork that was one of the dinner choices. She held the edge of her skirt as she worked her way down a makeshift path, her heels sinking into the thin runner but not straight through to the ground below.

The runner came to an end and she'd nearly turned, closing the last few feet to the tent, when a man stood in front of her. She stopped, nearly stumbling at the sudden figure when recognition tumbled through her like an avalanche.

"Mark!"

He smiled, that soft smile she always associated with him. Gentle and kind, it was a mix of "aw shucks" and "I'm happy to be here." It was one of his most endearing qualities and memories of that smile had always left her with a small stab of guilt at how things had worked out.

"I had no idea you were here."

"It was a last-minute decision."

It struck her as off, but the gentle smile on his face and the happy sounds echoing from the tent blended, to the point she couldn't quite get a handle on what to do.

It was rude to ignore him. And while it was odd he was there, it felt equally rude to send him away.

"Well, what are you doing back here?"

He had a fresh beer in hand and moved closer, opening his arms for a hug. "It's been a long time."

It had been a long time. But whether it was the happiness of the day or the sudden relief that all the horror with Ray was behind her, Veronica didn't know. She only knew it was good to see him again. It was especially good to think they'd moved on. Past the end of their marriage to a place where they could be civil to each other and enjoy one another's company.

With open arms, she reached out for a hug, pressing a kiss to his cheek. "Let's go in, then."

Those were her last words before she felt the sharp prick on her arm. The pain had her stumbling back, the first aid kit falling from her hand, and it was in that instant that she realized her mistake.

He wasn't there under any sense of goodwill or celebration. The absence of any warmth or kindness in his grim smile was proof of that.

Instead, the sweet, gentle man was gone.

And in its place was a cold-eyed predator.

He'd never considered himself a big wedding guy, but watching his second sibling get married this year, Ace had to admit to a mountain of sentimental thoughts. His conversation earlier with Veronica hadn't helped. It had been years since he'd thought of that dumb longhorn and the even dumber situation he and Tate had gotten themselves into.

Even now, he could picture his brother's wide-eyed stare as he stood on one side of the fencing and a seriously pissed-off bull stood on the other.

"Where'd you go?" Tate's voice held all its normal poking, but his touch was light when he laid it on Ace's shoulder, in obvious deference to his injury.

"I told Veronica about that time you and I stared down a horny longhorn."

"I believe I was the one to stare him down."

"Right. And all those whispered endearments of yours that finally calmed him down."

Tate shrugged, before smiling. "What can I say? I've always had a silver tongue."

"For BS."

"It worked, didn't it?"

"That and the timely arrival of Binky and Gus."

"Oh, yeah. I forgot they helped."

Ace took a sip of the lone beer he was allowed that day. "They saved us."

"We needed saving?" Tate's grin never wavered. "I suppose we did, but I wouldn't have bet against us, either. If the guys hadn't come along."

"We were going to get that longhorn situated and fix the fence?"

"Sure we would have. You and me, big brother. We've made our way just fine." Tate nodded toward the edge of the room where Hoyt sat with Reese, the two talking to her mother. He then nodded toward Arden, in the middle of an odd, arm-flapping dance with several of their younger cousins. "All of us. Together."

"Now you're making your way with Belle. I couldn't be happier for you."

"We took the long way around. But I'm damn glad to have made it to this moment."

Tate's gaze drifted to the edge of the dance floor where Belle stood with a woman he recognized as her cousin and her small son. The boy's face was red and teary, and a quick scan indicated the reason was the hole in his knee and the cut visible through it.

Ace tipped his beer toward the trio. "Looks like we had our first wedding accident of the day."

Belle saw them watching and waved him over. He had no reason to think anything was wrong, but the tense set of her mouth had him moving, ignoring the stab of pain in his side.

"What happened here?"

"The dance floor did it." Belle gave an abstract smile for the boy before turning back to Ace. "Could you go see what Veronica got up to? She ran inside to get the first aid kit but I haven't seen her. It's been like ten minutes."

"She hasn't come back?" Ace was already scanning the room, not one single body wearing a pretty red-and-gold dress.

"No. And she knew he was crying so I can't see why she'd dawdle."

Ace fought the explosion of panic in his chest and sudden shortness of breath.

That thought.

The idea that had hovered in the back of his mind as he'd taken the pills the other night. What was it? What had bothered him?

His sister-in-law looked beautiful in her wedding gown and he hated to bring something sordid and ugly into her day, but as it all came clear he couldn't hold back. "Belle. The other day. The capture."

She glanced at the small boy who'd stopped crying and was now interested in what they were saying. With a pointed glance for her cousin, his mother took him to get settled in a chair. Belle waited until they were just of earshot when she nodded. "Yes. What about it?"

"It was one guy. Right?"

"Yeah. The guy who's already been identified and shipped back to Houston. The Rat King."

"What about the other one?"

"What other—" She broke off. "The peeping Tom at Veronica's?"

"Yeah. Where did he go?"

"That wasn't Ray Barnett? But we took down the shooter and—" She stilled, her hands framing her face. "I never followed up on that. I turned the case over to take my vacation days and I never followed up to make sure they weren't the same person."

"No." Ace shook his head. "This is not on you."

"Of course it's on me. It's my case. It's my family!"

Her admonitions were sharp and pointed and Ace tried to shut her down when Tate moved up beside them. "What's going on?"

"Veronica's missing," Ace said.

"I never followed up on the other guy." Belle turned, her eyes frantic. "The one peeping at her vet practice."

"Okay. Before we get too excited, let's grab Hoyt and we'll figure out what's going on." Tate pointed toward the caterer's exit, which was closest to them. "Maybe she's outside. Let's go look."

Hoyt was already on his way over and the four of them made their way to the caterer's entrance. Not only was it closer but the shorter distance minimized the well-wishers, and in a matter of moments they stood outside the tent flap, staring at the ground.

And the first aid kit that lay abandoned a few feet away.

Chapter 18

Veronica came awake on a hard, choking cough. Her mouth was fuzzy and dry and it was suddenly impossible to take in air. Panic filled her as she tried to catch her breath, coughs racking her body once more. She struggled to calm down — to find a way to breathe—and after a small trickle of air thought she might be okay.

Could be all the way okay if she could get some water.

With that foremost in her thoughts she tried to reach out, panic spiking once more at the ties that held her hands behind her back.

What?

"Oh, good. You're awake. If I had to listen to that endless snore of yours one more minute I might shoot myself."

Veronica's eyes adjusted fully to the dim light in the room and saw Mark in a hotel chair, his legs sprawled in front of him.

The wedding came racing back to her. Stumbling upon him on the path to the tent. Their quick hug and then the blackness. "What are you doing?"

"What I should have done years ago. You're a lot harder to kill than I thought you'd be."

Kill her?

Mark?

"But you're my husband." The words came out on a rough, raspy cough and she fought to catch her breath once more.

"Ex-husband. Or did you forget?"

Whatever he'd given her was quickly wearing off, the cold air swirling from the air conditioner warding off the fuzzy aftereffects. The air conditioner had been one of the biggest fights of their marriage, his insistence on keeping their house like a freezer an ongoing irritation.

Not much had changed.

"I haven't forgotten anything. But I obviously missed more than a few clues."

"I know." He smiled again and how she ever imagined those lips could curl into something gentle was a mystery. "It's funny, isn't it? You were so busy being unhappy and pining for your cowboy you missed every single clue I practically waved in your face."

He laughed, the sound empty. Soulless.

"Sure, babe, go to work. Work all you need—I support you." He waved a hand, his devious grin never fading. "Need me to cover off a few afternoons a week at your office? Happy to. Just give me access to that pharmacy cabinet in case a shipment comes in."

Oh, God.

The muzzy-headed feeling faded fully as she ran through his remembered comments. She had given him total access to her practice, even going so far as to give him a spare set of keys.

"A locked vet practice is a mighty fine place to store a shipment of kilos." He laughed. "And you never knew. You were so damned busy being miserable and running to save your precious animals you never even knew."

She had done that. Had done all of that.

For all the insistence that she'd fallen in love and moved on, she hadn't. Not really. She'd taken the first smooth talker who'd come along. The first opportunity, really, to run away from Ace.

And in the running had fallen straight into the trap of a madman.

Ace paced the kitchen, his side burning like hellfire. Veronica was gone. Taken.

They'd questioned several wedding guests milling around outside the tent, asking if anyone had seen her. A few mentioned seeing a woman who looked too tipsy being walked to the parking lot, the man carrying her drooping form claiming she needed fresh air. Only when probed on the man's description, all that had come back was medium build, dark hair, slender frame.

The man Ace had seen peeking in the vet practice had been larger and blond. He wasn't a heavy guy but "medium build with dark hair" didn't fit the bill. It didn't help that few of the guests knew Veronica, either. But he did finally get an affirmative when he mentioned the color of her dress.

"It's possible Ray had several minions working for him." Belle paced the kitchen, her phone in hand as she covered the mouthpiece and her dress swishing in her wake as she walked a path through the floor.

She'd already called the Houston PD asking for known associates of the Rat King and had also pulled her own deputies out of the wedding, pressing them into action. Several had already taken off for town, using the description of the man with Veronica in hand as they canvassed for anyone who might have seen anything.

Now she was back on the phone, pressing one of her FBI contacts for help.

"She's amazing," Tate whispered, his gaze tracking her continuously since they'd come into the kitchen. "She never gives up."

"I'm grateful to her. To you." Ace laid a hand on his brother's arm. "This isn't how this day was supposed to go."

"Maybe not, but we'll take what we've got and we're going to see that Veronica gets home."

Ace wanted to believe his brother. More, he wanted to believe that the cool competence Belle had shown from the very first seconds they realized Veronica was missing was going to see them all through this.

But what if it didn't?

Especially if they had no freaking clue who'd taken Veronica.

No one had called, taunting them with answers to the kidnapper's identity. Nothing had turned up on the known-associates list. And none of them had any idea who met the description of the man who took her.

"What happened?" Veronica's father hollered as her parents flew into the kitchen, grief etched so deeply into their faces Ace would have sworn they'd each aged ten years since the Friday fiesta.

"Esteban. Marcelita." Arden stepped in immediately, putting an arm around each of them and leading them to the table. "Come over here."

Ace tried to offer comfort but her father wouldn't sit still. "Who did this? I thought that bad man was caught. This was supposed to be all done for my Veronica." Esteban's eyes filled with tears. "Who took my little girl?"

The pressure in his chest was oppressive as Ace could do nothing but watch Veronica's parents suffer.

Just as he was.

How had they been so stupid, believing the threat was gone? To so quickly assume the issue had been dealt with, no further digging needed.

They were all paying for that oversight.

And Veronica paid most of all.

Although Mark kept her hands tied, he'd moved them from behind her back to the front and he clearly felt the room was secure. She was allowed to move freely between the bathroom and bed while he spent most of his time in another room, visible through an adjoining door. A gun she had no idea he owned, let alone knew how to use, had been brandished in front of her face after he'd retied her wrists.

A visible and determined threat to get her to cooperate.

Even if she had no idea what she was cooperating for.

They were in a hotel room so at some point he'd need to move her from this location to another.

Or he'll kill you.

The thought had whispered through her mind over and over as she laid on the bed, staring at the squat, square room.

Images of the wedding filled her. The happy excitement that had gripped the ranch as everyone awaited the wedding. They'd all believed the threat to her safety was vanquished with Ray's death. Even Belle had believed.

Belle. A happy bride, looking forward to her future.

Although Mark's actions had ruined the woman's day forever, she would move on to a future. A bright one, full of love and happiness.

Had she ever felt that for Mark? Even on their wedding day?

Whatever she wanted to lay at his feet—and kidnapping suddenly put the man in a light she never imagined—she'd made a choice. She'd gotten herself into this the day she allowed her love for Ace to be overshadowed by her own fear.

The day she'd stopped believing in the power of the two of them.

She wasn't giving up on them now.

Rolling from the bed, she marched to the bathroom, seeking solace behind the door. Mark had the advantage of surprise and the benefit of a gun, but she wasn't totally helpless. She had been married to the man and had lived with him for more than six years. She'd learned to placate him and how to sense his moods.

Now she needed to find a way to lull him into a sense of vulnerability. If she could suss out his plans, she could figure out her next move.

She wasn't going down without a fight.

Ace stared at the face of his phone, exhaustion a living, breathing entity in the kitchen. He'd long stopped thinking about the pain of his broken ribs. The throbbing, ever-present ache only serving to remind him of what hurt worse: the haunting, visceral pain of Veronica's absence.

They'd gone through who knew how many pots of coffee, the kitchen door swinging with all the people who'd come and gone from their home. Belle and Tate had long since changed out of their wedding clothes, both now dressed for action. No one missed the gun strapped to Belle's waist, a clear signal she was in full cop mode.

"Keep calling." Arden tapped a piece of paper on the table over the top of her laptop.

"Nothing's turned up." Ace stared the wall clock, now reading 3:00 a.m.

"Something will." His sister determinedly stared at her computer screen. "Something has to."

Reese had suggested the idea around midnight. She took the guest list for the wedding—a spreadsheet that held every guest's cell phone—and suggested they all start making calls. They had no idea who might have been taking a photo at the right time, but it was worth a try. It also ensured there were another hundred and fifty people around the Pass who had their eyes open for Veronica.

The endless stream of photos that had begun flooding Arden's email hadn't turned up anything yet. Not enough people knew Veronica or had spent time with her. Hell, she'd spent so much time hovering over him and fussing on how he felt he hadn't done a very good job of introducing her around, either.

Hell.

He slammed back from the table to pace. Her parents huddled quietly in the living room, their heads bent together. Veronica's sister Maria had come over to join them, with Valerie planning to head over in the morning. Everyone was there.

Everyone except Veronica.

He so desperately wanted to believe all these people focused on finding her could bring Veronica back, but he'd lived in Midnight Pass his whole life. He knew the land and the terrain and why it had always been a favorite of drug runners and smugglers. The craggy, rocky land around the border hid any number of trails and traverses. Places people could hide to do their unsavory deeds while everyone else slept safe in their beds.

It had brought the dead body to their land back in the spring. Those crosses cut deep in the earth had allowed Russ Grantham to pass back and forth unseen, his murders hidden from view. And they'd likely been the way Veronica's kidnapper had gotten onto Reynolds land.

Unseen.

The steady itch to go out on his own, canvassing the ground with Walter, had remained high through the night. Hoyt had already sent out a team of hands, all equipped with heavy flashlights to move about the ranch, but his brother had convinced him to stay at the house.

If a call did come in, he needed to be there. A half-truth, Ace knew, at best. It also kept his battered body in place, under everyone's watchful eye.

To hell with that.

He'd already changed into riding clothes, tears choking his throat as he removed the tie Veronica had fitted around his neck. He was ready to move out.

He needed to find her.

The knock on the door was followed quickly by a grizzled head peeking in. Tabasco Burns caught his eye immediately. "Ace."

Ace waved the older man in, surprised to see their resident bar owner this far out of town. "Come in."

Tabasco had a few days' worth of gray scruff on his face and beer stains up and down his T-shirt, which advertised a local brew. "I'm sorry to bother you so late but I need to tell you something. I know Miz Veronica is missing. Few people came in tonight and mentioned it."

His heart hitched in his chest at the idea Veronica's disappearance was already making the rounds. The speed was expected, but it didn't make it easier to think of her kidnapping as casual conversation at the local watering hole. Pushing aside the sheer resentment at the idea, Ace focused on the man he'd never seen outside the Border Line. "It's not too late. What's going on?"

The room grew quiet, every anxious face focused on Tabasco. He nodded his head around the room, adding a wink for Belle and Tate.

"I don't want to rile anyone up and I try not to think things about the people having a drink in my place."

Belle moved beside Midnight Pass's favorite proprietor, her hand gentle against his forearm. "Sometimes people come to bars to get lost. It doesn't make you a bad person for noticing. Or for giving them a space to do the losing."

"'Suppose not." Tabasco nodded. "I don't forget many people, either."

Under normal circumstances, Ace had always found Tabasco's grizzled features and odd views on the world refreshing. Charming, even. In that moment, all he wanted was answers. His impatience was nearly out when Hoyt laid a hand on his shoulder, giving him a light squeeze.

Ace leaned into his brother, barely aware of doing it, when Tabasco's shuffling words paid dividends.

"I was pulling a round of beers for Missy to serve when I caught sight of an old face coming in. Hadn't seen him in a long time and I couldn't remember his name but

I knew he was familiar, you know? I was about to raise my hand in greeting when something stopped me."

"Did he do something?" Belle's blue eyes were flat and focused, all cop, as her vision never wavered off Tabasco.

"Met up with another guy. The two were stiff and formal but you could see they knew each other, you know? I didn't recognize the other guy, but the one I did know kept nagging at the back of my mind. Where I knew him from."

"What did he look like?" Belle pressed.

"Medium build. Not small but not big, you know. Sorta slight. Black hair."

"Bingo," Hoyt whispered, his voice low. His hand never wavered off Ace's shoulder, but that squeeze came once more.

"Who was he with?" Everyone in the kitchen, from Ace and his family to the few deputies who had been working with Belle, all stilled.

"Bigger guy. Blond. Didn't recognize him as a local."

"That's good, Tabasco," Belle affirmed. "These are the guys we're looking for. The medium build matches the description of who took Veronica."

Tabasco shook his head, clearly perturbed. "Problem is, he's familiar but I still can't place him."

"It's Mark." Maria stood in the entryway to the kitchen, her tearstained face set in certainty.

"Mark who?" Belle asked.

Ace beat Maria to the answer. "Veronica's ex-husband."

Light edged the drawn curtains of her room, drawing her eye as Veronica woke up. She had no idea when she'd fallen asleep, the lack of anything she could use as a weapon ensuring there wasn't a bedside clock in the room. If she had to guess, exhaustion had finally tipped her over somewhere past midnight, but the bright light now suggested morning.

Mark had already had her overnight.

Her ex-husband had kidnapped her.

Like a brick to the head, that reality hit her once more.

As if she'd conjured him up, he came through the adjoining door to their rooms, throwing a wrapped breakfast sandwich at her feet. "Eat."

The scent of carbs and bacon were enough to get her stomach rumbling, but she was confused where he'd gotten breakfast. It was still hot and she hadn't been tied up so he could go get the food. She might not know what his endgame was but there was no way he'd have kidnapped her only to leave her unattended in the room.

"Where'd you get this?"

"Don't worry about it."

She had no idea where the bravado came from, but did know she wasn't going to have very many shots to find out what was going on. Sinking into the bland voice she used to use over dinner, she unwrapped the sandwich, fumbling only slightly with her bound hands.

"This seems like a crude way to get my attention. We haven't even spoken in almost two years."

He sneered at her. "Time well spent."

Her question was nearly out when Mark continued on. "I was free and clear of you. Our time had run its course and you running away after the incident in your office left me the space to take my business to the next level."

His business? "Free of what?"

"You think most guys running drugs are lucky enough to have a wife with a pharmaceutical stash? All nice and legal like yours."

"You're a drug runner?"

"One of the best, baby." He eyed her across the room, his gaze devoid of any warmth. "And your office gave me the cover I needed to move the merchandise. To work my way up in the organization. To prove myself."

The answers are like successive gut punches, one worse than the next.

Even as the strangest sense of freedom came over her.

She didn't love him, but he hadn't loved her. Not one bit. He'd used her. He'd obviously seen her as an easy mark and, in those months after breaking up with Ace, she was.

But she wasn't that simpering fool any longer. And she wanted answers. All of them.

"And you knew I was going to be held up that night? At gunpoint?"

He had the gall to shrug. "Collateral damage, you know. I figured I'd play the grieving widower if I needed to. But that wasn't my goal."

Goal? The absolute nonchalance in his tone was the worst, but now that she was in it, Veronica wanted to know everything.

"What was your goal?"

"I wanted to move up. Getting those morons out of the way—the ones who held you up—were the end game."

"And once they were gone you didn't need my practice anymore, either." Or me.

"Nope."

"And the Rat King? What about him?"

"He's a tool, too. A passionate believer in the cause." Mark snorted. "The cause is money, nothing more. Believe it or not, that fool actually wants to be seen as some sort of king."

"So why now? Why suddenly come back?"

"You have what I want."

If he'd untied her hands and let her go, Veronica would have been less surprised. "What do I have?"

"You really are clueless, aren't you?"

"Obviously, since I had no idea my husband was a psychopath."

He struck, his hand flying through the air so her sandwich went airborne. "Stupid bitch. I'm a businessman, not a psycho."

The move was such a surprise—such a radical departure from the man she'd known—Veronica could only stare at the pile of English muffin, egg and bacon littering the floor near the bed.

Who was he?

And how had she never seen it?

All that time, living under the same roof, and she'd never seen any hint of his behavior. Hadn't even seen it during their divorce proceedings.

"Do you think I want to be here? I was happy to be rid of you. And then you had to go and take it."

"Take what?"

"The kilos. Prime, grade-A heroin, run up from South America. It's been sitting in your pharmacy cabinet for two years."

What was he talking about? She did regular inventory of her pharmaceutical stock. She'd have known if several pounds of heroin had suddenly found its way into her business. "I don't have any kilos. Anywhere."

"Liar!"

The sudden violence, flinging her sandwich, had nothing on the monster who seemed to morph before her eyes. The subtle, unobtrusive man she'd known had vanished.

In its place was a brutal, soulless figure who seemed to rise up before her beside the bed.

"You know where it is." Mark dragged the gun from behind his back and pointed it at her head. "And you're going to take me to get it."

She had no idea how she was going to magically produce illegal drugs she didn't possess, but her mind was already whirling with the possibilities. He wouldn't kill her until he had what he believed he'd come for.

Now she just had to figure out what in her medical supply could be used against him.

Ace sat in his truck, drumming his hands on the steering wheel. Hoyt sat beside him, ostensibly as backup but no doubt there to babysit. "This is a waste of time."

"It's a start," his brother said, calm and collected. "And it's better than sitting in the kitchen, swilling another cup of coffee."

Tabasco's visit hadn't turned up much motive, but the confirmation of Mark's presence in the Pass and his meeting with the second guy who Ace had seen nosing around Veronica's vet practice were enough to put everyone in motion.

There was no way Veronica's ex-husband was back for a visit. Especially not one where he carried her off pretending she was drunk. She was drugged. And now they had to figure out why.

Belle had been running whatever information she could find on Mark Stewart and, as of the point they left the ranch, hadn't found a thing. The man had no criminal record and strong, if consistently bland, marks at his job at an accounting firm in Houston.

Which had left them all even more in the dark than before.

Why would he suddenly come after his ex-wife?

Although he and Veronica had danced around the subject, his own frustration with her marriage contributing to that, she hadn't indicated any lingering feelings for the man. Nor had it seemed as if they'd stayed in touch postdivorce. She'd resumed her life in the Pass. Mark had stayed in Houston. The end.

Or not.

Which was why he staked out her business, far enough away to avoid the police who didn't want him there and close enough to see what was going on.

"Want to go in?" Hoyt opened the glove compartment and eyed the handguns they'd placed in there when they left Reynolds Station. His voice was low but there was a lethal thread of anticipation in his tone.

"To Veronica's?"

"Yeah. I know a way in."

"Cops'll never let us in there." Ace practically spat the words, the stern warning from his new sister-in-law an hour earlier still ringing in his ears.

"Cops don't need to know."

Ace knew his brother had developed some serious skills in special ops and the sudden light in Hoyt's eyes suggested he'd not forgotten any of them.

"I'm a liability."

"Which is why you're going to leave the hard stuff to me. But I know you can't stay here." Hoyt turned to him. "I know what it's like to wait outside. I had to wait for Reese while she was under lockdown inside her classroom and it nearly killed me."

"What if Veronica's somewhere else? If we're hiding in there we won't know."

"Let's take our chances. You saw that guy nosing around the practice. Where else are they going?"

Hoyt had a point and Ace was so desperate for action—any action—he was willing to take his brother up on the idea. "The cops are all over. It still won't help us get inside."

"They're taking turns. And trying to stay unobtrusive." Hoyt pointed toward the unmarked car sitting down the block. "Manny'll circle the block in about two minutes. In the meantime, Belle's been working to get snipers on the roof across Main. You and me'll go in the back while they're changing over."

Ace's hand was already on the door handle. "Let's go."

Although she was still hungry, Veronica was grateful for her lost breakfast sandwich fifteen minutes later. Mark had dragged her from her hotel room, through the adjoining door into his own. A guy was waiting for them both on the other side, and at the row of guns and ammunition he'd laid out on the bed, Veronica's stomach roiled in fear.

There was enough there to take out all of Midnight Pass.

And anyone who dared to get in their way.

Next to it all was a small duffel bag, it's slight shape upright on the bed, clear there was something in it.

"We get the rest of the kilos and then make it to the drop point," the tall, blond guy Mark had called Rocky said, tapping a hand on the duffel, suggesting "the rest" would be added to whatever they already had.

"Yep." Mark's attention shifted to her. "She's going to lead us right to it."

Her mind whirled with possibilities, mentally cataloging everything in her pharmacy cabinets. Several drugs came packaged in large boxes but the moment Mark held one he'd know there wasn't anything hidden inside. They'd be too light. She'd toyed with the idea of telling him she did have the drugs and had already cut them down to more manageable packets to stuff into various hiding places, but that wasn't likely to do her much good when she couldn't produce a single packet of anything.

And now there were two of them.

Her initial idea, to get a syringe full of sedative, had been the closest thing she had to a plan. It was only about half guaranteed to work but at least it would have been something.

But with two of them? And all those guns?

No way.

That bleak thought and the increasingly bleaker one that she'd never see Ace or her family again accompanied her as Mark perp-walked her out to his waiting SUV.

Ace's estimation of Hoyt's skills rose several more notches as the two of them snuck into Veronica's practice and closed the back door behind them. Hoyt had taken him around the long way, past the businesses on Main that flanked hers, and had them in the back door in a matter of moments.

"Lockpicks?"

"Small souvenir from the good old days."

"The government let you keep them?" Ace asked. He wasn't arguing but didn't think lockpicks were a standard takeaway when one left the service.

"I prefer to think of this in the camp of 'what they don't know won't hurt them.' And I consider them suitable payment from an arms dealer who believed himself untouchable."

Not for the first time Ace understood his brother had seen and done things that were unimaginable to the average person. For as much as it scared him, he was proud, too. "You're one scary son of bitch."

"I was. Once upon a time." Hoyt grinned one of his rare smiles. "Now I'm just mad and determined and hoping to have a few good stories to tell my kids."

"This one had better have a happy ending."

Hoyt laid a hand on his back, the grin gone. "There's nothing I want more."

Ace felt the edge of his handgun press into his spine where Hoyt had laid a hand and took subtle solace from the shape. They were armed. And if they were lucky, their instincts proven correct, they'd have a shot at Mark.

Once inside, they headed for Veronica's office and crouched behind her desk, eyes on the locked pharmacy door.

And settled in to wait.

Veronica eyed the confines of her practice, the familiar hallway and subtle scent of disinfectant strangely welcoming. She had little idea of how she was going to survive this, but the familiar surroundings went a long way toward making her think she might have an advantage. A slim one, but it was home court all the same.

With even further evidence of his advance planning, Mark had produced her keys. They'd been inside the ranch house in her purse, of no use to her during the wedding, but he'd slipped in undetected and found them, anyway. He'd even laughed as he held them up, the heavy ring jangling with the movements. "Same key ring with that stupid grinning penguin. Just like always."

He pointed toward the heavy security door that closed over the pharmacy. "Go. Now. Open it."

The temptation to dawdle was strong but he'd already proven he had little patience. She was going to need to move as fast as she could. She'd even considered dragging the steel door down on top of him as an idea.

In the moment, she admonished herself. *Take the shot you get the moment you get it.*

"Move." His gun didn't waver as he pointed it at her head. "Get it open."

Where she'd hoped he'd take the keys and act, he obviously wanted her in front of him. Crouching, she did as he asked, working the lock at the base of the steel door. It snicked open and she gripped the cool metal handle to lift the door.

Veronica gauged the heft with her ability to slam it down, but the tight tie over her wrist limited her movement. She'd never get it closed on him.

Mark reached behind her and flipped the fluorescent lights, illumination filling every corner of the room. He pressed the gun to her back, forcing her forward. It was only when both of them had crossed the threshold that she recognized their mistake.

The man who'd come with Mark had his gun up, pointed directly at Mark. "Drop the gun."

Mark's mouth dropped, his gaze frantically racing to the semiautomatic weapon pointed at his midsection. "Now."

Ace practically leaped out of his hiding place. Would have if it weren't for Hoyt's steadying hand. They used no words, but Hoyt gave a determined shake of his head. A silent order to stay put.

It took everything in him to remain still, but Ace did as instructed.

Hoyt knew what he was doing. Ace had to believe that. Had to believe *in* it.

Hoyt had already shifted his focus at the obvious double cross playing out before them.

"What is this?" Mark asked, disdain and fear curling his lips and forcing a slight tremble.

"What does it look like? I want the drugs and I'm leaving."

"I brought you into this."

"And I'm changing the rules." The other man moved forward, the gun never wavering, and slipped the duffel bag off Mark's shoulder. "I'll be taking this now."

Mark's frantic gaze roamed around the pharmacy. "But there's more."

It was then that Ace finally understood the ruse. "There isn't anything more. I cooked that up to get these." The man tapped the bag at his side with the hand that wasn't on the trigger. "I just needed to get these beauties you smuggled over the border so I could get on my way."

"But you said she had them!"

"She has nothing." The blond guy laughed. "She never did."

Although Ace couldn't see his face, the build on the man holding Veronica matched the one he remembered, skulking around her practice. The Peeping Tom. As scared as he'd been the day the bastard had been looking in the windows, it was nothing compared to the ice cold fingers that ran up and down his spine now. "She just had the good sense to leave your sorry ass."

"But the…the drop point?" Mark fumbled over the words.

"I'll be making that one all by myself. With the kilos already had. The ones you just handed over to me this morning."

Whether it was instinct or simple knowledge of the inevitable outcome, Hoyt moved. Without hesitation, his brother lined up his shot, the guy falling to the ground from a direct head shot before Ace could blink.

Veronica used the chaos to move and Ace was already out of the office toward her when he realized his miscalculation.

He stood between Mark and Hoyt, denying his brother a solid shot.

And without hesitating, Mark moved, dragging Veronica under his arm.

Veronica struggled to process what had just happened, the heavy sounds of gunfire still echoing in her ears. Mark's double-crosser had nearly made it out with the bag of drugs when Hoyt had suddenly rose up like an avenging angel.

And then there was Ace, there, before her. In motion, his gaze displaying every ounce of his determination to get to her. Only now Mark had her back under his grip, his gun stabbing her collarbone with painful thrusts.

Her head spun with the chaos, even as Mark screamed over and over, "Get back! I'll kill her!"

Ace had already moved, giving his brother a clean shot, but instead of forcing a standoff, it only had Mark's hand shaking harder, the gun pressing over and over in tight jabs against her skin.

How had this happened?

And how was it possible she'd married a man, believed she'd loved him and never known he was running drugs? The situation was dire, but somewhere deep inside a small fire began to burn.

"Who *are* you?" she asked.

The words—so calm, so controlled—had a strange effect on the room. The tension that gripped everyone, including the racing adrenaline that seemed to be the only thing fueling Mark, changed.

Shifted.

Like those last moments when an animal you were convinced would attack shifted gears and stood down.

"I'm the man you should have given more credit to."

"I guess I should have." She kept her voice quiet, even as the pressure of the gun loosened just slightly enough to suggest her words had sunk in.

But it was the calculated risk, after her gaze drifted over Ace and Hoyt, that she went all-in. At Hoyt's subtle head nod, Veronica moved.

She pushed hard on the gun as her head slammed back, into Mark's chin. "But I really think I should have given more credit to myself."

Ace saw it unfold. Saw the change that came over Veronica as she confronted the man she'd once married. Saw the genuine shift in Mark's behavior as a result of her questions.

Most of all, he saw the truth that had haunted him since the day Arden came home with the news of Veronica's marriage.

If Veronica had loved Mark—and he was increasingly convinced she never really had—she didn't any longer.

The lull in Mark's aggression—so faint as to be nearly nonexistent—put Ace in motion. Veronica's push on the gun was just enough to further upset Mark's equilibrium and Ace took his shot.

He ignored the gun strapped at his back and went on sheer animal instinct instead. Leaping forward, fueled by the yawning pain in his ribs, he went after the enemy.

While the space between them wasn't more than a few feet, the gap between him and Veronica seemed endless. But Ace did have enough of the element of surprise to see him through.

Mark instinctively shifted backward at the intrusion, the movement and Ace's war cry as he leaped seemingly a sensory overload. Veronica moved immediately, her hand slashing down on Mark's forearm to dislodge the gun, and Hoyt came up to flank the rear, his own screamed curses at Ace's sudden impulsive action echoing off the cavernous metal cage of the pharmacy.

The gun clattered to the ground, Ace and Mark tumbling after it. Mindless with the fear that had gripped him for nearly twenty-four hours, Ace reacted in a haze. He slammed Mark's head into the floor, using the leverage of both weight and the lingering element of surprise to stop the threat.

In moments, Hoyt had the situation in hand—Mark's gun kicked out of range and their hostage pressed against a wall, nowhere close enough to reach for the gun of his fallen comrade.

Or double-crosser.

Belle's voice came next, hollering through the open back door of the clinic. Hoyt hollered back an all clear, but none of them could have predicted the avenging angel who came through the back hallway, stopping short at the tableau spread out before her.

"What in the hell are you doing here?" Belle demanded. Her gaze tripped between Ace and Hoyt, even as her gun never wavered in her tight grip.

"We couldn't wait," Ace said, unrepentant.

"I can see that." Belle scanned the ground, her gaze settling on Veronica. "You okay?"

"I am. I'm sorry I ruined your wedding."

His sister-in-law shrugged, her smile broad. "I told Tate he was marrying me, job and all."

"And he's a lucky man at that," Ace interjected as he struggled to his feet. "The luckiest of men."

The disgusted fish-eye that came winging back suggested Belle wasn't going to be all that quick to forgive. "Those ribs hurt?"

"Like a bitch."

"Good." She nodded hard. "Now go kiss her and take her home and tell her you love her. Please."

Ace grinned, ignoring the grunting and screaming coming from Mark where he still lay under Hoyt's steady grip. "I already did that."

Belle leaned in and pressed a quick kiss to his cheek. "Then get out of here and do it again."

Veronica navigated out the back door of her clinic toward the parking lot. Things looked wildly different than when she'd walked in, convinced she might never see daylight again.

Might never see Ace again.

She supposed that fact might sink in sooner or later, but for the moment, she was happy to breathe fresh air.

Even happier to hold his hand.

"I thought I lost you." Ace tugged on their joined hands to stop her forward progress.

"I thought you lost me, too."

"I can't believe Mark was behind it all along."

It was going to take some time to process it all, but between his boasting back at the motel and his shouts at Belle that he was the mastermind behind a drug ring in Houston, she'd begun to piece it all together.

Along with the reality that he'd been played as easily as his mark, Ray Barnett.

He'd used her Houston practice as a front, running drugs through her pharmacy. He'd done it just long enough to make it up the ladder with his band of thugs and thought he was headed for the big time.

Mark had been the one to manipulate Ray Barnett, teasing the man about his loss that night in her office in Houston. It was just the trigger Mark needed to set everything in motion. Get Ray in place to scare her and put him in position to get into her practice for the extra kilos.

Only Rocky had been the mastermind in the end.

Because the supposed kilos were just a ruse. One to get the stash Mark already had so Rocky could make off with it himself.

She'd never believed there was honor among thieves, but the triple cross was beyond shocking.

Veronica shook her head, the reality of the monster she married still not sunk in. "I never knew. Never even had a clue."

"It's hard to think someone you loved was capable of that."

"I didn't love him."

As soon as the confession was out, she knew it for the truth. She'd fought it for years, some small voice inside suggesting it was a personal shortcoming not to love her husband.

Only it wasn't.

She hadn't loved Mark and that was on her, no matter how twisted his ultimate behavior.

But loving Ace. That was on her, too.

"I love you, Ace Reynolds. I have from the start. Every stubborn inch of you."

"I love you, too."

"I never should have run away from us. Or convinced myself that our volatility was a shortcoming."

His eyebrows lifted, those gorgeous green eyes as vibrant as emeralds winking in the sunlight. "You mean you want to fight with me?"

"Fight with you. Make up with you. And everything that comes in between."

He moved in, wrapping his arms around her. "I'd rather think about all the fun that comes after." He nuzzled her neck. "You know. When we make up."

"I want that, too." She lifted her head, her gaze never leaving his. "I've never stopped wanting it."

"I guess it's official, then."

"What is?"

"You're stuck with me."

"And you're stuck with me." She lifted her head and pressed her lips to his. The kiss was full of promise and the passion that always arced between them. But even with those emotional jewels winking brightly, she felt something else.

Satisfaction.

She'd looked for some excuse—some reason—to explain her feelings for Ace. Feelings that seemed at continued odds with the impulsive and hot-blooded emotions he churned up.

It was only now that Veronica acknowledged that she never needed one.

She loved him.

They had a love that had remained strong despite the distance and now it would grow and thrive together each and every day.

Who knew love could make a person so happy? she wondered as she wrapped her arms around his neck and pulled him close.

Even better, who cared?

She was happy. Content. And she had a future with Ace Reynolds as big and as bold as their love.

Wild Horse Reynolds had found his place, under that big Texas sky.

Forever more Veronica Torres would say the same.

* * * * *

Don't miss the previous Midnight Pass, Texas, books:

Special Ops Cowboy
The Cowboy's Deadly Mission

Available now from Harlequin Romantic Suspense!

WE HOPE YOU ENJOYED THIS BOOK FROM

HARLEQUIN
ROMANTIC SUSPENSE

Danger. Passion. Drama.

These heart-racing page-turners will keep you guessing to the very end. Experience the thrill of unexpected plot twists and irresistible chemistry.

4 NEW BOOKS AVAILABLE EVERY MONTH!

#2159 COLTON 911: SECRET ALIBI
Colton 911: Chicago • by Beth Cornelison

When Nash Colton is framed for murder, his former lover, Valerie Yates, must choose between proving his innocence and putting her mother's fragile mental health at risk. As they fight to rebuild their relationship, they must learn to trust each other—and find the person trying to kill Nash.

#2160 DROP-DEAD COLTON
The Coltons of Grave Gulch • by Beverly Long

FBI agent Bryce Colton has dedicated the past year to finding serial killer Len Davison. When Davison becomes obsessed with Olivia Margulies, Bryce believes the man may be within reach. But the obsession turns dangerous, and Bryce takes the ultimate risk to save the woman that he loves...

#2161 THE LAST COWBOY STANDING
Cowboys of Holiday Ranch • by Carla Cassidy

Marisa has been waiting to kill a man who kidnapped her. When she hires Mac McBride to care for an abused horse on her ranch, she thinks there might be some good in the world after all. But Marisa's past isn't finished with her— and Mac may not be enough to protect her.

#2162 MATCHED WITH MURDER
by Danielle M. Haas

When multiple murders are connected to users on Samatha Gates's dating app, Detective Max Green knows she'll have information he needs. Neither of them expected Samantha to become a target—and now she has to share her secrets with Max to find the true culprit.

HRSCNM1121

SPECIAL EXCERPT FROM

⬦ HARLEQUIN
ROMANTIC SUSPENSE

*When multiple murders are connected to users on
Samantha Gates's dating app, Detective Max Green
knows she'll have information he needs. Neither of them
expected Samantha to become a target—and now she
has to share her secrets with Max to find the true culprit.*

Read on for a sneak preview of
Matched with Murder,
*Danielle M. Haas's
Harlequin Romantic Suspense debut!*

Samantha dropped her head in her hands. "I had the
same thoughts. I called the Department of Justice this
morning, and the woman I spoke with said I needed to
speak with the warden. I didn't get a chance to call before
Teddy stormed in. But I...I can't believe Jose is behind
this."

Max stared at her with hard eyes and an open mouth.

She wrapped her arms over her middle, not knowing
how to explain the conflicting emotions Jose still stirred
in her gut.

"I have to go." Max strode toward the doorway of the
kitchen that led to the foyer, his strides fast and furious.

She staggered off the stool and followed behind him
as quickly as she could. Her mind raced with a million
possibilities. Her bare foot touched down on the wooden
floor of the foyer.

Crash!

She whipped her head toward the broken window that faced the street. Glass shattered to the floor and something flew into the newly formed hole.

"Get back!"

Max's yell barely penetrated her brain before he scooped her over his shoulder and ran in the opposite direction. He reached the carpeted floors of the living room and leaped through the air. They crashed behind the couch and pain shot through her body.

Boom!

A loud explosion pierced her eardrums. The lights flickered and plaster poured down from the ceiling. Max's hard body crashed down on her. Silence filled the heavy air and Samantha squeezed her eyes closed and waited for this nightmare to end.

Don't miss
Matched with Murder *by Danielle M. Haas,*
available December 2021 wherever
Harlequin Romantic Suspense
books and ebooks are sold.

Harlequin.com

Get 4 FREE REWARDS!

We'll send you 2 FREE Books plus 2 FREE Mystery Gifts.

Harlequin Romantic Suspense books are heart-racing page-turners with unexpected plot twists and irresistible chemistry that will keep you guessing to the very end.

FREE Value Over $20
